Until the Ice Cracks

Jan Turk Petrie

ALSO BY JAN TURK PETRIE

No God for a Warrior:
Volume two of Eldísvík trilogy

Within Each Other's Shadow:
Volume three of the Eldísvík trilogy

Mankind has always had a strange relationship with foxes – weaving so many stories and fables around them. The fascinated male gaze has often fallen upon the female of the species: the vixen – so distrusted for her cunning savagery as a hunter and yet so beguiling in her lithe beauty.

Markús Guðjónsson (2053) '*Stories We Tell Ourselves*'

And so enter the vixen packs. Each cub would now imprint, from the moment its cute little eyes opened, onto an individual decoy officer to be trained and controlled and thus respond in an instant to their commands and theirs alone. What could possibly go wrong?

Andre P. Berteau (2070) '*The Way of Many Things*'

Decoy

noun, (dee-koi, doh-koi) *from Dutch: de kooi, literally: the cage.*

model or replica, esp wildfowl, traditionally used by hunters to lure wild birds within shooting range.

person used to lure another person or animal into a trap. Example: a police officer in disguise.

One

There are no stars out there tonight. Through the many layers of glass, Bruno Mastriano looks down on the unfamiliar, snowbound sector of the city, all laid out before him like the negative of its other half.

He's the last one left in the waiting area; in the window's reflection, a line of empty chairs is superimposed across the mountains in the distance. He drops his gaze to look at his face in the glass. Beneath his highlighted brow, his features merge into the night sky; there are shadows where his eyes should be.

Despite everything, he's admiring the effect, would paint himself like this if he could paint: his gaze both seeing and unseen. Hadn't he always been that figure – the outsider, the onlooker? People never fail to sense that there's something odd about him no matter how hard he tries to disguise it.

Left with no devices – not even his stud – Bruno can't guess at the time. The pain in his body has been building and at the same time it's become more localised to the back of his neck, his left shoulder and a broad diagonal band across his chest. He wants to take another of those painkillers but it can't be time, not yet.

That might have been it for him tonight – the end of everything on just some ordinary Tuesday night. The thought makes his stomach contract and the awful trembling starts up again; he has to lean in further to feel the solidness of the wall holding him back.

He watches his reflection shake its head. The two of them wouldn't have been out here in the first place if someone in his year hadn't lied to Krista Sigurðardóttir for some sick reason of their own.

He shuts his eyes but it's no good – it's there still, repeating over and over in his mind.

He'd been delighted, not far short of amazed, when she'd invited him back to her home. 'My folks are away,' she'd told him as they walked in. She hadn't wasted much time before showing him her grandfather's XKR Jaguar, untouched for years but fuelled up, just sitting in its pristine, heated garage like it had been waiting there for him, begging to escape.

'I heard you know how to drive one of these,' she'd said, fiddling with the ends of her ponytail the way he'd seen her do in the lectures they share, smoothing it down hand over hand. Right then and there he could have told her the truth.

She'd opened the door so he could sit in the driver's seat. Gripping the wheel that steers the machine, he'd been overwhelmed by all the past energy running through him. Krista had chosen that exact moment to get in beside him and he'd worried she might notice how much his hands were shaking.

Turned out the technique involved was easy enough. Next thing, they were out on the old highway and he was enjoying the roughness of the ride, having to wrestle the brute round the more difficult corners, loving the incessant bass from the Zor Savage track turned up high. Beside him, Krista had been singing along and not quite reaching the high notes. Fat snowflakes began to come straight for them out of the darkness; those old-style wipers were struggling to clear each new layer before it rebuilt across the screen.

They were approaching the very edges of the Free Zone with nothing – no lights or barriers – to stop them venturing beyond. Unconcerned, he turned the heating up to maximum. Krista was still squirming to the beat, her exposed thighs mesmerizing him. So many hitherto undreamed-of possibilities to distract him and so, yes, maybe for a while back then he'd forgotten there was no collision avoidance system on those old petrol vehicles.

Bruno props both his elbows on the windowsill though the movement stabs at his right side. It hurts more each time he inhales. Up this close, his breath mists the glass and then dissipates; for a moment he's fascinated by the way it blurs and then slowly reveals his mouth.

Damnit: even if he shuts his eyes it keeps playing on a loop.

I'm alive. His first thought – a primal concern – in the shock of utter and total darkness. *Am I? How do I know for sure?* He'd smelt the stench of escaping petrol – such a reassuring proof of life, at least at first. Then panic; a blind battle with the buckle of the strap restraining him; stabs of pain everywhere as he'd forced his weight against the door, freeing his legs to kick at it over and over until he could finally push it upright like a hatch; the ragged edges of metal had cut deep into his hands as he hauled himself out.

Bruno stares down at the bandages covering his hands like oversized mittens, at the blue strips wound round to keep them in place. It shames him now that he hadn't thought about Krista – not at first anyway; not until he was sure of himself, standing back and looking from outside at the way her granddad's upside-down car had become part of the tree.

The muscles in his legs start to twitch, willing him to act. He knows he has to get out of this room; out of this waiting around with the pressure building in his head.

He grabs his jacket, the chair teetering backwards but not quite falling. On his way to the lifts, his trainers are a squelching rhythm against the shiny floor.

Down on the ground floor, he searches his pockets for anything that might have been left behind, and, just as before,
finds nothing except that crumpled note and a spare credit log
he knows to be nearly at zero. He offers it up to the over-lit
machines and finds there's just enough to buy a bitter tea to
wash down the next two pills.

Then, with no obvious alternative, he takes himself straight
back up to the twelfth floor, back to sitting half out of that
chair, back to looking out at that grey-scale section of the city;
that sad reflection in the glass.

Succumbing to the dry heat and, despite the hardness of
the plastic and the awkward angle of his limbs, Bruno drifts
into sleep.

Two

From the darkness a lone figure materializes. Slender: the slightness of a woman; her breath rising to a misty halo around her head. The heels of her boots are striking the ground in regular, determined blows that ricochet off the derelict buildings on either side.

Already, she's so close his only choice is to flatten himself against a brick pier.

She passes him by unseen or unacknowledged. He exhales at last, could get away now and yet, drawn by curiosity, he follows. The stench of decomposition hits as she leads him into an alleyway. Up ahead, a streetlight illuminates the snow that's fallen in drifts across the pathway.

Hardly slowing her pace, she strides on through. On reaching clear ground, her footsteps ring out once more, hitting the pavement in the exact, same, jarring rhythm – she's announcing her presence.

He reads her thoughts: she's telling herself to forget the moves and counter-moves that have led to this moment. None of that matters now. She's even pleased to see those developing silhouettes – the burly figures solidifying at the end of the alley to block her way. More of them line up right behind. She doesn't falter, carries on walking towards them at the same, unhurried pace.

They advance to meet her, their differing statures high-lighted under the acid glare of the light. It's too late now: a mechanism has been set in motion like a toy wound to near breaking point before release, leaving no control over where it might go or what it hits. She is no longer responsible.

Closer with every step, her opponents are backlit, length-ened by their own shadows.

Loitering behind them in the darkness, he waits for what must come.

Like a starting bell, he hears the run of steel as she pulls her weapon from its sheath. The blade rises high in the air then flashes in its downward arc.

Weapons fire back; a burning cloud detonates all around her and yet that singular blade continues to rise and fall, scything a path through flesh; reaping and releasing cries of agony.

Until it stops.

Motionless, she stands upright in the midst of the carnage, bends her head to stare down at the slow, crimson tide coalescing around her boots. Her whole body shudders.

Seconds pass before she inhales again.

A skulk of vixens emerges from the shadows to surround her. One of them raises its snout, turns its ears and then the whole of its sleek head towards him. Its glowing retinas pierce the distance that separates them.

Blade still in hand, she straightens her back and then her cloaked head turns in his direction, seeing or sensing him there – the only witness.

He shrinks back. Though his line of sight is blocked, his mind's vision continues to watch her gloved hand wipe the gore from the blade before she hooks it into place at her back.

Looking up from their prey, ears pricked, the foxes wait. At her signal they part then slink away with their bloodied trophies, flowing out like mercury into the abandoned streets.

Under the streetlight, she throws off her hood to reveal a shock of auburn hair. Then she walks on.

Her footsteps resume the same, steady, heartbeat rhythm; each blow echoing down the alleyway as her outline softens and then dissolves into the night air.

Three

The room is in darkness, cold at this hour, though Nero Cavallo is bathed in sweat, his eyes rolling beneath closed lids.

His stud flashes red on the bedside table; its strident note bores a hole in his consciousness. Still wrestling sleep and more, Nero fumbles to attach the device to his ear and listen.

'On my way,' he says.

The shower coughs into life. Water jets programed to progress from hot to blood heat instead begin a sub-zero assault on every part of his body. Nero cuts it short, slaps himself warm and then air-dries while he rubs at his scalp and thinks through this change to his weekend plans. No time to shave. His mirror face tells him the dark rings beneath his eyes are becoming a permanent fixture.

A desolate collection of clapped-out partygoers are sprawled out in the expressway's pod, their smudged, sour faces averted. He can't help but smell their sweat, the stench of alcohol on their breath.

The train jolts a little as it emerges from the high tunnel and, once again, a vast sea of lights spreads out beneath him. Nero surveys the impressive spectacle of Eldísvík's ever-glowing, ever-growing Central Business District. On the skyline, he can just make out the bulk of G.Therm Corp with its plumes of steam white against the blue-black of the sky. The span of the new Hamrar Bridge is illuminated; its reflection dancing in the water as it broadens out into the black depths of the fjord.

To his right the Orange Zone is a whiteout; a permafrost ring that surrounds the southern half of the city. Above it all sit the snow-clad mountains, their peaks like giant, white-sheeted ghosts floating over the metropolis. He can just make out a pink glow on the horizon caused by the latest volcanic activity – the living heart in those mountains.

This is his city, or at least the one he is officially a citizen of, and yet, even after all these years, not quite home.

For a moment, he studies his own reflection in the window – judging himself as a stranger might. He'd say this person looks older – early forties even. Beneath the angle of his hat, his hair is merging into the dark sky.

The briefing had been an all-personal message and, well, brief. It seems one of the decoy agents, an unidentified female, has gone rogue. Initial evidence points to a single woman being responsible for nothing short of a massacre and, what's more, in the Double Red. It beggars belief that, working alone and at night, she'd been able to penetrate the very core of the exclusion zones. The woman, if indeed it was a woman, had shown extraordinary courage, or madness. More likely both.

Leifsson's administration will be quick to interpret what's happened as a lone-wolf scenario and they'll be keen to stick to that narrative unless any evidence to the contrary becomes undeniable.

To carry out a proper investigation, his department will need to conduct a thorough examination of the crime scene and that would mean entering those zones for the first time in his career. Will they be allowed in? The prospect excites and scares him in equal measure.

Fully awake now, Nero's stomach audibly rumbles. The workings of the Decoy Department have always been a bit of a mystery to the rest of DSD. Homicide has far fewer dealings with them than Organized Crime or Narcotics and even they are kept at arm's length from the individual decoy agents. All very cappa e spada – a cloak and dagger operation. Despite the present circumstances, Nero can't help but smile at the aptness of the expression.

The head of the young woman next to him slumps against his shoulder. Not wanting to wake her, he resists the pressure until, with a long intake of breath, she changes her position.

Each decoy must surely undergo regular psychological testing given the stressful nature of their work. Shouldn't someone have noticed the first hints of insubordination or psychosis in this individual long before it came to this?

He requests a summary of the archived material on the Decoy Initiative and his left lens flashes with a steady stream of intel. Nero rubs away at the scar on his forehead – it's way too early for all this.

Since his superior's abrupt and unexplained departure, Nero is, by default, Homicide's most senior officer. This will be his first time in charge of a high-profile case. It isn't going to be easy with such a depleted team. Ordinarily, they'd do thorough background checks on all the victims but getting any kind of information on the people she'd just slaughtered is going to be a challenge.

Reaching his halt, Nero steps down into a snowstorm. It still surprises him that the weather in this city can change with the blink of an eye. Every day you had to be prepared for all and every eventuality. Walking on, head bowed against the weather's assault, he switches to audio and a faster narration speed.

It's a mockery of a coffee. Nero hates buying it from the yawning all-night vendor; hates more those re-cy cups that survive like cockroaches. He mourns his usual espresso.

'Enough. Basta!' he says, to the narrator in his ear. The coffee man looks up. 'Sorry, I didn't mean you.' The man continues to scowl.

Giant snowflakes are turning and spinning, catching the light spilling into the street from the glass atrium of the DSD building. Nero wishes that, for a short while at least, the district heating didn't always melt them on impact.

Inside it's all noise and jostling. As they funnel into the lifts, he bumps into Rustler. 'You look like death warmed up, Cavallo,' Rustler says, not bothering to stifle a yawn. 'Smart money says this is all crap. Just a drill to keep us on our feet.'

Nero soft-punches Rustler's ample gut: 'Got a fair point, I'd say.'

'If they're right, I'll be first in the queue to throttle our illustrious governor.'

Like always, Nero's insides lurch as the lift drops. With everyone else, he shuffles along the corridor into Central Administration and then on into the largest of the briefing rooms.

The air inside is already stale and dense with sweat. Nero recognises a few people from Communications and Public Relations and is more than a little irritated that the governor has seen fit to brief all departments together. They're wasting valuable time here.

Leifsson himself is standing in the centre of the line-up waiting to brief the room. Aside from the usual expensive tailoring, the man is wearing his best cometh-the-hour expression. The Tech boys have been busy – there are multiple shots of this gore-fest on the walls behind the speakers; none of it easy to swallow on an empty gut.

The boss waits for the commotion to die down. Full head of hair, six-eight and tight-bound like salami – since the recent, hurried departure of the Chief of Police, along with his three most senior officers, Leifsson is proving more hands-on than a dockside masseur on a Saturday night.

A loud cough from the governor and the thirty-five men and women in the room fall silent in the same beat.

'Apologies for the wake-up call, folks.' Leifsson doesn't bother to sound sincere. 'As you can see, we had quite an incident at approximately 03:00 this morning.' He turns to the images on the wall behind him. 'These are the first visuals available from East Nineteen – right inside the Double Red. The next few have been enhanced. If I run the sequence on, you can see human remains being dragged out into the Orange Zone, and finally deposited right here in the Free Zone – in the heart of our city.'

The complex schematic behind him shows a mass of body parts along with their final resting places.

A politician's long pause. 'The exact number of dead is uncertain at this stage. Forensic officers along with clean-up crews are working through them as fast as they can.'

He waits to aid digestion. 'All available satellite images suggest that one of our decoys illegally crossed two zone boundaries and was then –' he gestures to the horror show behind him, 'singlehandedly responsible for all this.'

A severed foot looks like it is rooted in Leifsson's left ear. Nero wishes he hadn't noticed; he turns away to hide his amused revulsion.

'The decoy in question is, or would appear to be, female, of slight build and an estimated 1.65 metres tall.' He beats the lectern with his fist. 'Not only did this individual contravene strict standing orders but her vixen pack ripped these people to shreds.'

Leifsson's voice slices through the resulting commotion. 'Due to our common interest in apprehending this decoy, we've been able to establish communications with certain PCI's – for the uninitiated in the room that means Persons of Considerable Interest – within the Double Red. I'm pleased to say a temporary truce is currently in operation to allow us to carry out our investigations.'

He shrugs to wipe the sweat from his forehead with his shirtsleeve. 'Okay, so first off, we need to have some idea how this whole thing could have happened.' Like a seasoned compere, he turns to introduce his line-up. 'Most of you will know Dr Arthur here – our Chief Psychologist. He works closely with our Decoy Training Department.'

Dr Arthur gives a mock salute. Unfortunately, the movement triggers an auto-zoom behind him into what looks like a section of liver.

'And this is Dr Magnúsdóttir from the Institute of Biological Research, along with her assistant Dr Ramirez.'

Magnúsdóttir half raises a hand; she doesn't bother to smile. Dr Ramirez looks like a sheep in the headlights.

'I've asked them here in order to address some of your more pressing questions.'

Dr Arthur is first to jump on this cue. His round, hairless face is reddened by the rosy glow coming from the gore right behind him. 'As yet, we have no idea how this individual could have slipped through our extensive background and psychological testing.'

The man must be well into his fifties but still his thin voice carries little natural authority. 'I'd like to remind everyone here that our lengthy and rigorous assessment procedures mean only the most outstanding 2% are accepted onto the full training decoy programme to begin the imprinting process with live animals. Less than half of these individuals will display the remarkable skills and perseverance it takes to become a serving decoy.'

Hagalín, Leifsson's deputy, cuts in from the side: 'Okay, so we get that these people are the best of the best, but we haven't heard a thing yet about these rogue vixens. In my opinion, they could pose far more of a threat to law-abiding citizens. I mean, how come these fokking animals are now tearing people limb from limb?'

Dr Magnúsdóttir raises a finger to answer then waits for

the requisite attention. Nero has met her a couple of times before, though only briefly. She seems even tinier standing next to Leifsson. Though she looks older, he knows she's only in her late-forties. Her clothes are neat but willfully unstylish and the severe cut of her grey hair is certainly doing her no favours.

Magnúsdóttir waits for complete silence. When she finally speaks, her voice is barely raised, forcing them all to lean forward as they strain to hear her. 'Let me begin by explaining that *if* the imprinting processes is carried out *correctly* with each and every individual decoy, the implanted wolf genes ensure that each vixen will obey their every command.' Though clearly agitated, she's careful to keep her delivery slow and calm. 'They must work together to achieve an outcome that is *always and without exception* dictated by their pack leader: the decoy.'

Someone in the back – Delaney from district two – raises a hand. 'Remind me again – why is it you use only female foxes?' He sneaks a conspiratorial smile to his cronies before adding: 'Have you got something against the male of the species, Doctor?' There's some sniggering around him.

Magnúsdóttir knows better than to respond to innuendo. Her sigh is all exasperation. 'The short answer to your question is that, as with so many tasks that require a subtlety of response, the females are simply much better at doing precisely what the decoys require of them.'

There are a few chuckles from the audience while Magnúsdóttir takes a long, steadying sip from the water glass in front of her. 'Our vixens must also display a particular aptitude for self-sufficiency when "off duty", as it were, and so remain unobtrusive to all but the most expert of observers.'

Nero is frustrated that, so far, he's learning very little. It's time someone insisted on an unequivocal answer to a question. Projecting his voice to its fullest, he asks: 'Working in the Homicide Department, we understand *human* frailties only too well. If these vixens are, as I understand it, trained to use only necessary force, how come this pack disemboweled these double-bad men and then spread their remains around a dozen zip codes?'

Dr Magnúsdóttir's head is shaking before he's finished. 'I would remind you that, at this time, it's unclear what their precise role was in this incident. However, if, as the evidence suggests, the vixens did predate these bodies, I simply have no idea how this could have happened. It *should* be utterly impossible for them to override so fundamental a part of their training.' She looks at the governor. 'We laid down all the necessary procedures for *your* Training Department to oversee. If followed *correctly* and to the letter, I can categorically state that such behaviour will never occur.'

She performs a sharp, accusing turn to glower at Dr Arthur.

Arthur raises his shoulders and his voice to meet her challenge. 'Let me assure you all that, without exception, we at the D.T.D. meticulously adhere to and record all stages of each individual animal's training – exactly as prescribed. Both the vixens and the decoys undergo the *precise* programme of testing and reinforcement you yourself approved, Dr Magnúsdóttir – to every last detail.'

After glaring at Magnúsdóttir, Arthur turns to the governor. 'With absolutely no exceptions.' Nero notices the man's hands are trembling. Is this from anger or could it be something else?

Magnúsdóttir's slight frame stiffens though she's doing her best to look unruffled. Without raising her voice an iota, she says: 'The possibility of one vixen slipping through the regime we recommended has been calculated as vanishingly small. The possibility of the entire pack turning like this is, well – ' She raises both hands in appeal. 'It's just not possible.' She waits a beat. 'Unless – '

Nero doesn't buy her apparent spontaneity of thought; this all sounds a bit rehearsed. 'Unless this decoy managed some-how to introduce a regime of parallel training. Conceivably, these animals could have been drilled to execute – '

A few sniggers from her audience prompt her. 'Pardon me – I should have said *perform* a more extreme change in behaviour, which could be switched at her command,' she snaps her fingers, 'between what Jung termed in humans as "the persona" and "the shadow". Putting it in layman's terms – from Dr Jekyll to Mr Hyde.'

She doesn't quite hide a smile of admiration. 'To date, it has never been shown that animals can, as it were, compartmentalise in such an extreme way. To attain this behaviour with a whole pack would be a formidable challenge.'

She takes another sip of water – creating a dramatic pause. 'In my opinion, this is not something an untrained individual could achieve without assistance from someone with expert knowledge. In any case, it's hard to imagine how such an alteration in these animals' training regime could have remained undetected by a single person in Dr Arthur's team.'

Dr Arthur's reedy voice cuts in. 'That inference – or should I use the word accusation – is entirely speculative and completely unsubstantiated.'

In the uproar that follows, Chan – the trainee only recently assigned to bolster Nero's homicide team – holds up an unsteady hand.

The governor silences the room and then nods his consent to her question.

'Can I just ask why you can't find out which of the decoys was in that area at the time? Or alternatively, use satellite data to track this woman's subsequent movements?'

Someone groans.

'No, no – that's a fair question.' Leifsson smiles down at her. 'Who here would like to enlighten our young friend – Chan is it?'

Nero cringes at the man's condescension. Lúter, his sergeant, obliges with an answer. 'The decoys have to operate deep undercover, so they can't be discovered and then targeted. Official knowledge of their locations would jeopardise that.'

Leifsson can't resist taking over to demonstrate how well briefed he is. 'Sadly, this has proved necessary to prevent any *leakage* of information to the undesirables operating in the Orange Zone.'

Rustler doesn't squander the opportunity to gripe. 'Back-tracking through satellite images ought to be doable but our department's budget has been cut and cut again. Our sat-coverage is a joke. The data available to us has more black holes than deep space. The good citizens of the Free Zone would piss their pants if they only knew–'

Leifsson interrupts. 'Let's all try to focus here. We have people working on this as we speak. However, this decoy seems to have known the exact time to make her move.' He glares at Vasiliev – Rustler's boss – before he asks: 'Did she just get lucky?' Leifsson points a suspicious finger at the room. 'Or did she already have precise information about the satellite coverage in that area at that time? Knowledge that enabled her to hide her movements before and after the event.'

He gives his audience a wry smile and then wags his finger. 'In any case, folks, she slipped up.'

Behind him, multiples of one single image fill the entire wall. Leifsson stands aside to draw attention to the outline of the grey and grainy figure caught off to one side. The woman's bright red hair is clearly visible.

'As you can see, the light levels were particularly poor,' the governor tells them. 'This image is as clear as we can make it – although that's still being worked on. We were unlucky with the angle and, of course, the hair could be a wig.'

The briefing goes on for a further twenty minutes, though Nero learns nothing more. People around him are beginning to get restless.

Sensing the developing mood of his audience, the governor plants both feet apart like he's ready to hit a winner down the line. 'The Decoy Initiative has been one of the most successful crime-fighting programs in our city's short history.'

The man puffs up his impressive chest. 'It's undoubtedly made the Orange Zone safer for the people living there and, in turn, it's helped to make Eldísvík one of the most peaceful and secure cities in the world today.' He looks at his audience from right to left. 'I have every confidence that, working together, we'll catch this insane woman before she can do any more damage.'

The lectern almost topples as the governor strikes it with his fist. 'This administration will not tolerate acts of sedition. We will show no toleration for any attempt to undermine the security and stability each and every one of our citizens has a right to enjoy. Ladies and gentlemen, I thank you for your attention. And now I leave you to get on with the job of catching this damned woman.'

Nero shakes his head. Leifsson's up for re-election in the summer and couldn't resist this opportunity to tone up his rhetoric. Turning to go, the governor raises his fist again in a defiant salute – a gesture worthy of an old-style communist.

As the room empties around him, Nero continues to stare at the single, blurred image of the decoy, at the slightness of her silhouette. She wanted to be seen, of that he has no doubt. That red hair glows in the greyness that surrounds her; how frail and vulnerable she would appear to be if you didn't know better.

He observes a moment's silent respect for this woman's outstanding bravery. His stud buzzes with a new data download and then bleeps softly to indicate visual mode is available. He's seen enough. If they don't stifle this particular initiative, they all might end up simmering in the same pot.

Four

The down-force frees Nero at the last second. Lift doors open onto a confusion of day-shift workers. He weaves a way through their noise and insistence to exit the building. He walks rapidly, his footsteps splattering melt-puddles edged with the building's fugitive light.

The sky is a dark lid over the awakening city. Though the freezing air stings his face, it's a welcome change. Despite regulations, Nero removes the stud from his ear and drops it into his breast pocket. The snowfall is lighter than before – a few delicate flakes dancing in the wind.

He strides on against the wind, begins to enjoy the sensation of loosening his limbs and untangling his thoughts. Early-shifters pass him, each one preoccupied with their stud messages.

Further on, he passes a line of shopkeepers tugging up heavy grills to reveal their colourful enticements. An ancient street-cleaning machine trundles past, spraying and sucking into every corner, as it searches out yesterday's detritus.

The dark lozenge of a patrol vehicle approaches him silently from behind, then glides on down the central reservation. It comes to a halt at the junction before turning left and disappearing amongst the high-rises.

The café's steamed-up windows help to soften the drabness of the city in winter. Better for having eaten, Nero stares straight ahead while savouring his second espresso. He likes to sit here at his usual table and let everything swirl around, go whichever way it chooses, and then lean back to let it settle into a fuller picture. It's always better to take this time-out somewhere he can't be accused of idleness.

Every few minutes the dragon sounds from the coffee machine rise to dominate the room before subsiding into a brief and fragile silence. He breathes in the wholesomeness of fresh baking while staring at nothing, unaware of how time is passing.

There are obvious places to start their investigation, but he'd be surprised if this decoy hadn't already thought of the obvious. The crime scene in East Nineteen has been a no-go for longer than he's been in the force. It's known to be the headquarters of the legendary Pearson syndicate and their extensive operation; this decoy chose to take her grievances to the very top.

Nero swallows the remains of his coffee then sips at the water that his body prefers. He keeps coming back to what Dr Magnúsdóttir had said about the training of this particular vixen pack – surely that has to hold the key to this investigation.

Two brown eyes are watching him from under one of the empty tables – four-year-old Joey in hiding from his mother. Behind the counter, Lucia is too busy with her work to have noticed his absence.

Lucia smiles over at him and then breaks off from her task to come over and clear his table. She offers to get him something else. He sees her concern that the small room is now beginning to fill up and every seat is needed.

She's right – he's been sitting here too long. As he gets up to leave, Nero bends to pick up a stray toy soldier and slip it into the boy's sticky grasp.

Behind the mountains, the sun hasn't yet risen. The sky has now cleared and the moonlight seems at odds with all the artificial lights; it's producing a strange tension in the air.

While walking back, Nero attaches his stud and his left eye begins to scroll through the waiting intel. He listens to the account of the sergeant in charge of the maglev armoureds. The sergeant's name is Ramón. In the small hours, they'd been ordered to transport and then guard the team from Forensics as they ventured into the Double Red. He describes at some length their struggle to get the vehicles to hover above those crumbling, pockmarked rails. Ramón had reconnoitered the kill-zone himself. His formal report, like the prelims from Forensics, paint an ugly picture.

Virtual and actual reconstructions of the victims are still in progress. Nero studies the schematic showing the routes of the various body parts and the pattern of dispersal.

Though the physical clean-up has been completed, it will take far longer to erase people's memories; to forget that severed foot abandoned on a walkway or the human spleen hanging from an air vent, to close their eyes and not still see that clump of hair, still attached to its scalp, clogging the street gully.

Sleet comes out of nowhere to sting his face. Up ahead, the lights of the DSD building shine through the sculptural planes of the atrium: the visible tip of the labyrinthine construction below. The building was meant to be reasonably inconspicuous when it was constructed in the late 40's. At the time, the bulk of the population still drove by in their individual vehicles hardly noticing a thing. Once the city became totally grid-locked, everything had to change. Walking past it now, all the steel barriers surrounding the place would hardly fool a fool.

The lobby's ret-scanners give Nero's world a rosy hue for a couple of seconds. He swears aloud when his lift lurches and, not for the first time, comes to a halt between floors. Maintenance spending is too invisible to be high on Leifsson's list of priorities. Nero presses every button and waits. After a few minutes, there's a gut-wrenching drop before it slows for the final two floors.

Someone has finally fixed his name to the top of the glass door. He notices they've spelt Cavallo with only one l.

The only thing he can say about his new room is that it's functional. Nero sits down at his desk and again wonders exactly where he should start. He can see Kass approaching, the glass in her spectacles streaming the corridor's overhead lights. Her full name is Arnfríður Kassöndrudóttir. When she joined the department four years ago, she'd told everyone to just call her Kass. Is she hiding behind those thick frames of hers? He once asked her why she wore them. She'd laughed it off. He remembers her exact words: "I've learnt not to trust anyone with a laser aimed at my face."

Kass gives the open door a token knock as she enters. She's piled high with a stack of cardboard folders, 'I've collected some background on the Double Red, Inspector.' She dumps it all on his desk.

'On paper?' Nero can't hide his amusement.

'Well, you know me – I like to be thorough.'

'Okay.' Nero shows some respect. 'Anything that says boo?'

'This stuff goes way back – some of it's not even in English; you'll have to pass them through the translator. The murder scene – if that's what we're calling it – is in the very first area to be designated Red, which was way back at the end of the 30's. The exclusion zones were then extended and redefined in 2049.'

She hands Nero a crude paper diagram of the area. The zone within a zone looks like a dark red pupil in a pale red eye: the eye is looking to the left.

'It was built way back as high-rise housing for the workforce with connecting alleyways. Then a recycling company bought up the whole area.' She opens the largest file and spreads out some of the documents. 'The directors at the time were Messrs Thomas, Keen, and *Pearson*. They flattened a central section but left some of the surrounding buildings as offices and cheap accommodation. These reports suggest drug processing and wholesaling; forged documentation; small-arms warehousing and so on.'

'A veritable smorgasbord of delights for the career criminal,' Nero strokes the growing stubble on his face.

'It's hard to see why the prosecutors back then wouldn't green light prosecutions with all this evidence available. I'm smelling a bit of a rat here.'

'I guess there's no point in us going down that particular tunnel, Sergeant – not after all this time. Let's fast-forward to the past few decades.'

Kass switches from paper to her stud's log. The blue light from the Holo-Pro plays across her pale, upturned face. 'Couple of patrolmen were murdered there way back in 2041. A handful of arrests during the mid-forties but each time charges were later dropped. Same pattern over and over, until it was finally designated Double Red. The Decoy Programme classified it as a point 0.1 from the start, which roughly translates as "we give up". Last night was the only *reported* incident in that section since its classification.'

Staring at that faded red eye, Nero focuses out for a moment before jumping to his feet. 'Thanks for that.' He waits for her to meet his gaze. 'Look, Kass, personally, I think it's essential to examine the crime scene for ourselves. I'll be asking for volunteers to accompany me into the Double Red.'

Nero rubs the same spot on the forehead while he outlines his plans: how he believes they can enter and, more importantly, leave both zones with the minimum of risk. 'Let me be clear: I'm giving each and every Homicide officer a genuine opt-out on this one.' Her skin is so pale he can see the veins running underneath. 'No photon will be held to your head. I mean, it could be–'

'Please count me in, sir,' she says.

Nero nods. 'Good. Thanks, Kass.'

He bundles up the heavy documents from his desk into her arms. 'In the meantime, get onto Foster, find out how they're progressing with access to the Defence satellite images. I'm guessing the co-operation will be minimal for something they're likely to classify as a "civil" crime.'

Lúter and Rashid stand side by side in the cramped space. Rashid's recently shaved his curly hair to stubble. The man's broad neck supports a wide, square jaw and yet his eyes seem almost feminine in their dark liquidity.

Nero has no sooner started when Rashid interrupts. 'I want in on this. Absolutely.' He whistles long and low. 'The woman took it to a double red, alone, and still survived. I got to see for myself where all this mayhem went on.'

'So we'll be going in there quietly but not covertly?' Lúter's pale eyebrows knit together, his slightly pockmarked face is all concentration: 'And you're saying our exposure before and after will be kept to the minimum?' He keeps his hands clasped behind his back until Nero has stopped talking.

Nero waits while Lúter continues to stare at the floor for a moment. Then he raises his head and gives Nero a thin, determined smile. 'Okay, you can count me in, sir.'

'I can see you have reservations and that's understandable in your situation.'

'Like you, Inspector, I'd hate to become a target. The people out there have just lost their colleagues – their close friends perhaps; they might welcome the opportunity to take it out on somebody.'

'You're right: it's a considerable risk and not one I'd try to minimize. You've got your family to consider. I'd completely understand if you wanted to pass on this.'

'No,' Lúter says, 'I've said I'm in and, if you don't mind, I'll stick to my decision.'

On his way back from Surveillance, Nero passes their new trainee, Chan, in the corridor. 'Can I have a word?' he says, shepherding her into his office.

Predictably, she is over-excited by the prospect of the recon trip. For a moment he thinks she might be about to hug him. 'Oh, and I've been reading up on these vixens,' she tells him. 'Do you know why they chose the red fox?' Before he can answer, she tells him. 'Because of their size; some can weigh around 18 kilograms and be more than one and a half metres from tail to nose.' Was he ever this keen? 'Once they'd escaped the fur farms, they bred like Dubia roaches, started colonising the countryside and from there moved into the city for its easy pickings. They've driven out all the poor old Arctic foxes. I feel a bit sorry for them. I mean it doesn't –'

Nero raises a hand and she finally stops talking. He sobers his own face, makes himself look into her extraordinary eyes. 'We'll be facing very real dangers out there, Constable,' he says. 'This is not a decision you should take lightly.'

His words do nothing to dampen her enthusiasm.

The corridor leading to Administration is over-run by earnest types in 3,500 credit suits. Nero waits in a long line to see the governor. Amie, Leifsson's PA, throws him a pained look as an apology.

When he's finally admitted into Leifsson's office, the governor remains hunched over his desk, his meaty hands supporting the weight of his head. He barely looks up. The stench of the man worries at Nero's nostrils.

'They assure me these damn things last for two years – minimum.' Leifsson picks up a stud from his mahogany desk and waves it in Nero's face like he's some errant salesman.

'Damn thing got so hot it's actually scorched my ear. Guess there might be a metaphor in that somewhere.'

When he turns his head to the side, Nero obliges him with a concerned look, though he can see nothing amiss. The governor waves him away.

Nero has to wait out another techno-rant before he can run through the details of his proposed recon of the crime scene.

Leifsson remains distracted. 'Sure, go take a good look – but easy on the heroics and try not to lose anybody, Cavallo. They tolerated Forensics earlier; don't go doing anything stupid to antagonise the natives.'

With a brief nod, the governor agrees to his request for an armoured vehicle.

'As you know, there's almost no contact between individual decoys and our department,' Nero tells him. 'It would be useful if one of their decoys could accompany us. If we're to figure out how this could have happened, we really need to understand more about their working methods. We need to understand what it's like to– '

'Okay, okay – I get your point, Inspector.'

Leifsson pours himself a glass of what looks like water but isn't. 'I don't need to remind you it goes against the usual protocols. I'll do my best – speak to the Commanders myself. Even if they agree in principle, it might prove impossible at such short notice.'

Another shrug tells Nero that, in any event, Leifsson has little faith their activities will turn up anything of significance but, as always, the man isn't averse to covering all the bases to protect his own backside.

In the same spirit, Nero runs through his choices for the recon team. Should he have included Chan after all?

On that topic, the chief's response is predictable. 'Ah – that girl who asked awkward questions in the briefing. And you're choosing her for operational reasons, right? And not because of the woman's more obvious attractions?' His large hands mime a crude outline of Chan's supposed anatomy. 'I mean—'

'Her evaluations, so far, have been outstanding,' Nero tells him. 'I just assumed you wouldn't object to the department nurturing new talent.'

'Okay, okay Cavallo – take her with you if you want, just spare me the mission statement. I'll buzz you through the satellite stuff once the military have released it.'

Done with him already, the governor activates his monitor's Holo-Pro. 'Should be a piece of cake once we have those to track her subsequent movements and locate her current position. There'll be no need to involve your department in the arrest and, before you ask,' he gives Nero a long look, 'I'll make it clear they should use only *necessary* force.'

He peers through the projection at Nero. 'Would you believe the damn media are already swarming over this. So much for News Management – this place is a bloody sieve. I'm told social media is buzzing with suggestions that the decoys themselves are the result of in-utero modifications.' He throws up his hands. 'Apparently, they're reckoned to be some kind of hybrid of man and animals – or so the theory goes. These nut-cases actually believe we're using goddam chimeras!'

The governor's face contorts. 'Oh, and then we have the Neo-Reds. I kid you not – they're calling this woman an *Avenging Angel.*' Leifsson does that parenthesis bunny-ears thing with his fingers that Nero loathes. 'At the same time, they're expressing moral outrage over close-ups of the body parts found in their own backyards.'

Leifsson shakes his head. 'I have the SSAS on standby. Once I've heard from Defence they'll go in. With luck, we'll have her in chains in time for the early evening briefings.'

Such a swift outcome would, of course, give the governor's poll ratings just the boost they need. Leifsson will be sure to freshen up, change his crumpled shirt and exorcise that shadow haunting his chin. The old pro will look humble enough to disguise the high he's riding on by modestly praising all the officers involved.

Leaving the governor's office, Nero finds he's hoping the military will refuse to supply those satellite images. It must be all the pheromones circulating in Leifsson's office that now have *him* thinking like a second-rate politician.

Five

Blinded by the intensity of the light, Bruno senses someone or some *thing* is approaching. Desperate to get away, escape into the darkness, he finds he can't move, not even a finger. The beam passes through his clothes and skin, enters his blood and bones. His gut tightens; he can't breathe, his heart is mad-pumping in his chest. A low vibration is coming from somewhere underneath his feet, like he's aboard a moving vehicle. What can he taste? Something metallic. He swallows and instantly there's a shooting pain in his neck.

He shakes himself into consciousness, struggles to open his eyes and make sense of where he is – the chair he's in, the empty waiting room. How long has he been here? Under the flickering overheads every object glares back with too much clarity; even the bruises on his arms are turning a lurid rainbow of colours. The dry air has parched his throat and that rumble is still there. It could be a generator.

Not just a dream – no it had to be a warning; he's sure of that much. He tries to draw his body back into the chair but can't find a comfortable position, can't rest however much he twists around.

In frustration, he stumbles to his feet, rotates his left shoulder until it catches on pain. Only then does he recall the full horror of what's happened. Oh God. If he could just bend over and make himself retch: puke up everything that feels so bad, so rotten, inside him and then straighten up to a different reality than the one he's stuck with right now.

What time is it? Anything could be happening to Krista in the meantime. Why haven't they come to find him? Someone must know if she's okay or not.

His mood turns to anger and then determination. He strides to the end of the corridor, unaware of that involuntary curl of his fists, checking for any open door, peering into the dimmed-down wards where all he can hear is snoring.

There's no one around. He carries on searching until he's walked the whole length of the corridor to the lifts.

Back on the ground floor, it's still busy, though not packed out like it was earlier. He's forced to stand and wait in front of the main desk for the duty administrator to get off her stud, shifting his weight from one foot to the other in his impatience.

'Can you help me, please?' he pleads, when it's clear she's finally finished. She's twisting a strand of hair, prepared to give him only half her attention. Bruno repeats Krista's name several times; explains how he's been waiting for ages, swallowing back the self-pitying tears that are rising in his throat.

'And you are?'

'Bruno Mastriano: a friend. I was with her in the vehicle. Driving it. I need to know how she is.'

The woman's long look sizes him up. Finally, she nods an acknowledgement and puts in a call. The conversation goes on for some time and consists of numerous repetitions of "okay" and "no?" on her part. She even laughs out loud and long at something. 'You're kidding me, right?'

'See you later,' she finally concludes, hanging up to straighten her face in an instant and fix him with her tired, brown eyes: 'Okay, your friend's had her op and they've taken her up to Recovery.'

His relief is uncertain; he can't begin to relax without knowing she's going to be okay. 'So can I go and see her; just for a second?'

'Next-of-kin only at the moment, I'm afraid. And I'm guessing that's not you, right?' She looks away, already done with him, and begins to tidy some files into a stack. They're near the zone limit but what kind of rubbish hospital still uses paper records?

He stays exactly where he is, refuses to budge until she looks up at him again. 'Your friend's parents have just arrived and they're in with her. I'm guessing you're not going to be flavour of the month. Best thing you can do, son, is to go home and get some rest. Check in tomorrow: see if she's up to having other visitors.'

She picks up the stack and, clutching them to her ample breasts, walks away.

In that instant, Bruno is no longer angry: just dejected, rejected. He has no alternative except to do exactly as he's been told and leave the building.

Without a functioning stud he has no expressway pass, no credit line – nothing. Better then to start walking, keep moving until a solution comes to mind.

Bruno trudges on past security at the perimeter fence, right away from those lit towers. Beneath each streetlight the snow sparkles up at him. Ice particles are hitting him almost horizontally, stinging his cheeks and soaking his hair. He's forced to wipe his eyes repeatedly; it's a struggle to keep the bandages dry. He buttons up the strap at his neck then stuffs his exposed fingers into his pockets as far as the dressings will allow.

Nothing seems to be open, not even the scruffy drinking den on the junction with its groaning sign swinging wild. From its painted surface, a skinny dog stares down at him. 'You and me both,' he says, crossing the road.

They don't seem to have street signs this far out. The snow is so heavy he can't see any landmarks. Head down, Bruno concentrates only on getting through this. By the time he reaches a wider track, the bottoms of his jeans are soaking wet and water is creeping into his shoes.

It's some time before he stops again to look around. In the normal parts of the Free Zone, the ones he's familiar with, underground ducts melt the snow almost before it lands. Here, it's filled up the pitted tracks stretching out before him in all directions.

Everything seems less than real: the blank-faced, frozen-in-time buildings make him feel like a bit player on a movie set. Bruno doesn't know this sector at all; he can't even tell if he's now crossed into the zone boundary. Right now, he doesn't care much, except that he has to make a decision about which direction to head in.

As if on cue, a splashing Mitsubishi Tokugawa approaches. He can't see the occupants through its blackout windows. He gets the sense that he's being surveyed. Perhaps he should raise his thumb for a lift – like people used to.

Bruno is relieved when it moves on. He's shivering so much it's difficult to concentrate. Does he know anyone who lives this far out? What about Juri's mate, Keith? He'd found a crazy-cheap place that might not be that far from here. For his moving-in party, they'd caught the expressway to the last station on the line. Bruno can only remember waking up at noon the following day with his brain still wired and his limbs corpse-stiff from sleeping on the floor with only his rolled-up jacket for a pillow. There's no way he can check Keith is still living hereabouts, never mind find the address. Damn it, Juri would know straight away.

What was the name of the district? It was something like Haxaborg or Hugaborg? Looking towards the skyline, he still can't see a thing past the falling snow.

Then he's back to thinking about Krista; about how, once the patrolmen had got her out of there, she'd seemed perfectly all right. Sure, she was shaken up and there was that long cut on her leg and plenty of bruises, but otherwise she'd seemed okay.

As gently as he could, for both their sakes, he'd put his arm around her. When she'd squeezed his damaged hand, he'd winced, almost cried out. Then he'd felt the connection that told him of her relief, though she hadn't spoken a word.

The two patrolmen just wouldn't let up with their questions, going over and over everything while he worried about the car he'd just totalled and how much it might have been worth.

New lights had approached – more medics arriving in one of those cool ambulances with independent interior suspension. They'd set off for the hospital and he'd been distracted by how fast the thing could go; even on the rougher parts of the highway the interior stayed completely stable.

They'd talked about their lucky escape and how it would have been much worse if they'd hit that tree straight on. Yes, he'd been enjoying the ride, the excitement of it all, hadn't noticed at first that Krista had gone quiet. The medics asked her if she was okay and she'd said something about feeling dizzy.

The banter had stopped instantaneously, their expressions turning serious. Everything sped up, the blue lights danced in circles over the snow while the woman held a sensor against Krista's arm.

They'd wheeled her in ahead of him and more people came rushing over. Krista mumbled something about pain in her stomach and how it was getting worse and then how one of her shoulders really hurt. The doctor in charge kept rubbing at his chin, like he was stuck for ideas. He made Krista stand upright, even though she looked like she might faint, while he checked and rechecked her blood pressure.

A new doctor arrived and started asking the same damned questions. Bruno couldn't hear her answers because they'd drawn a curtain round her: a barrier to keep him out.

After a few minutes both doctors had emerged, walking off a little way, glancing back over their shoulders in Krista's direction while they conferred. The older one soon hurried back to her bedside and this time Bruno had heard him say too many positive things: 'Good. Yes. Right, that's fine. Well done,' in a tone you might use to reassure a small child or someone a bit simple. 'We're going to move you now, see if we can't make you a little more comfortable.'

They'd wheeled her bed over to the lifts, the doors closed and then she was gone. Bruno could only stand and watch the floor numbers rising.

'What about me?' he'd asked of no one in particular. 'I've got pain in my shoulder, in fact all over the place; why aren't they taking me up there too?'

The fat orderly had only smiled. 'Your results are all fine, young man. You'll feel a bit sore for a few days, that's all.' She'd dropped two of his pills into a plastic cup. 'These will help.' Wagging a finger, she'd said, 'Remember – you really mustn't drink any alcohol at all while you're taking these.'

'So, what's wrong with Krista? Where've they taken her?'

The orderly had leant in conspiratorially. 'Between you and me, the doctors are worried she might have some damage to her spleen.'

'Really?'

'Yes, really. They think your friend's shoulder pain might be caused by referred pain from her abdomen.'

He'd taken the meds from her, wished he hadn't dropped Biology so early; he had no frigging idea where a spleen was or what the hell it did.

'There's no chance of anything serious happening? I mean, she's not going to die or anything stupid like that, is she?'

Passing him some water, the orderly had said, 'If they're right, they will need to operate.' Seeing his panic, she'd squeezed his forearm. 'Your friend's in good hands. I'm sure she'll be just fine. Fortunately, a person can survive perfectly well without a spleen.'

Right now, out in the sheer density of this snow, Bruno's feeling strange: not exactly himself that's for sure. It might be down to those bloody pills. How many has he taken? He can't remember. The chattering noise in his head is coming from his teeth – they're knocking together like he's a cartoon character.

A flash of memory – that red-brown streak caught in the headlights for less than a second. A fox had leapt into the road; its eyes glowing, its head turning to stare directly at them. *That* was why he'd swerved: a bloody reflex.

He stops walking and stands quite still reliving the moment – the instinctive choice he'd made to preserve life. How fokking ironic; he kicks at the snow.

The wind is cutting right though his clothes. His anger begins to abate. He senses he's being watched: that somewhere in the shadows more than one pair of eyes are trained on him. At any moment someone or something could leap out at him. 'Come on, for Christ's sake get a grip here,' he urges himself out loud, pulling his body together and hunching deeper into his clothes. Which way now? Keith's place must be roughly south from here. It's not much of a plan but it's the only one he's got.

He turns left. The scattered apartment blocks he passes are all in darkness, every blind drawn tight. In one or two he sees a telltale flicker of light. Should he knock on one of those doors in the hope of being admitted? But no one sane would welcome a strange man into their home after dark. This island used to be full of stories about the Hidden People: normally invisible elves or trolls who live parallel lives alongside humans. He's heard lots of tales about how they come to the rescue of lost travellers and give them food and shelter for the night.

Bruno can't be certain how long he's been walking: time is playing lots of tricks on him tonight. As if on the ground in front of him, he keeps seeing Krista's ashen face through the hole in that shattered windscreen. That patrolman keeps repeating his warning. *'Careful now, this is petrol: it only takes one spark and it's boomf!'*

All at once it stops snowing. As the air clears he thinks he can make out someone else's half-filled tracks. Bruno begins to follow them. The full moon emerges from between the clouds to reveal the distinctive shape of the human footprints along with lots of smaller ones that must have been made by animals. Could be dog's prints or more sodding foxes. One beast had trotted almost in a straight line, while the rest cross and then re-cross the footprints. Further along their tracks diverge and they go their separate ways.

Shit, this isn't right. None of this is right. He almost cries aloud in frustration. If only he could already be on the other side of all this walking, already telling his mates this story. It would begin with something like: I did the stupidest thing…

He's taken more than a few wrong turns that's for sure. Miscalculated. At the moment he's heading towards a lit-up security block. This must be all wrong; he needs to focus – needs to reverse everything.

Though his legs are weary, he makes himself turn around. Fifty metres further on, there are more footprints. This time, they lead him down a long, narrow walkway between high walls. The end comes into sight and he's relieved to be out in the open again. More lights run alongside a security fence that surrounds what looks like a derelict factory block. There are dark star shapes on the broken windows. A dilapidated sign – *Sveinsson & Kjarval Ltd* – towers over a razor-wired entrance gate. Some distance away from the glare of the lights, he notices the lock on a propped-up section of the barrier fence is hanging loose.

At least this building might offer some kind of shelter for the rest of the night.

Pain stabs at his chest as he squirms through. Inside the fence, there is nothing but virgin snow in all directions. He trudges around each building in turn looking for a way in. At last he finds a door that's slightly ajar. Wincing with pain, he pulls on it until the gap is wide enough to squeeze through.

Inside, it's pitch black. He breathes in the dusty, damp air, the stench of urine and then, further on, the musk of animal spray. Unable to see more than shadows, his bare fingers feel their way along the side of a rough wall. Broken glass crunches beneath his feet.

After a few metres, the darker shape of a doorway swims before him. He passes through this into a short passageway that leads to an enormous space with moonlight shining through a row of high skylights. The floor is strewn with more broken glass along with a fresh dusting of snow. On the far side he sees a door.

This time it's locked. Beside it there's an old-fashioned keypad lock – of all things. He holds his bandaged right hand over the grid of numbers and letters and tries to empty his mind of all conscious thought, concentrates only on visualising the hand that's about to unlock it.

The hand belongs to a woman. Using her index finger, she depresses each key in turn. He enters her mind, follows as she presses each digit one after another.

R 7 7 H 3 9 0 1 8 B

No wait – that last one was the letter below – C

He repeats the sequence and then depresses the handle.

The door opens.

It's a small room; its window is still intact. The air in here seems warmer – although that could be wishful thinking. There's just enough fugitive light to pick out the large no-ticeboard that's covering most of one wall: a scattering of rectangular documents are pinned to it. To one side of that, he can see something that's raised up – it's a bed of sorts.

Bruno is shivering almost uncontrollably. What was the name of that girl in the stories who slept in other people's beds? Goldie somebody?

He doesn't hesitate, doesn't concern himself with who might normally sleep there and why. He flops down in relief and pulls the rough covers up and over his half-frozen body.

Six

All of them turn towards the low moan of the approaching Sentinel: the smallest and quietest of the department's armoured maglevs. Externally, it has the simplicity of a raindrop on a spider's web, but this belies the wafers of various compounds bonded together to give it a near impregnable shield.

They need to get going. Nero knows that Leifsson must have yanked on a few chains, and quite hard, to fix up their rendezvous with a serving decoy. The plan is to rendezvous with the decoy in Sector Three: inside the Orange Zone.

Bulked out in their full-body kit, the team takes several minutes to cram themselves inside. Once the hatch is down, they feel the vehicle rise up and pull away. Nero's read-out shows their first destination point is Ytragil– the Orange Zone's main conurbation.

Late afternoon and the light levels have begun to drop, along with the temperature. The Sentinel continues its ethereal glide along the magnetic grid. While they're crammed together in its underbelly, it drifts past block after block, progressing through the centre of Ytragil and towards its outer suburbs.

Peering through their narrow visors, they scan for trouble. Since Nero's last visit to this sector, it's looking worse than ever.

A red light brings them to a sudden jolt and the vehicle's

narrow window freeze-frames on a run of splintered grey hoardings. Nero looks out directly into a young woman's face. Her expression seems to hold a complete understanding of exactly how wretched it is to be shivering in that snaking, hunched-over queue, waiting to be sold the basic essentials of life.

The bus takes a few seconds to cross their path.

They move off again, wafting slowly past a magnificent snow-topped building that must once have been the focus of community pride; its many windows are all boarded up.

'This is awful. I mean, I thought it would just be a little rundown but it's much worse than that.' Chan shakes her head. 'I suppose I never imagined their lives–'

When no one else speaks, she falls silent.

Another ten minutes sees them clear the built-up area and break into open countryside. Their second destination point is the middle of the narrowing valley. They are very close to the Red Zone border, with the bad weather closing in. There's nothing much to see outside except the tops of reeds poking up through the drifts.

The vehicle pitches a little and then stops. A lone man approaches. Mid to late sixties, dressed in grubby taupe and hunting green – his neglected appearance helps explain why the Decoy Programme has been so successful.

The driver flips the hatch and the man pulls himself in beside them with surprising ease and a current of bitter air.

'You can call me Harris,' he says.

Nero supplies the introductions.

They continue on their journey, but now the Sentinel has to slow to walking pace in order to negotiate damaged sections of the grid. Nero keeps looking at the decoy's worn clothing, trying to spot the exo-skeletal layer. There's nothing – except the slight giveaway of that extra width of the back of the collar that conceals the hood; you would have to be up close like this – within striking distance – to spot it. The body armour they're all wearing is standard DSD issue and so much cruder.

Without turning round, Harris says, 'You're right, that is the only weakness with this outfit.' He extracts a woollen scarf with a thin laugh. 'But I've developed this high-tech solution – as you can see.'

'I'd like to know more about these vixens,' Nero says. 'Exactly how do you keep them under your control?'

'Imprinting – so common and yet so extraordinary. I become their pack leader from the moment they open their tiny eyes. Oh, what power it gives us – at times I feel almost God-like. An age of wolf evolution tells them I'm their uber-parent and they must follow my lead.'

'But hasn't science already interfered with their nature?'

'Yes, of course it has. How could we humans resist all that marvellous tinkering? However, the imprinting instinct is so basic – so vitally important – it survives all. I have no difficulty in signalling them in manually or with a high-frequency whistle. Without fail, they always come to my assistance when needed.'

Nero senses there's something he's not being told. 'But you've had other problems?'

'You see, Inspector, how much poorer we'd be if we couldn't use our instincts? You're right to suspect that all is not as simple as the bio-geneticists would have us believe.'

The ripe smell of the decoy's street clothes is becoming almost overwhelming. 'In what way?' Nero asks.

'I can only speak from my own experience – well, mainly. The biggest problem I've encountered is in getting them to fully disperse. It's crucial to our survival, to all our disguises, as it were, that they behave exactly like ordinary feral foxes when "off-duty".' He puts air quotes around the phrase. 'They must spread out away from me and, more crucially, away from each other.' He takes a piece of cloth from his pocket and blows his nose. 'Having implanted the full pack instinct, we then demand they drop that behaviour when we aren't around.'

'And they find this difficult?'

'Yes, of course they do. Wouldn't you? We have to teach them over and over this dual behaviour pattern. It can be a struggle for them to know exactly what is expected of them at any given time. It's a big ask, as they say.'

Nero's silence gives Lúter an opening. 'What about aggression? Do they find it difficult to back down once they're roused?'

'No. They've learnt to follow my lead with that.'

'And what if you didn't tell them to stop. Would they just keep attacking?'

'It's never arisen. I set their behavioural perimeters when they are cubs. They know I'm boss, so they back off when commanded. My vixens have never, ever, crossed a line beyond my control.'

'Can you tell us more about some of your outfit's other properties?' Chan asks. 'I mean, I know it protects you, but does it affect your strength or your physical prowess?'

'You mean does it make me Superman?' Another laugh, this time with more edge. 'Well, my dear, it helps me carry the shopping.'

Nero gives him a long look.

Harris clears his throat. 'In answer to your question, Constable – Chen was it?'

'*Chan,*' she corrects him.

'Well, Chan, this suit, along with regular and specific exercises, means my strength is approximately twice that of a normal person. However, at my advanced age, that's less impressive than it sounds.'

'So, age has increased your vulnerability?'

'Inevitably. It means that my decoy days are numbered, if that's what you're getting at. I don't mind telling you I'm looking forward to my retirement. I plan to move back into the Free Zone and spend some of my hard-earned credits. I'll find a quiet spot; nothing special – somewhere too boring to be anybody's turf.'

Like an actor finding his stride he continues, 'I was delighted when my commander asked me to meet with you all today. I had thought I'd have to carry on with my work for a while longer, but now that I've met you all, I won't have to. This is it for me – the end.'

For the first time Nero understands just how seriously this has blown Harris's cover. The Commanders must have selected him because of his age. Unknowingly, he's precipitated this man's retirement. The schematic tells him they've crossed the border into the Red Zone.

'So, tell me, when a decoy retires, what happens to their pack?' Lúter's question suggests a possibility Nero hadn't thought of.

'A perceptive question, Sergeant. We can't just turn them loose, can we? That might cause mayhem.' He sighs, 'I'm afraid they're all *humanely* – oh what a word that is – *terminated*. It's the only option.' His voice remains level. 'Without exception. Nothing else for it.'

Lúter leans in. 'Couldn't they be reassigned? Or just released, set free into the wild?'

'How can they be released when they're already free?' When Harris shakes his head, his hair hardly moves. 'You see, they're what you might call *customised*. They're *my* vixens and could never be operated by anyone else. Free and yet captive. Death is their only true release. But isn't that so for all of us?'

Nero can see they're almost there. He should concentrate on what's about to happen once they leave the steamy confines of this cabin.

As Harris turns away, Lúter nudges Nero, directing him to look at the back of Harris's grey hair. His black roots are showing through.

'I also have a hat,' Harris says without turning round.

At the intersection, the Sentinel swings eastwards under a steel grey sky. A little farther on, it slows right down and then sinks onto the track. The pilot releases the hatch. One at a time they step down into the mud a mere two hundred meters from the edge of the crimson pupil of the Double Red.

Although the grid out here had long ago been disrupted by sabotage and decay, they could have gotten nearer but Nero wants to retrace the route used by the decoy.

'Here be dragons,' Harris says as the Sentinel moves away. The armoured will use the cover of an old bus station while the pilot awaits Nero's summons.

Once it is out of sight, a profound silence descends.

They approach the SOC following the high walls of a derelict shopping mall. The snow here is much sparser on the ground – the result of geothermic heat coming from somewhere. It's possible the original ducts are still in place. At the end of the block, Nero signals for them to turn right. Up ahead, high, rusting gates still guard the main entrance.

They cross the old bus halt, its fragile boards creaking under their weight. The space in front opens up. His scanner is picking up no sign of humans in the immediate vicinity.

'This really is a damned– ' Rashid stops, distracted by a flicker from one of the many shattered windows looking down on them. Along their length a crazed mosaic of sky offers no further clues.

Harris dodges into the lead. 'What a wonderful place this is, ladies and gentlemen,' he says, both hands held high in the air. 'Another world – which is also your world, in a way.' He gives a little snort of a laugh.

Nero scowls; this man's retirement is long overdue. Rashid is lagging behind to cover Chan's back. Nero understands his instinct to protect might be more about her gender than her inexperience. It doesn't matter to him either way.

They draw closer together as the buildings crowd in. Entering an alleyway, they are forced into single file. Nero's shoulder protector scrapes along the rough surface. All this blockwork was laid in the ambition and enthusiasm of another time. Now every surface is coated with a greyish deposit. His monitor tells him it's volcanic ash.

The reek of decomposition is everywhere. It can't yet be from this morning's corpses. The sweet sickliness of the smell coats the back of Nero's throat – the scent of alien territory.

The walls of the alleyway climb up to dwarf them. Underneath a fine sprinkling of snow, pale yellow guano has collected along the chamfered bricks running along the top.

Everything feels like the trap it is.

'Make sure your weapons are inconspicuous,' Nero says. 'We don't want to precipitate any action, but you're all free to respond to any incoming.' His words are for Chan – the others don't need to be told.

Harris is in his element enjoying what, despite his words, must surely be his own first foray into a Double Red. 'Don't worry, Inspector,' he says over his shoulder, 'by now my vixens will be close.'

'Very reassuring, Mr Harris,' Kass says, sharing a look with Nero.

The ground becomes clear of snow. His wrist monitor tells him they're approaching the kill-zone. Lúter signals his attention to a thin trail of what must be blood running along the paving near the foot of the wall. Cellular analysis confirms it. Nero is uncertain whether they are coming or going.

Abruptly, the alley broadens out into a central area festooned with ravens. The birds all fly off as one to colonise the drooping wires just above their heads. The rats are more reluctant to leave.

Nero is furious that no attempt has been made to secure the main crime scene after Forensics had pulled out.

Treading with care, the homicide team fan out. Blood has fused into the surface of the pockmarked tarmac creating patterns of deep red that extend to an area roughly the size of a stickball court. Inky patches show where the snow has melted on impact. Fresh bird droppings are layered on top.

Amongst this, the forensic team – with their hands full – have left a large number of small, fleshy deposits. Nero is reluctantly reminded of a Jackson Pollack painting he'd once seen on a school trip.

Forensics had chalked around the remains before removing them, but the outlines are less clear now. Nero tries to join the dots. He counts fifteen shapes that appear to be limbs but only one possible head. Could these vixens have acquired a taste for human brains?

The rats have overcome their initial reaction and are moving back in. Rashid throws a few stones and they retreat but only halfway back.

'Quite a war zone!' Harris says. 'There couldn't have been anyone left standing.'

'You're mistaken, Mr Harris,' Nero tells him. 'You're forgetting the one individual who definitely survived.'

Seven

A bright red dot is dancing unsteadily across the back of Rashid's head. It drops down to dot the "I" in the word POLICE emblazoned across Chan's back.

Nero strides forward to block its path. Laser sights: that means this particular weapon is at least thirty years old – though no less lethal. He spins round to face its source somewhere in the mass of windows arrayed against them. His right hand crawls towards his photon. He sees a slight movement at a curtained window on the sixth floor.

The red dot on his chest is extinguished. Behind the billowing curtain, a shadow lingers. Nero out-stares the splintered pane but it offers him nothing more.

On either side of him, Chan and Rashid are engrossed in their work.

'Okay folks,' Nero forces his voice level. 'Let's get this done before our truce expires.'

He checks the windows again and is satisfied there appears to be no current threat. Taking in a few deep breaths, he walks back to the section he'd been scanning before.

The tarmac shows a great many scorch marks – telltale signs of the weapons discharged. Signature residues look to be mainly photon, but a few are laser and there's even some damage from bullet-firing arms. Nero continues to look for any physical evidence that may have been overlooked.

Treading with awkward care, he matches the holos from forensic with the outlines he's seeing on the ground. The body count is still unclear but, together with the reports from the clean-up teams, the current estimate is eight, possibly nine, males and one female. The decoy's odds had been ten to one. It's unlikely they'll establish original identities on any of the dead, although even bad guys get toothache. DNA and bone analysis will solve the corpse jigsaw and fill in the ethnicity and hometown boxes but probably not much more.

Looking up, he surveys all the hardware assembled along the roofline. He raises his monitor to stream the images back to DSD, pretty certain they're seeing the sensory organs of the operation but unable to identify the equipment in the falling light. Immediately, his monitor bleeps to indicate that the connection with base has just been terminated.

This is not a good sign; they've been permitted to enter, but have they been given an exit pass?

He walks over to the outer edges of the staining. Rashid seems tempted to fry the rats standing their ground only a few paces away. Surely the man needs no reminding that such a gesture could prove his last.

Chan seems to be holding up well, methodically capturing data the way she's so recently been trained to do.

Kass has stopped her work and is staring at one of the houses. Nero follows her gaze. Someone has recently painted one of the front doors a pale turquoise; there are intact curtains at a few of the unbroken windows: an interesting attempt at gentrification that seems unlikely to catch on.

Satisfied that the others are preoccupied, Nero squats down. He takes off his gauntlet and holds his bare hand a centimetre above the surface. He looks around once more to check no one is watching before he shuts his eyes.

His fingers begin to tingle as his mind connects with the ferocity of the conflict that took place here only a few hours ago. He feels it then – the strength of one person's determination and, in an instant, understands that this is only the first step of a crusade. Her focus here was so completely on the task in hand that, try as he might, he can glean nothing more.

He replaces his gauntlet and straightens up. Considering the strength of the opposition the decoy faced here, he doesn't fancy her continuing odds. This victory was extraordinary – she struck at the very heart of the enemy's operations despite all the surveillance. For this first and only time, the woman had the element of surprise on her side.

He must ask Harris about the exact properties of the exo-suit and its ability to withstand this volume of firepower.

Harris, where the hell is Harris?

Nero does a one-eighty and spots him way out on his own moving towards a metal hangar. 'Harris!' he calls out at a pitch just below a shout. 'Harris! Get back here now!'

No reaction. Nero's pretty certain entry into that steel-encased building is beyond their access permits. 'Right now, Harris!'

The decoy continues his unhurried pace. Rashid breaks off and starts running towards the decoy. Before he can reach him, Harris turns. His face contorted with anger, he makes a sudden open-handed gesture.

Nero sees a flash of brown-red fur disappear behind a building to his left.

Harris walks up to Rashid waving an accusing finger in his face. 'You should have known not to do that, you fool!'

The hand Rashid has clamped around his weapon looks unsteady.

'Back off, Sergeant!' Nero yells, moving in between the two of them. 'I said back off.'

Rashid reluctantly turns away, the anger in his face still undiminished.

Nero leans into Harris. 'Stay with the team, d'you hear? You put us all in danger going off like that.' He locks eyes with Harris, waits for the retreat. 'You got that?'

'Look over here, Inspector,' Chan says. 'There's something lodged in this fissure.'

Kass and Lúter fall into sentry-mode while Nero goes over to examine her find. Her monitor beam is lighting up a bright yellow object that is wedged deep into a crack. In their hurry to depart and with their hands full of body parts, forensics had clearly missed this.

'It's reading inert.' Chan's ungloved hand is already moving to retrieve it.

'Wait.' He touches her arm. 'It's always best to double-check with a different machine.' He adjusts the scan depth and then passes his own monitor across the object. It too insists the object is harmless. A wider sweep assures him there are no further objects planted in or around it.

He nods. 'Analysis confirmed.'

'Then may I, sir?' Her wrist is as slender as a child's.

He should insist on being the first one to touch it. Once it's contaminated, the object will be useless to him – at least in that way.

Nero capitulates: 'Try with your gauntlet on first.'

When her grip fails, he allows her to remove the glove. Her bare fingers reach down into the crevice. For a few minutes she works at freeing the object. Slowly, she pulls it out and then holds it up for them all to see. It's a battered, plastic duck. The others mime their applause.

'Bag it up, Chan.' An unnecessary instruction. 'Well done.'

While the team continues their work, Nero keeps a closer eye on Harris, aware that, during their stand-off, he'd been the one to look away first. The decoy has reined in his behaviour a little but is still ranging wider than Nero would like, making the most of an opportunity unlikely to present itself again.

They continue the scanning operation. A few minutes pass and then Kass holds up a tiny fragment of cloth – another thing forensics missed. Initial readings indicate a reinforced garment of the type used by decoys.

Lúter then bags up some other, as yet unidentified, particle.

They've now completed the SOC grid. With little more to be gained, Nero orders the withdrawal.

Hardly pausing to wait for their departure, the ravens rise up from the wires: a mass flapping of wings intent on resuming their gory picnic.

On the return journey, Nero is sullen. What they've learnt toady is not enough to justify the risk he'd taken with six lives. They've had no intel yet from the military's satellites, but if, or when, they've tracked the decoy's subsequent movements, this little foray will have been in vain.

At least Chan is coming away with a trophy. He'd been right about her potential. Analysis of the bathtub duck is unlikely to reveal any physical clues – it appears to be identical to millions of others that are widely on sale.

None of them can have missed the significance of her chosen signature object. Hunters have always lured real birds traditionally by using decoy ducks. The plastic duck's glaring artificiality suggests a warped sense of humour at play.

Eight

'So, Mr Harris, each of you is assigned to a particular sector but not to a specific area within it?' Nero wants to be certain of his facts.

'That's correct,' Harris says. 'Inside its perimeters we're allowed free movement.' The man carries on looking out of the window like a tourist trying to savour a last view of another land. 'We sub-divide the territory between us on what you might call an ad hoc basis – though that too must be changed irregularly and randomly.'

'So you have contact with other decoys?'

'Yes – a limited amount.' Harris stiffens. He finally meets Nero's gaze. 'Before you ask, I am not prepared to go into further details about exactly how we communicate with each other, Inspector.'

Nero shrugs. 'Okay – so let's broaden the discussion a little: tell me, why do any of you do it?'

'I can only speak for myself.' Harris removes his hat to scratch his head in a silent-movie parody of a man thinking. 'In my case, I assure you it's not for the pay – though I'll admit the substantial rewards are a lure for some. I'd have to say, for me it's that final moment when the hunted become the hunter. In the guise of the weak and vulnerable, we lure them to us and then turn the tables on them – a form of job satisfaction that is, sadly, all too short-lived. They mostly turn out to be petty criminals, minor drug dealers and/or pimps. No real PCIs, I'm afraid.'

'But you're not working alone, are you? You must have to call in other departments once you've made the arrest.'

Harris sighs. Looking down to study his soiled fingernails, he says, 'We rarely need assistance to disable them. Unless they're entirely off-grid, as it were, it's easy enough to skim their identities and then fine them from their credit logs. After that, we tend to just let them go and hope the shock and expense puts them off.'

'So – do you think it works?' Rashid asks.

'Maybe those particular individuals go on to choose the path of righteousness, but I doubt it. I'd say we're a fairly effective deterrent in the short term. We keep the mean streets surrounding the Free Zone safer, help to stop inward migration of the wrong type of citizen.' He snorts. 'Even if the people we arrest mend their ways and choose a new line of work, the Orange Zone continues to throw up an unending supply of desperados ready and willing to take their place.'

Harris keeps peering at Chan as if something about her is bothering him. 'Of course, if you look in the other direction, you'll notice how the *Red March* is continuing inexorably – we decoys are aware of how powerless we are to delay its progress.'

They drop Harris off on a small patch of wasteland in Section Five – just inside the Orange Zone. The air in the cabin immediately freshens with his departure. The decoy stands back as the sentinel rises up, then gives them a mocking salute. When Nero looks back, the man has already disappeared.

They cross into the Free Zone and at last he can take off his helmet and visor. The others follow suit. Lúter's flattened hair is sticking up at crazy angles. Rashid guffaws.

'What?' Lúter asks.

'Nothing.' Rashid chuckles and shakes his head.

Finally guessing the reason for their laughter, Lúter rakes his blond locks back into place, though he misses a few spikes at the back.

Their laughter continues well beyond the joke.

Above the glowing light from the city, darkened clouds have folded themselves into deep furrows. Nero looks out over the familiar streets. Arcs of warm light are radiating a welcome from every cafe and bar. Pedestrians are weaving their individual paths with practiced precision. Although this calm orderliness is in one way reassuring, the contrast with where they've just come from is a jolt.

Nero slides opens a vent and the hum of the city intrudes; the sound of the expressway taking the last of the workforce home and the first of the evening drinkers out on the town.

The latest intel contains no satellite images from Defence. Leifsson must be livid that there's nothing for him to boast about on the evening news briefing.

All things considered, the recon could have gone worse – after all, none of his team has been killed or injured and between them they have managed to bag some new evidence, which might yet prove useful to the investigation. This decoy's deadly little joke – choosing a plastic duck as a signature object – is definitely significant.

They alight in the bay underneath DSD Headquarters and make their way up to the equipment store. Nero is careful to follow all post-mission protocols to the letter before he dismisses them.

He's the last to take a shower. With his hair still damp, he walks out into the middle of the team's loose circle and a tight conversation.

'For me, it's black and white – simple as that,' Lúter says. 'As a catholic, it's hard not to translate it into those terms.'

'I understand what you're saying – I just don't see things in that way,' Chan tells him. 'Surely history teaches us the possibility of other ways – other methods.'

Kass tries to bring the discussion back to earth. 'Seriously – those decoys earn every penny. For me, the rewards would have to be out of this world to do that job. Even then, I'm not sure I could contemplate spending the best part of my working life out there.'

Nero extends his arms around the nearest shoulders and gives them a squeeze. 'I just wanted to say it again – well done everyone. You all did a great job out there today.' He looks at each in turn. 'Right now, I think we all need something to eat and drink.'

Further down the corridor, he can see the governor's office is in darkness. Leifsson must have gone home, probably to freshen up a little: his essence-of-polecat smell is unlikely to prove popular with the media. Right now, the man is probably in his private gym wrestling with weights and his limited imagination as he attempts to come up with a positive spin on the day's progress.

Nero lets Rashid lead the way to the exit and then follows them down the long, dimly-lit corridor that leads to the out-side world.

Nine

She hears it first; then sees it looming towards her out of the gathering darkness. A small smile to herself: it wasn't difficult to guess his choice of this particular spot; Harris still hadn't quite mastered the habit of no habit. A small but significant weakness, perhaps the single way he fails to obey orders.

The approaching sentinel comes to a halt and settles onto the track. Harris springs from it with his usual dexterity and then stands to attention with a parody of a salute.

The mag floats off, pulling its sound behind it.

Harris doesn't move; perhaps he's adjusting his vision. She can almost smell that old, weather-weary coat with the missing fifth button, that silly joke scarf he's hung onto doggedly. On good days, they can still fool themselves their band of decoys own these streets together.

This is not a good day.

Harris has started walking. She knows his pack will soon catch his scent and follow. For the moment nothing else moves; no nearby curtains twitch. Earlier, she'd had little to entertain her but the comings and goings of the dull, limpet-like residents left behind in this no-honest-mans-land. Outside, they went nowhere. Inside, they hid behind rows of cheap locks, which, given the slightest blow, spring apart like zippers. All it takes is one good kick.

From her vantage point she continues to watch Harris. He's an expert at showing passivity, could fool anyone with that act; and yet he must know. There's still time to break cover, try to persuade Harris just once more. They are eighty metres apart when they should be side-by-side. She gets ready, stretches her limbs to pump blood back to muscles that have been inactive for too long.

Curfew begins much earlier at this time of the year. There's barely a half hour left. He's out in the open, making his way towards the spine road. In her heart she knows it would be useless to try to stop him.

Instead she follows, keeping a steady distance. If he senses her presence, he doesn't acknowledge it in any way.

The gap between them increases. For a while he almost disappears from sight but then he emerges from the scrubland – allows his silhouette to stand out against the ridge. The darkening sky hangs upon his back.

Her outfit's layers protect her from the weather, but tonight she can feel the chill in the air. Does he know she's there? Would it change anything if he did? The Commanders expected them to survive being unknown, uncared for, unacknowledged; she won't let that be Harris's fate.

Up ahead, Harris is quickening his pace. A few sparse lights wink on and then begin to leak their thin pools of hollow reassurance. She finds it impossible to imagine that other time when, at this hour, these same streets would have rung with the sound of children arriving home from school.

The breeze already betrays the sound of their approach; they'll be upon him in a few moments and yet Harris is intent on closing the distance. He must hear them coming just as she does. They both know they'll hang back – wait until he's past this row of low-rise apartments. They will want no witnesses.

A cold sweat breaks over her back as Harris reaches the crescent of abandoned and boarded-up shops.

Time and choices condense into a hard, immutable nugget.

They come in swiftly, encircling Harris and then hanging a uniform distance away.

She's as close as she dares. He holds himself upright before them, unbowed. As they emerge from their vehicles, she sees his head turn as he looks along the ranks, from one heavily armoured man to the next.

'I knew you'd come,' Harris says, without expression. Of course, he knew: hadn't he told her more than once that this would be the fitting and only possible end to their employment, that logic dictated there could be no other?

The intruders remain set in their circle, silently regarding Harris. Time elapses, stretches beyond the confines of their location.

An expectant hush split by a grating sound as the final hatch opens and a man steps out.

His raised voice carries, 'I know you will understand the necessity for this. There can be no alternative, no exceptions. Before we commence, we would like to thank you for your services on behalf of the city.'

Without being signalled in, Harris's vixens emerge from cover to encircle him. Their heads turn towards the enemy, eyes glowing red in the headlight trained on him. Harris bends down to stroke the pelts of the nearest.

Her throat swells but she remains anchored by their promise – the final vow she solemnly made to him.

'Make it swift for them, Commander,' he says.

'We'll make it quick,' the man says, retreating. 'For all of you.' He climbs back into his vehicle and slams the hatch shut.

Simultaneous flashes of light and explosions of sound rip the air apart. Though she has to block her ears, she refuses to look away.

It's been hours but still she hasn't moved. The sickening smell lurks on in the damp, complicit air. Another wave of disbelief overwhelms her; she can see nothing except the terrible images seared onto her retinas.

At last, she truly knows them by their deeds. Military strength protons for God's sake: they should have known, or perhaps didn't care about what would happen when they allowed him no time to remove his ecto-suit. Encased in what had once protected him, Harris was roasted alive. He'd staggered towards them, wrapped in flames but still somehow upright. When they continued blasting, he became a man of steam and oil. His blackened skeleton finally fell and disintegrated; the vixens had already powdered into carbon.

Instinct for self-preservation had kept her from running into that final circle of hell. Once most of them had departed, a small detail had been left behind. They'd taken a long time cleaning up the scene before they left, satisfied that they were leaving no traces of their deeds and their culpability.

The bleached-out stain she now creeps towards is all that remains of Harris.

A strange, misted quiet descends. All those listening will fervently deny what just happened. She vows to remain indelible – the one true witness to his death and his life.

Ten

Bruno wakes to find the upper half of his body propped against the wall. How long has he been asleep? Hours? Days even? It's still dark but at this time of year it doesn't get light until after 10:00 and daylight lasts only five or so hours. He's still cold but not like he was before. There's a damp corruptness in the air along with something else that smells metallic. Underneath the various layers covering him, he's fully dressed – hadn't even stopped to remove his wet shoes.

He can't feel his lower limbs. Harnessing the strength in the rest of his body, he swings his numb legs over the edge of the bed until his feet are resting on the floor. He needs to stand up, walk around a bit until the feeling comes back.

The numbness begins to wear off. It's replaced by burning, throbbing pains that shoot up and down from his ankles to his thighs. He breathes through the worst of it and, after a while, it settles into a profound, muscular ache.

Surely it must be time to take the next dose of those pills. It's quite a struggle for his bound-up hands to reach down into his jacket pocket. His fingers fix onto the cap of the container – at least he hadn't dropped them. Shaking one of the pills into his bandaged palm, he aims for his mouth and chucks it back, swallowing hard. The second one's trickier; it catches on his dry tongue; he needs several attempts before he can get it down.

Once he's confident his legs will bear his weight, he takes a few faltering steps towards the window. For the first time he registers the metal grid barring his exit. Moonlight slips through the gaps throwing a striped pattern along the adjacent wall. He's surprised that his breath isn't steaming white in front of him.

Bruno looks out through the glass into the glow of the whiteout. He can just make out some half-covered tracks in the outer yard. In this light and from this angle, he can't tell whether they're the footprints of animals or humans. In this sort of weather, old folk are fond of warning anyone who'll listen that a Fimbulwinter is coming – a winter that will precede the end of everything on earth.

He grips the bars to muster his strength then limps across the room to the door. Partway there, a sound stops him dead. A mumble of voices is coming from somewhere inside the building.

Overwhelmed by a sense of impending danger, he backs away towards the sanctity of the bed. Both his hands touch the bedframe and a jolt like electricity shoots up his arms into the centre of his chest. He's engulfed by a terrible burning sensation – has to break free, force his stuck-fast hands to release their grip on the metal.

Once his breathing has subsided, he looks down at his bare fingers expecting them to be seared by the heat like meat on a barbeque, but they remain unmarked. The bandages around the rest of his hands remain a grubby white. He explores each finger in turn and can find no blisters or scorch marks.

So what was it he felt? He finds he already knows the answer to that question: it was a woman's intense and overwhelming anger, unadulterated by any residual humanity; the sheer strength of her emotion making it impossible for him to tell who, or what, it might have been directed at.

Oh, God, if that's her out there, he's probably dead already.

He needs to get out of here. With luck, he might sneak

past them, get to the outer door and take his chances out in the open.

But what then? He could freeze to death before he can get help. But if he stays put and she finds him in here, in this bizarre parody of a bedroom, how angry will that make her? If he can get out of this room, at least he won't need to explain how he knew the entry code.

He walks back over to the door, presses his ear to the slight gap above the lock and listens again. A conversation, possibly an argument, is going on some distance away. He can hear a man's questioning tones and then a woman answering him.

Could be some lost couple sheltering from the weather. It doesn't seem likely anyone would be out this way on a date. No, the chances are it's her. And, if that's true, she's not alone. He'll be up against the two of them; there could be more.

They can't know he's in here. While they're busy arguing, he should leave this room, which now seems more like a jail cell.

He grasps the handle, turns it as slowly and quietly as he can. It won't open. Again and again he tries, pushing all his weight against it at the same time. The bloody thing won't budge. It's locked from the outside – which makes him a prisoner.

Damnit! He tries to project his thoughts through the door onto the keypad hoping his mind alone will depress the same sequence of numbers and letters. It doesn't work.

Can he climb out of the window? Those bars look old – they might be rusty enough to give way. But what about the noise? There'd be no better way of broadcasting his presence.

What if he calls for help? If the people out there hear, they'll come and let him out. He can even tell them the code. At least there's a chance that way. In this weather, who else is going to stumble into this abandoned building by accident?

If it *is* really her out there, wouldn't it be better to face her? He'd rather meet his fate like that than endure a slow, lingering death like some animal in a trap.

He hears footsteps approaching. A second later the handle before him rotates and the door opens. There's nowhere and no time to hide from the two shadowy figures standing there in front of him.

Bruno reels back.

They don't attempt to come inside, don't appear to show surprise; they merely stand there looking at him.

'I'm glad to see you've made yourself comfortable.' The voice is synthesised but still sounds like a woman's.

The shorter of the two figures takes a step towards him. He steps backwards. 'Well now, Bruno, like I said to my friend while you were sleeping, it really is quite remarkable how very ordinary you appear to be. If they hadn't given you those brain scans at the hospital, we might have taken you for an ordinary, lost teenager and never guessed your little secret.'

She releases a parody of a laugh. 'You know, I'm quite excited – this is my very first sighting of a telepatico – in the flesh that is.'

Bruno's never heard that word spoken aloud though he's always known it – exactly what it meant and what it made him.

'Che figata! My very own telepatico.' She repeats it again like a sting then moves closer one slow step at a time – a slight figure shrouded in black and yet so full of menace.

The other person slips past Bruno to stand behind him; legs planted apart, hands folded across the impressive width of his chest.

Bruno's eyes are drawn to the shadows directly behind the woman. The dark shape of an animal emerges, and then another and another; their massed bodies entirely blocking the exit. For a moment he's held in the rhythm of their low, collective breathing; in the stench of damp undergrowth emanating from the raised fur along their backs.

In front of him, the cloaked figure gives another weird, electronic laugh – the pitch grating in his mind like a migraine.

'Have you heard of a place called Pingelap?' she asks.

He shakes his head. Right now, there's no possibility of escaping.

'No – I thought not; not many people have. It's a tiny atoll in the pacific where around 20% of the population can only see in black and white. Imagine that. Must be like being in one of those old films.'

Another sound that might be a sniff or a sneer. 'Way back, a tsunami wiped out all but twenty of the island's inhabitants; subsequent interbreeding resulted in the original genetic defect.'

He feels like a fly being played with by a spider. 'Achromatopsia they call it – a fancy term for total colour blindness.'

While his attention has been on her, like they're playing grandmother's footsteps, the animals have been slowly advancing towards him, their white muzzles and chests clearer now, their eyes shining with reflected moonlight.

She comes closer. 'Some people claim foxes can only see in black and white but that's not true.' Her hooded head rotates from side to side. 'Though I'll grant that their colour vision is less developed than in most humans.'

A deafening, bird-like scream from the nearest fox sends a jolt of fear through Bruno's body. A second animal repeats the call. The whole pack is almost upon him; the edge of the bedframe presses into the backs of his legs.

The woman makes a hand gesture and the animals retreat by the smallest of degrees.

'In this sort of light, my vixens really do come into their own. They're able to detect the slightest movements, can see many more shades of grey than you, or I, ever could.'

She leans in towards him and, as he can back away no further, he falls back onto the bed.

'Where was I – ah yes – the way genetic variations in a confined community become more pronounced. I believe the same thing occurred in a tiny, Italian village in the Julian Alps near the Slovenian border. Ring any bells, Bruno? Of course the kindest explanation is that it stemmed from them drawing together away from foreign outsiders – that famous Italian patriotism.' Another diabolical laugh sets his teeth on edge. 'We might agree to be polite and leave incest out of the equation.'

Like a switch has been thrown, he finds his fear begin to mutate into anger at the slur intended on his mother's family; at having to listen to that synthesised voice lecturing him, at the confidence that's oh-so-easy when you have someone outnumbered and at your mercy. Well fokk her!

'Of course, it took a few more generations before the attention of the scientific world was drawn to this handful of people who appeared to share such *extra-ordinary* abilities. That's when that perfectly straightforward Italian adjective – telepatico: so often whispered in the other nearby villages, underwent a sort of linguistic trick and became a brand new noun. A label, as it were, for this new variant of humans that some regarded as rarities and others as aberrations – mutants.'

Bruno's face is level with what he judges to be her stomach area. If he butts her now she won't be expecting it. But then those damned foxes of hers will be upon him before he can do anything else. On top of that there'd be her silent companion to deal with.

'A new minority group had now been successfully labelled. But the question was what to do about them. Or with them. As always, it all depended on your point of view. Some people thought they should be preserved and studied – the same method that had already failed to conserve most of the world's endangered species.'

He might as well try it; this woman is clearly a total psycho; she's never going to let him go. Doesn't he already know exactly what she's capable of?

'Other people suggested a kind of captive breeding program. And then there were others who grasped all the possible advantages of these remarkable powers–'

Her right hand is reaching for something from behind her back. 'Reading minds. Precognition. Couldn't their genetic material be extracted to create a new breed of super-humans?'

He curls his fists then bows his head ready to aim for the bitch's stomach. He'll drive the wind right out of her. There's no way he's going to sit here and take this crap, whatever happens.

'Although I don't share your abilities, I know exactly what you're thinking now, Mr Mastriano. You're thinking that you might be able to overpower me – take your chances.'

In one swift movement the blue arc of a blade comes to rest a centimetre from his neck. Moonlight is glinting off the steel edge poised ready to decapitate him. It doesn't waver.

Bruno holds up his empty, bandaged hands in surrender.

She steps back as she sheaths the sword. 'How flawed we all are – how quickly our thoughts turn to violence, eh Bruno? Don't feel too bad – despite all your astounding gifts, you stand no chance against such a powerful instinct.'

Her hand goes to the side of her head, to roughly where her ear must be and then she gives a short chuckle before adjusting something on the side of her neck. 'Your people couldn't win,' she tells him, her voice now that of a youngish, almost pleasant-sounding woman. 'What am I saying? Whether through precognition or mind-reading your people *could* win; from the smallest game of chance to the big international lotteries, the movement of the world's commodity prices, insurance markets, political battles. . .'

Another chuckle, like she's really enjoying this. 'On and on it went – all those new possibilities. Oh dear, what a threat to the established world order you and your kind posed. So few in number, and yet how you seemed to threaten everything we thought we knew about the way the world works. Those authorities who chose to act believed quite sincerely they were doing so for the good of world order, that they had no choice but to neutralise every, single, last, one of you.'

Her glove comes towards him. It's a shock when she grips his chin and turns his whole head one way and then the other, scrutinising him. 'Forewarned as they were, your people none-theless stood little chance against such overwhelming odds.'

When she lets go of his chin, he continues to feel the im-pression of her grip. 'Of course, it was always rumoured that a handful managed to escape, finding anonymity amongst the many in the endless, northward flow of so many refugees.'

Her gauntlet is in his hair, moves it to one side in a gro-tesque parody of a motherly gesture. 'And now here you are, the still-living proof. Such an ordinary-looking young man with literally nowhere to go. My dear Bruno, I really do think it's time we unlocked your full potential.'

Eleven

Leifsson is studying his reflection, practising the man-of-the-hour expressions he likes to project. The dark circles around his eyes can be easily disguised with a dab or two of Light Up. Right now that's the least of his problems.

'We can still use this thing to our advantage. Although we need to be careful things don't start...'

The whine of Hagalín's voice always seems to flick a line of switches to *Off* in his brain. He cuts in, 'I'm fully aware of the dangers.'

'And I'm just saying – we'll be fine if we stick to the basic message–'

'Yes, I'm already there, thank you Hagalín.' Hadn't he answered questions on every conceivable angle just this morning? Of course he knows what their continuing message needs to be. His statement will be straightforward enough; it's the Q and A he dreads. Better if he announces up front that there's a limited time for questions. At least that way he'll look like he's too busy solving the problem to talk about it. It's already been a long day –and he's not feeling at his sharpest after only three hours sleep and a failed ten-minute power nap.

His press secretary, Eivin Davey, has drafted the statement; he just needs a quick read-through to make it his own. Normally, he likes to add a joke or something to lighten things up

– but not today. His body is buzzing from too much caffeine. Just time for a leak and then he'll read through the speech in make-up. He needs to make damn sure they don't make him look as tanned as they did last time – they just need to tone down his natural ruddiness.

He likes to edit his script in the small dressing room set up behind the main auditorium. Walking in, the penetration of lights further darkens his mood. A girl comes in with her bag of tricks and gets to work on him. He can vaguely recall this one's called Fliss. Or was it Flick? It's some daft name like that. Slim enough though there's not much shape to her. When she leans in, he can smell her scent-disguised body odour.

My fellow citizens. Did that sound too plonky – a tad insincere? Perhaps he should come straight to the point: *Good morning, folks.* No, more formal – *Good morning, ladies and gentlemen. Many of you will be alarmed at the recent events in the city.* No, that was saying that alarm was the emotion they should feel. *Recent events may have caused some of you to feel a little concerned.* He scribbles in the correction.

The girl begins by making his hair look more calm and collected. She's certainly good at what she does.

The coverage of recent events from some quarters has been somewhat hysterical at times. Better – it doesn't tar them all. *Let me lay the facts before you.* Yes, the next bit's good – Eivin has pitched it just right. Nothing to hide, straight talking, trusting to their common sense.

She keeps dabbing with that powder puff. 'That's enough,' he tells her. His skin now shows about the right balance of indoors and outdoors. The girl continues to fuss until he tells her to leave.

The Decoy Programme is one of the most successful crime fighting initiatives. Yes, let's remind them how good they've had it. De da, de da, de da. Nice touch about the full force of the law, situation in hand. Good; good – yes, that ought to do nicely.

We are fully in charge of the situation. Arrests have been made.

Should that be arrest? – he didn't want to make it sound like some enormous conspiracy. But then the one lone avenger bit sounds far too heroic. *Arrests have been made. I'm afraid we are unable to give more details at the present time.*

Okay, then he'll add: *I'm afraid we only have time for one or two questions.* No – that's two afraids. *I'm sorry, ladies and gentlemen, we only have time for a few questions.* Yes, that would use up most of their available air-time – the gap just before the big game starts.

Leifsson can hear them assembling in the auditorium – the muffled clamouring for the best seats and angles. He'll wait for Hagalín to warm them up a little before he steps out there. Not that the damn man is much good at it. Truth is, he'd been obliged to appoint Hagalín as deputy after the man did so well in the Primaries. Given his obvious limitations, it's extraordinary the man could have risen so far on little more than family money and ambition. If he does his job properly, he'll begin by reminding them how they're all batting on the same side.

The girl knocks and comes in to tell him it's nearly time – as if he needed telling.

He hears Hagalín ask them all to find their seats and settle down. Whilst the man's droning on, Leifsson checks the mirror – nothing is caught between his teeth, his hair is still very much in place. A final deep breath, and then, as always, he touches the photograph of his mother for luck.

His opening statements are well received – he notes a good deal of nodding amongst the assembled commentators. The tension in his shoulders relaxes a little. Yes, they all seem to be on-side. He's conducting the mood music and they're buying his major theme; everything's well in hand and under control. 'Let me assure you we are fully in charge of the situation,' he tells them. 'Arrests have already been made. We're unable to give you more details at the present time.'

He wraps it up. Looking at their faces, he feels confident he's managed to pour oil on these particular troubled waters. It helps that he's got to know most of them over the years. There's Linda on the left and Gary over there and then there's Katla just down the front.

He starts the Q & A and they jostle for supremacy – arms raised like the keen kids in class. He takes the first from Katla.

'Governor, some people are saying that this *Cloaked Avenger* is showing us the way we should have tackled the situation from the start; that a state can never properly function without *all* its streets under its full control. This lone female is showing us all that, if we have courage, we can–'

'Just hold up one minute there, Katla.' Leifsson is determined to put a stop to all this neo-religious claptrap before it takes hold. Swallowing his growing anger, he says, 'It seems to me that you're literally playing devil's advocate here. These commentators – these deluded theorists – are, at best, naïve. The ordinary citizens of Eldísvík can't begin to comprehend the difficulties our security forces face every day in order to keep them safe in their beds at night. If they're stupid enough to be taken in by individuals peddling their deluded ideas and absurd suggestions – all this nonsense that's being bandied about – it could *potentially* put at risk the peace and stability we all enjoy. Such loose talk can inflame weak-minded individuals into actions, which ultimately jeopardise the rule of law. I can assure you folk that is *not* going to happen – not on my watch.'

Katla begins to interrupt but Leifsson is not having it. He thumps the podium. 'As we speak, that murdering, traitorous bitch is still on the loose out there. Who's to say she won't turn her attentions to the folk in the Free Zone next?'

Gary is raising an arm to speak. 'So, Governor – you're admitting this woman is still at large and that, so far, despite the efforts of the various security forces, she has evaded all your efforts to capture her. What is there to stop her striking again, anywhere she pleases – maybe even tonight?'

The question exposes the full extent of his gaff. For the next quarter of an hour, sweating profusely, Leifsson tries to extricate himself from the consequences of that one moment of unguarded folly.

He strides back to his office, a look of confidence still plastered on his face. Eivin and Hagalín push themselves straight in behind him.

As always, Eivin is full of reassurance. 'On the whole I'd say that went well, Governor. I think we made all the points we needed to.'

Hagalín stands further back. 'It was a good performance, Erik.

A great one under the circumstances. I'm sure it's put paid to all that "Lone Avenger" crap. Wouldn't you say, Eivin?'

'Yep, I think you nailed it, Governor. I think that should silence the critics.'

Leifsson's heard enough. 'Okay, gentlemen, thank you for your help. I just need to use the bathroom, if you don't mind.'

They walk out all smiles.

So, it was as bad as he'd thought. Well, after tonight, he'll make sure that drusla – that Katla whatever-her-name-is – will be off the briefing list from now on. Damn Hagalín and his endless nit-picking. Damn his lack of sleep. Why did it all come down to such basics in the end?

He retreats into his private bathroom, pours cold water into the marble washbowl and splashes it on his face. Stripped of the effects of Light Up, he instantly looks older. The weight pit has given him a body that defies the long line of rotund farming stock he's risen from, but that lineage of round, blunt-nosed faces still haunt his own.

His new stud buzzes with some early reaction stuff. A lurid projection is superimposed onto his reflection in the mirror. GOVERNOR REASSURES CITY. Below that:

SUSPECTS STILL AT LARGE. Another one comes in hard on its heels: LEIFSSON'S DECOY PROGRAMME LIES IN TATTERS.

The meeting he's scheduled with the Commanders is in twenty minutes. Before that, he'll get Eivin to wade through all the media reactions and send him a summary – no punches pulled.

He's surrounded by incompetence; even Vasiliev is proving less than persuasive with those halfwits from the military. The damned media has grasped the potential implications of this thing far better than the military appear to have done. Rustler might be more up to the task then Reeve. Perhaps the Commanders will step in now.

He longs for uninterrupted sleep. Just a quick half hour would refresh the nauseating staleness in his head. Inside his small safe he locates the pills that should help him stay on top. Why hadn't he taken them earlier? He washes three down with a half litre of fortified water from the fridge. Staring at his own reflection mixed with images from the growing media storm, he waits for the feel-better to kick in.

Twelve

It's early for the governor to be out and about. Irritated by the man's unannounced intrusion, Nero nonetheless offers him the only chair.

Leifsson declines with a dismissive wave of the hand. 'So – did you learn anything at all from yesterday's little excursion or was it just a waste of time?'

As always, the man seems to commandeer the space and most of the air being pumped into the room.

'Well, having seen the scene with my own eyes, my first thoughts are that to survive that battle, the woman must have amazing physical strength and agility. Looking at some of the hardware they have there, it's difficult to believe she was able to get so far before being challenged. Unfortunately, no attempt had been made to secure any remaining evidence once the forensic team departed. By the time we got there, it was heavily polluted by rain, scavengers and Lord knows what else.'

Leifsson looks beat and beaten. Despite the harshness of the overhead lights, the man's pupils are dilated.

'So, did you find anything?'

'We managed to retrieve some evidence that warrants further investigation. When we got back, the labs had closed so, at the moment, I'm still waiting on their reports.'

Nero allows a dramatic pause. 'We found something of real

significance which they overlooked.' Remembering Leifsson's remarks at their last meeting, he adds, 'I say *we* – in fact, it was Chan who found it.'

He picks up the bag containing the plastic duck. 'The decoy left this signature object. It was well hidden; her little challenge for us.'

'So what's the significance?'

'I'd say it shows a classic need to communicate, claim the credit and deny any potential imitators. She brought it with her: a cool calculation, which shows a strong belief from the outset that she would prevail against the odds. The duck itself is her little joke.'

Leifsson looks blank. 'I don't get it. Are we supposed to feel sorry for her kids because Mommy's not always there for bath time?'

'I'm guessing it's a tad more complicated than that,' Nero says. 'This woman's a professional decoy. We all know that hunters use decoy ducks to lure in wild ones but, clearly, this one wouldn't fool any bird for a second. This suggests a degree of cynicism not just about her work but about the incompetence of others. Such an attitude towards authority ought to have been apparent during her various assessments. So, either the psyche testing was incompetent or she's immensely skilled at disguising any telltale reaction – including the physiological ones. That, in turn, suggests she must have made an intense study of interrogation techniques.' He holds the duck up a little higher. 'In effect, she's mocking all the people she's managed to fool.'

'Is there some good news in all this?'

'Not really. If you want my professional opinion, given this degree of premeditation, I'd say she's highly likely to strike again. And soon.'

'Fokk me!' Leifsson shakes his head. 'This bitch must be one hell of an operator.'

The governor may not be at his most articulate today, but at least he finally understands the nature of their adversary. Nero tries to muster some pity for the man's predicament – right now the house is shedding bricks around the poor guy's ears. 'I'm sure we'll get some leads from the samples we brought back,' he tells him. 'And before the end of the day, the pathologists should be able to give us some more information about the victims. I must say, so far, the spread of ethnic backgrounds suggests a degree of inter-racial cooperation that would be impressive in any organisation.'

'Cut the smart stuff, Nero.'

He's seldom seen Leifsson so disconsolate. Looking into his eyes again, he can see the man has clearly exceeded the recommended dose of something. Better not to antagonise him any further – no sense in poking a wounded bear. 'I'm going to have a chat with Dr Arthur, the head of Psychology–'

'I know who he is, for fokk's sake.'

'Okay, so I'm hoping he can expand the psychological profile we have of the lady so far. I'm also seeing Dr Magnúsdóttir to get more of her take on the situation.'

He lets that sink in. 'It's clear this decoy had to put in a lot of extra hours with the pack, right from the off. Perhaps between the two departments we might get some signposts. We'll need clearance to look at the personnel records held by the Commanders. Oh, and for the record, I was planning to take Chan along – she took a major in psychology from the Institute.'

The silence that follows suggests his plans meet with Leifsson's general approval. Nero can't resist asking, 'What about the military – had any luck with those satellite images?'

'Do you think I'd be sniffing around in the sodding basement like this if we had?'

Leifsson turns towards the door and then stops. 'You know, Nero, you could try to make this place look a little more homely. Put a few photos of your family and friends on the wall – that sort of thing. Oh wait – I forgot, that doesn't apply in your case, does it?'

That last remark had been unwarranted but Nero refuses to rise to the bait.

The governor walks out. Head down, he heads towards Vasiliev's office.

He watches the man's unusually slow progress. The back of Leifsson's crumpled jacket has a thick thread protruding like a smoldering fuse.

Thirteen

At the lift doors they are greeted by a pungent, chemical odour; its acid tang immediately catches in Rashid's throat bringing with it the memory of nausea. The images in the pathology reports had been nothing short of grizzly.

Rashid looks over at Chan; how will she hold up when faced with all those mangled leftovers in the flesh? 'I'm really not sure what Inspector Cavallo expects us to add to the intel they've already sent through,' she says. 'There must be other areas we could be–'

'The man believes in being thorough,' Rashid tells her. 'You're part of his team now, so you need to respect his methods. Besides, no report can tell you everything. Some things inevitably get overlooked.'

'But surely nothing of any real significance?' The woman's tenacious, that's for sure. She seems annoyed but perhaps that's just to cover her other feelings. Her cheeks have a little more colour, adding to her undeniable beauty. 'I can't imagine–'

'Tell you what,' he says, 'why don't you see if it pays off before you go off on one.'

She opens her mouth to respond, but then holds it back. As they near the door marked "Mortuary", she looks a little less solid.

He knocks before entering. 'Don't worry, Rashid, you won't

disturb anyone,' Jue Hai says coming forward to greet him with a handshake and several pats to his back. The pathologist looks thinner and more careworn than the last time they met.

'Good to see you, mate.' Rashid squeezes his shoulder. 'You still owe me another shot.' Though the pathologist is only in his late thirties, he notices more grey hair around the man's temples.

Rashid turns to Chan, 'Constable, this is Dr Yew, pathologist and all round genius.'

'What can I say?' Jue Hai shrugs. 'It's true.' He looks at Chan. 'Ni hao, nei giu mut ye meng?'

'I'm sorry, I don't speak Cantonese,' she tells him, to the man's obvious disappointment. 'Chan Jie Ning,' she finally says. 'But you can call me Constable Chan.'

Her smile is too late to turn the remark into a joke; Jue Hai nonetheless gives her a broad smile in return.

'So, with everyone running around after this decoy,' the pathologist says, 'this must be a good time to rob a bank – though I don't suppose people do that anymore.'

The air temperature drops considerably as he leads them through to the main autopsy room where a number of sheeted trolleys have been arranged in two columns running down the length of the room.

'So, I suppose we should take a look at these bodies,' Rashid says, surveying the prostrate ranks laid out under the unforgiving lights.

'*Remains* would be a more accurate description,' Jue Hai says. He walks them over to one of the tables. 'It's quite a collection.' He looks directly at Chan, 'Not a pretty sight, I'm afraid.'

Her face is unreadable.

The pathologist pulls back the first cover to reveal a collection of body parts only roughly arranged to resemble a human body. Ten years in the force, and Rashid has only witnessed this level of carnage after a train wreck. He looks away until he can still his stomach's reaction. Alongside him, Chan seems composed.

'Meet "Boris",' Jue Hai announces. 'Bone analysis shows he was raised in an agricultural area near Poltava in the former Ukraine but has lived in this city for the past twenty years. Evidence of long-term drug abuse – mainly crack and G.R.S.K. Approximately thirty-nine years old. A big man – I'd say a fraction over two metres judging by this one intact femur.'

The pathologist's hand hovers above what is left of a thigh. When he points to a severed eyeball, Rashid almost gags.

'We've matched his tissue to this eye. As you can see, it's blue. Let's assume the other was the same colour – heterochromia iridium has an incidence of less than one per cent.' Jue Hai is showing off now. 'Last meal unknown due to total lack of digestive organs. Evidence of wounds from a very large knife or similar bladed weapon, which were inflicted before the animals began their work. There's a tattoo here on his left wrist.'

Rashid peers at it. 'Would you say that's a lion?'

'Yes, but it's an amateur job. Ink analysis shows it's Ukrainian. No match to any cartel mark we know of. Muscular development shows he was right-handed, so he could have done it himself. Though his head's still missing, judging by his body hair, I'd say his hair was probably dark. As you can see, we've identified his left ear. Regular sort of shape, no sign of any piercings. These three limbs were found near the crime scene – if you're calling it that – but this section of his torso, the eye and the ear were deposited in the single red. All these other bits and pieces were found further out in the Orange Zone.

Rashid remembered his task. 'What can you tell us about the weapon she used?'

'It's hard to be more definitive. There's so much additional damage that it's impossible to identify it with any accuracy. If more parts come in, we may find cleaner edges to the wounds.'

'This eye – have you tested it against retinal recognition records?' Chan asks.

'Of course,' Jue Hai says, pulling an exaggerated frown. 'The data match came up blank.'

The pathologist covers the remains before leading them across the room to the next table. 'Over here we have "Fatima", the only female – although even that was difficult to be certain about at first glance due to a total absence of primary and secondary sexual organs.'

He pulls back the cover. 'She's about thirty-five years old. Height around 1.75 metres. Born in Cairo, moved to Istanbul in her early teens. Hair black – going by what was still attached to this section of her neck. DNA suggests an Afghani father. She'd spent some time in America in the last ten years, but calcium levels show she's resided here for approximately the last six. No evidence of drug abuse. The arm's muscle pattern suggests possible military, athletics or dance training. That upper jaw was found down the road in Hail Park.'

'Dental records?' Rashid is still hopeful.

'No matches found, despite traces of a root canal abscess about a year ago – she decided to suffer for her art.'

Rashid notices the curve of her fingers with their delicate, pink nail-gloss. His eyes travel up the arm past the numerous puncture wounds and then onto the obscene cornucopia of flesh and veins that appear to be reaching out for their missing shoulder. He thinks of the lost embrace of a mother, or a lover, or a child and is unexpectedly moved.

Revealing each set of body parts in turn, Jue Hai continues his round until they're standing before the last table. 'And finally, this is "Carlos" – the proud possessor of the only complete head so far recovered. It was left behind in the kill zone. Blade wound to the back of the neck where it was severed. This damage here came from the teeth of *vulpes vulpes*: the red fox.'

'So good they named it twice,' Chan cuts in.

Both men manage a smile. 'Due to their selective breading, we know the teeth of these vixen packs tend to be slightly different from those of regular feral foxes,' Jue Hai tells them. 'From what we've seen so far, I'd say the animals from this decoy's pack were mainly responsible for the injuries to the upper body areas on each victim. In this case, to the face itself.'

Looking at Carlos's severed head, Rashid finds it hard to imagine those mangled, grey-tinged features had ever been animated.

'Images have had to be sent to the techies for reanimation before we try to find a facial match. No easy task, as you can see. Right now, I'd put his age at approximately 40. We know he was born in or around Mexico City. We're just waiting on the deeper bone analysis. And, before you ask, Constable Chan, no retinal records. Dental work is extensive – we're checking for a match internationally.'

The pathologist looks at Chan again. 'It's extremely unusual, at this stage of an investigation, for us to have no precise ID match on the victims. For obvious reasons, we're more hopeful with this one. By the end of the day, we should have his name.'

Rashid is relieved when Jue Hai finally pulls the cover back over "Carlos".

'You say the vixen pack may have concentrated their attack on the head and upper body,' he says. 'Might they have been trained to target those specific areas?'

'I would think so. I'm surprised more heads haven't turned up yet.'

'Maybe it's symbolic,' Chan says. 'You know, to rob them of their individuality, their identity – reduce them to little more than meat.'

The pathologist nods. 'Yes, perhaps.' He leads them over to his desk. 'We asked the university's Mammal Research Unit about the distribution of the body parts retrieved do far. Their report contains information about the usual pattern of urban fox territories, which helps establish a picture of the distribution between the feral sets. You should receive this simulation.'

The pathologist boots it up. 'As you see, this shows how many other predators, besides the vixens, were responsible for the spread pattern established so far. Professor Jameson thinks it likely that the decoy's pack backed off quite quickly and that this then allowed other foxes, feral dogs and then smaller mammals and birds to predate the carcasses.'

'I think we should continue to use the term *remains* rather than *carcasses*,' Rashid says.

Jue Hai acknowledges the correction with a slight bow of the head. 'I take your point – a slip of the tongue.'

'This decoy showed no respect for these people, alive or dead,' Chan says. 'The woman must have a psychopathic personality.'

'Possibly, but we have yet to establish exactly who these particular victims were. When we know more, we'll have a better idea of whether they were strangers to her or whether they were specifically targeted,' Rashid tells her.

Chan bows her head, emulating Jue Hai's gesture of apology but without his sincerity. Rashid lets it go. To his right, he spots the bagged evidence from the team's recon on a table. 'Did you get anything more from that little lot?'

'I was about to come to that,' Jue Hai says. 'The small fragment of clothing you recovered appeared to be *similar* to the composition of the standard decoy's exo-skeletal cloth.'

'When you say *similar*, do you mean just that these can vary slightly, or was there something unusual about it?' Rashid asks.

'I didn't carry out that particular analysis. It is more the field of my colleague Jóra – Dr Bjarnadóttir. It might be better if you speak to her directly.'

'Can we have a word with her now?' Rashid asks.

When Jue Hai goes off to find Bjarnadóttir, they're left alone. He's aware of all the bodies, in their industrial shrouds, surrounding them on all sides. Chan is silent. 'Are you okay?' Rashid asks.

'I expect you thought I would be more shocked,' she says. 'The truth is that, when you have lived through a civil war, you have seen many such sights. I wish I could still feel the sensitivity for the dead that you have. When you've– ' Her voice wavers. 'When many members of your family have been killed right in front of you, even though you might have been very young at the time, it stays with you.'

'I didn't know.' Rashid is uncertain whether it's appropriate to put an arm around her shoulder.

While he's deciding, a tall, elegant woman comes in with Jue Hai. 'This is Doctor Bjarnadóttir,' the pathologist says.

'Nice to meet you,' Rashid says. The scientist looks to be in her mid-forties though she could be younger. 'I understand you want to talk to me about the cloth fragment,' she says.

Rashid nods. 'I assume you compared the fragment we recovered with a regular sample of the exo-skeletal clothing?'

'Yes. Perhaps you'd like to see for yourself the differences we found?' Bjarnadóttir walks them through to an adjoining room. She pushes a button, which rotates the large instrument on the desk. The machine continues to adjust itself until, finally, it projects an image. 'Please,' she offers. Her Icelandic accent is slight and hard to place.

Rashid and Chan step forward together. The instrument makes a further adjustment before the image is simultaneously projected into their eyes.

'As you can see, the two materials are similar. Notice the grey fibres from the reinforced material and the way it's attached to the other fibres that would have formed the outer layer.'

'So the exo-skeletal layer has been fused to a different outer fabric. That must be normal, surely? They don't all wear the same clothing, after all,' Rashid says.

'You're right, of course,' she says, 'But look more closely at that exterior layer.'

'I see what you mean,' Chan says. 'There is something very different about it – a strange quality to it. A luminescence.'

'Very good, very good.' Dr Bjarnadóttir is almost jumping up and down. 'That's exactly right.'

Now Rashid can see it too. The first projection is replaced by another. 'This is the same sample further enhanced by a factor of twenty – it needs to be interpreted for our crude human eyes. Now we see it more clearly at the sub-molecular level, the difference is undeniable.'

'So what exactly is it that we are looking at?' Rashid asks.

'That's the thing,' Dr Bjarnadóttir says. 'It's a substance that's entirely new to me. As you are no doubt aware, a large amount of this city's wealth comes from rare earth elements – more especially the heavy ones. I myself began my career in the mining industry. So, without false modesty, I'd say I know all there is to know about europium, gadolinium, terbium, lutetium, ytterbium and yttrium and so forth.'

Confident that she's established her credentials, there's a pause before she adds, 'But this particular substance is something quite different from anything I've encountered. I'd rather not speculate about its properties and possible function until I have heard back from the various universities I've sent these images to.'

'You're saying that this is an *unknown* substance.'

'Not just a regular unknown substance yet to be identified, I'm saying that its structure, at molecular level, is unknown to science. As far as I am aware, this is a substance previously unknown to mankind.'

'Surely not from outer space?' Rashid pulls a face – this is getting out of hand.

'I can't say at this stage. With all the global expense poured into near-planetary mining over the last twenty years, I could speculate that it's some undisclosed material retrieved from those missions. Or, alternatively, derived from the remains of an asteroid fallen to Earth. It must have been developed in a highly secret facility, which has, so far, chosen not to share its findings with the scientific community.'

'Who could afford to fund such a project these days?' Chan asks.

'It's normal for that sort of pioneering research to be carried out in secret,' Rashid says, 'for commercial reasons, but are their obvious candidates?'

'Unfortunately, I don't even have the beginnings of an answer. I've contacted some of the world's leading authorities. Let's hope they can help us,' Dr Bjarnadóttir says, turning off the projection. 'In the meantime, I'll leave you to speculate about why they would go to all that bother and expense.'

Rashid walks back along the corridor with Chan. 'So, as if we didn't have enough to figure out, we can now throw into the mix that this decoy was possibly wearing a totally new, unknown material.'

They reach the lift. 'Perhaps she really is an Avenging Angel,' he says. 'Or an alien come here from another planet to show us the error of our ways?'

'But still carrying a large knife or similar weapon?' she reminds him.

'Ah, but that could just be for symbolic reasons; you know, like the scythe that Cronus used. Or Odin's sword.'

They step in and the doors close. Chan turns to Rashid, 'You were right, Senior Constable, I did learn a lot today.'

Rashid smiles back, relieved to be once again breathing air that had only circulated amongst the living.

Fourteen

She pulls back her hood and Bruno finds himself staring at a normal looking woman, though in the half-light, with her pallid skin and the shadows around her eyes, she still looks a bit like a cartoon alien.

She removes one of her gauntlets and a small, delicate hand emerges. (What on earth did he expect?) 'I think it's time we became properly acquainted,' she says. As if they'd just met under ordinary circumstances, she extends her hand towards him. Her fingers are very close to his, but she makes no attempt to grab his hand. 'I believe all it takes is one touch.'

'I won't,' he says. 'But thanks all the same.' He's still trapped on the bed. He moves his bandaged hands behind his back and holds them there as if protecting a precious object from her grasp.

'Oh dear, it seems I haven't made myself sufficiently clear. Look around you, Bruno; I think you'll agree you're somewhat outnumbered.'

Illogically, he checks to confirm the continuing truth of her claim. Trying to sound calmer than he is, he says, 'Look, I'm just an ordinary student who got lost. I really have no idea about all that other stuff you were talking about.'

'You're suggesting this is a case of mistaken identity?' She shakes her head. 'I suppose you had to try.' Her mouth falls into a parody of a smile. 'However, if that were the case, I'm afraid we'd have to kill you right now.'

She carries on staring at him. Unblinking, enjoying the hold she has over him. 'I thought you and I might reach an understanding,' she says, 'seize this opportunity to discover where our mutual interests lie.'

She nods his attention towards her companion. 'I'd rather keep this civilised, but, if you force us to, we will use an alternative means of persuasion.'

'What exactly do you want from me?'

She begins to pace before him like an animal considering its prey. Then she stops dead. 'I realise I'm jumping the gun a little here – I confess, I have a tendency to do that.' She gives him another long look. 'You must be wondering how on earth we found you. Perhaps you're not aware there are distinctive anomalies in the brains of all telepatico? Apparently, these occur within the sensory cortex and the temporal lobe – unique activity patterns that show up quite clearly as abnormal during a routine brain scan. Luckily for you, young man, we have friends at the hospital.'

Bruno remembers having a load of tests, but this still sounds like bullshit. 'None of this makes sense,' he says. 'Even if what you're saying is true, I was just wondering around out in the snow; I could have ended up absolutely anywhere. Why would I have willingly walked right in here?'

'Well, since you ask, it's time for a little confession. The pills you were prescribed had a certain loosening effect on your thought processes. The rest of it wasn't down to anything we did – well, not directly anyway.'

She holds up both hands in a gesture of innocence. 'Of your own free will, you made a series of choices,' she says. 'Each one drew you closer to us. You willingly followed the trail we set in the snow.' Her laugh contains more menace than amusement. 'Doesn't that tell you something? Those extraordinary instincts of yours led you directly to us. You might even call it fate,

Bruno. And now your destiny is inextricably linked with ours.'

He looks past her towards the door. From their small tics and low growling, he can see the foxes are becoming restless. Not a good sign.

'Animals can always sense when something's not right about a person,' she says. He nearly misses the hand signal that sends them back into a crouching retreat. Their eyes are still trained on him.

The light suddenly diminishes and everything before him turns grey except her hair, which has turned the colour of congealed blood. 'Our crude combination lock was a small test,' she tells him. 'It got you in here. If we hadn't raised the temperature of this room while you slept, you would probably have succumbed to hypothermia. That fact alone ought to convince you that your interests are better served by co-operating with me.'

Without looking, he senses her well-built companion has moved closer and is standing near enough to overpower him in a single movement.

'Just think,' she says, 'if we hadn't intervened to prevent your test results reaching official attention, in the blink of an eye, the ACC–'

'The what?'

'You haven't heard of the ACC – the Eldísvík Commander's Committee?' She tut-tuts her disapproval and then wags a superior finger in front of his eyes. 'You young people really should take more of an interest in the political structure of your own state – you need to understand where the real power lies.' Her face is a pale, floating oval. 'Without our intercession, an alert would have been triggered and an automatic protocol would have swung into action. The Commanders would have dispatched a unit to the hospital and, right now, you'd be in custody. The very best you could hope for would be permanent containment.'

He can only just make out the hand she's extending. 'You

see, their knee-jerk response is to neutralise all and every possible threat to the status quo. Once you understand the situation as we do, I'm certain you'll appreciate the reasons behind all the little interventions we're planning. There's no need for that perplexed expression, young man; I suspect you already have more than an inkling of what I'm talking about.'

The hand is almost touching his chest. She's so close he has no choice but to breathe in the same air she's exhaling. Her last meal must have been fish. 'I'm sure you've heard the expression: the means justifies the ends, and it's true in this case,' she says. 'In fact, I'm so confident you'll agree, I'm willing to allow you inside my own mind.'

He recoils at the thought of sharing her all-consuming hatred for a second time and yet it would be an advantage if he understood exactly what this woman is planning to do. Behind his back, his hands are already loosening their grip on each other.

'I can sense you're eager to know more,' she says. 'Come on, Bruno, it must be crystal clear that there's only one deal on this particular table. Let's just shake on it, shall we?'

He wants this to be over, is so tempted to acquiesce. Instead, he plays for time. 'I can't do it. Not like this, it won't work. I need to concentrate and I can't do that when I'm dying of thirst. Not with you standing over me like this and him right behind me with his foul breath warming my ear and all those fokking foxes getting ready to tear my head off.'

From what he can see of her expression, it's clear this isn't helping her anger-management issues. He stands his ground. 'I'm sure even you must agree this is hardly the most relaxing of situations.'

She folds her arm but otherwise doesn't move an inch, just continues to glare at him: used to being in control, being the one calling the shots.

At last she takes a step back. 'I take your point.'

A slight movement of her hands is enough to make the

animals behind her rise as one. Each slow limb at a time, they begin to back off until, finally, they're subsumed into the corridor beyond. Bruno has no doubt they'll remain only metres away; eager for the swift gesture that will call them back in here and straight upon him.

Turning towards her mute companion, she says: 'Fetch a hot drink and some food.' The man hesitates, seems about to say something but instead he leaves the room.

'I haven't got time to play games,' she says, practically spitting the words in his face. 'In case you have other ideas about how this is going to work, let me spell it out for you: after you're fed and watered, there can be no more stalling. I'll come back alone and we will begin. Once you fully understand the situation, you'll appreciate the urgency.'

Like an apparition, she exits the room in one flowing movement to leave him staring at the closed and fox-barred door.

It's a relief, at least, to be able to move freely again. He goes across to the barred window and stares out at the abandoned yard; at the silvered peaks where the snow has drifted up against the walls. There's no way out; he's their prisoner. No cavalry is arriving to rescue him. From the light levels, he guesses that the sun is about to begin its shallow arc across the sky. All the footprints that encircle the building are beginning to melt and merge together. The weak sun will soon obliterate any remaining traces of his footsteps.

Fifteen

Nero walks the short distance to The Institute for Biological Research. His appointment with Dr Magnúsdóttir is at 11:40.

A strong wind is scattering the low, grey clouds and assaulting him from the gaps between the buildings. He pulls up his collar. People are pouring out of the ground-level walkways. He watches them act out their parts of stud conversations, unaware of the fact that the same technology being used in the device to interpret and transmit their words is also being used by the Z team to monitor each and every conversation.

The hourly Zeitgeist briefing is always available on Nero's stud. It is currently showing elevated levels of safety concerns along with heightened anxiety indicators. Sanford's unfortunate outburst at the press briefing has stoked a growing panic; in the last 24 hours there has been a ten-fold increase in orders for personal security equipment. The share price of Safe-T and Garrison has rocketed. It's not long before the election and the prospect of defeat is coming towards Leifsson like a runaway maglev. It wouldn't have happened to a nicer guy.

Arriving at the institute, Nero is bleeped into Dr Magnúsdóttir's office. She stands to greet him with a handshake. The physical connection instantly makes his hand tingle. 'Inspector Cavallo,' she says. 'I see you're exactly on time.' Up close, she seems even smaller. Aside from the grey skirt and sensible boots, she is wearing a plain white shirt and what looks like a genuine wool jacket.

'Dr Magnúsdóttir,' he says, looking about at the stacks of books taking up most of the free space. 'I hope you don't mind me asking you a few questions.' So many heavy books have imbued the air with the musky odour of old wood. If he were to shut his eyes, he might think he was in an old forest.

'I've sent you all the information that could possibly be of use,' she says. 'My assistant told me of your rather old-fashioned preference for face to face interviews.' She gestures towards her books. 'As you see, I'm something of a traditionalist myself.'

'I won't take up too much of your time, I just wanted to clarify a few things about these vixen packs.' Concentrating hard, he finds he can read some of her more superficial thoughts.

'Fire away, Inspector.' *Cavallo – isn't that the Italian for horse? Looks self-possessed, confident – somewhat overly so.*

'I've studied the simulation provided by the Animal Behaviour Unit at the university,' Nero says, 'and I'd like to know more about how these vixens behave when they're off-duty, as it were.'

'I'm sorry, Inspector, I don't quite follow.' *He keeps looking at my hair as if it bothers him. Perhaps he sees it as unusual for a woman to have little interest in her appearance. He's probably speculating about my personal life – my sexual preferences.*

'Well, as I understand it, though the indigenous Artic Fox tends to have large territories, the more urban living Red Fox ranges less widely and their individual territories are usually hexagonal in shape.'

'You've done your research, Inspector. Fascinating, isn't it, that these creatures should emulate other patterns found in nature, most famously, of course, the structure of beehive.' *Seems fond of straying off his own path. Well, he's in my territory now.* 'Oddly enough, the family structure of the Red Fox varies considerably: sometimes they practice what you might term polygamy, sometimes polyandry – which is the reverse arrangement.'

'That's very informative, Dr Magnúsdóttir,' he tells her, 'but could we get back to the question of their territorial behaviour? I believe Red foxes normally defend their ground against incomers. They scent-mark the boundaries with urine and this demarcation line tends to be respected by adjacent family groups. Is that correct?'

'It is, Inspector.' *So, he's persistent. Some women might consider him attractive. He likes his hair short – perhaps to control its natural wave, or does he like the way it follows the blunt contours of his head. A firm, squared-off jaw – beard growth that's rather too prolific.* 'The same pattern of scent-marking is repeated throughout the animal kingdom. In crowded cities such as our own, the behaviour of humans is, in some ways, not that dissimilar.'

'So just how do these rogue, off-duty vixens fit into the picture?'

'An interesting question, and one that greatly occupied us at the beginning. We choose vixens not just for their superior protection instinct but also for their skill at remaining undetected. For any animal this requires sophisticated judgment. You could say it takes the fabled stealth of the fox.'

Though it's a poor joke, he dutifully smiles.

'In the case of our vixens,' she says, 'once fully trained, it becomes a near-to-natural behaviour pattern, second nature, as it were–'

'Forgive me for interrupting, Doctor, but what I'd really like to know is: as they are all females and outsiders, when they are not on-duty how do they manage to live peaceably inside other fox territories?'

Is that stare meant to intimidate me? No pupil dilation evident in either direction – we both understand that much at least. Not the slightest attempt to look away. He's hoping I'll find this unbroken eye contact disconcerting.

'During our feasibility research, we tagged a dozen of our vixens and followed their behaviour,' she says. 'We were surprised to find that other foxes – both the Red ones and their more elusive Arctic cousins – treated them as if they were a separate species. Somehow these animals sensed the differences the wolf genome implant had made. Possibly because they had observed their tendency towards pack behaviour, possibly due to a change to their odour we ourselves can't detect.' She sits back in her chair, relaxing into lecture-mode. 'Once the feral foxes recognise this difference, they tolerate what you might describe as their parallel existence.'

'So they aren't regarded as a threat?'

'It would seem not. We introduced a feeding procedure, which reassures other predators that our vixens posed no danger to their own food supplies. Our vixens are able to colonise their own areas and from these they can come and go unmolested – provided they return to claim their space within a day or so.'

'So, does each pack have its own distinct territory?'

'Not exactly.' *Does he see himself as horse-like? A stallion maybe? The man's dogged, that's for sure. Perhaps he's Inspector Cane da Caccia: the hound dog running at the horse's side.* 'Unlike wolves, they spread out and tend not to stick too closely together. Each individual vixen has its own territory adjacent to that of the rest of their pack. On a more practical level, the decoys are thereby able to track them down and feed them within a central geographical area.'

'So there is a direct link between each decoy and their pack's particular off-duty area?'

'Yes, Inspector, your conclusion is correct. But as we don't monitor the movements of the individual decoys or their vixens, it's hard to see how this helps you in your search.' *Here is your bone, Inspector Cane. You won't find much meat on it.*

'So you think we'll be unable to track and locate this decoy?'

'That is your job, Inspector, and not mine,' she tells him. 'The task may be impossible without further satellite intelligence and I understand that the military haven't been especially co-operative in providing it.'

'You think we won't be able to find her without their help?'

'In my opinion, that's a distinct possibility. Unless, of course, she makes a mistake.'

'Do you think the decoy herself is likely to be feeling safe – confident she can't be traced?'

Pure instinct this time – just a sniff in the breeze. 'My main expertise is in animal behaviour, Inspector. It's impossible for me to guess with any accuracy how this decoy might be feeling. However, I will say that, despite every effort, she remains at large. She may well feel safe and elated by her victory. She's experienced an extraordinary triumph and is, most likely, enjoying the sense of success that brings.'

Nero lets the silence between them continue. It fails to rattle Magnúsdóttir.

Eventually, he clears his throat and asks, 'Do you have a theory as to how she was able to get through the screening process laid down by your department?'

She sighs. 'As I stated during the initial briefing – and again in my report – it *ought* to have been impossible. I'm certain your Decoy Training Department have been remiss in some way. I understand they've suffered financial cutbacks recently. There may have been an attempt to save money by using less-qualified staff. Or perhaps this is a case of over-worked and overstretched officers making mistakes. I'm sure this happens in every department – even in your own.'

'But your institute oversee the programme in order to make sure they adhere to the agreed procedures.'

'We do some limited monitoring, but not a sufficient amount to guarantee no mistakes will ever be made,' she says. 'Sadly, we ourselves have insufficient staff to ensure this.'

Recognise the blind alley for what it is, Inspector Cane with no caccia to follow. You are hardly a match for such an adversary. 'Talking of which, I have various pressing matters to attend to, if that is all, Inspector?'

She stands up. This time her handshake is more of a quick clasp. Nero walks towards the door and then turns. 'Leifsson may well have to fall on his sword after this,' he says.

'Yes, I think you may be right. His performance during last night's briefing was truly dismal; no doubt he will have to pay the political consequence before too long.'

'Seems a bit harsh though, don't you think?'

'I think a respect for tradition is not the only thing we have in common, Inspector.'

'I don't quite follow what you mean.'

'I'm sure we both recognise weakness when we see it.' Her grey eyes are shining. 'I wish you luck with your investigations,' she says, turning away.

Her parting words resound in Nero's head as he leaves the building. The woman's distain for him and his investigation had been clear enough. There had been far more but, so far, she'd been able to hide it from him. One thing that was certain – he'd just been set a challenge.

He takes a little detour and heads towards his favourite deli in order to buy a couple of turtlitts. The cakes are a small weakness, the nearest he's found to the homemade fritters his grandma used to make for carnivale. Their subtle amoretti flavour will go perfectly with his coffee – when he next has time for one.

Sixteen

Kass and Lúter return looking far from happy. 'How did you get on over there?' Nero asks. Now he's managed to beg a couple more chairs, he gestures for them to sit down.

They remain on their feet. Lúter is the first to answer his question. 'Doctor Arthur wasn't there but we managed to interview the head honcho in Psychological Assessment: a Dr Bob Fuller. After that, we questioned Arthur's deputy: a bloke called Uri Haim. Both of them were at pains to tell us the department had already carried out a thorough review to see if there could have been any omissions or glitches in their procedures over the last ten years. No prize for guessing, they found–' he looks down at his log, '"no anomalies or exceptions to any of the department's established protocols".'

Kass finally flops down into a chair. 'The official line they're all sticking to is, and I quote: "We can offer no explanation for this decoy's abhorrent behaviour".' She peers at Nero from over her glasses. 'Everyone we spoke to seemed keen to remind us the Commanders hold the only records on serving decoys.'

'As far as they know, there are currently ninety decoy officers,' Lúter tells him. 'Haim took a guess that, at any one time, probably about a third of them are on duty – but that was just a guess. They have no way of knowing how they choose to operate.' He finally sits down. 'They're now only recruiting four or five new decoys each year. Both Fuller and Haim maintained this was no reflection on the decoys' effectiveness or performance. They claimed it was only due to recent cutbacks and what-have-you.'

'So, one or two of those ninety decoys could have already left the service and they'd be none the wiser.' Nero scrubs at the growing stubble on his chin. 'Did you get the impression that they were hiding anything?'

Kass looks over at Lúter and then shrugs. 'Hard to be certain,' she says. 'We were surprised at how readily both Haim and Fuller agreed to bio-feed analysis during their interviews. They didn't bat an eyelid. All their readouts appeared to be normal – no signs they were obfuscating or telling us anything but the truth.'

'Oh, and both of them denied any knowledge of a new material being used in the manufacture of decoy suits.' Lúter's frustration is etched into his face. 'We tried everything, boss, but they passed with flying flags and a brass band.'

'Good work all the same,' Nero says, getting to his feet with them. 'See if you can find out where Dr Arthur has disappeared to and when he's likely to be back. I think I'll go over there and interview him myself.'

As the two sergeants turn to go, he slaps them on the back. Over the years he's made it a rule never to attempt to read the minds of colleagues or friends and right now he'd hardly need to in order to hear the mood music. They leave his office with their heads down.

Nero sighs. Perhaps he should have that coffee now along with those turtlitts.

Later in the afternoon, Nero decides to pay Rustler a visit in his brand new capacity as Military Liaison Officer. 'Congratulations on your elevation,' he says.

'Take a seat.' Rustler barely looks up. The man's chair

squeaks in an irritating way as he continues to rotate it back and forth. Nero notes that every last trace of Vasiliev has already disappeared from the office. Rustler's personal effects are still in a box on the desk. 'I'm not bothering to unpack,' he says, reaching into the haphazard collection of his possessions to retrieve what looks like a child's juggling ball. Rustler starts to pass it from one hand to the other – over and over. 'I probably have twenty-four hours in this job – that's if I'm lucky. If this decoy isn't caught soon, Leifsson will be looking for another fall guy. What the hell can I do – my hands are tied.' Without warning, he throws the ball at Nero. 'Good catch,' he says. 'I'm glad somebody's reflexes are still working properly.'

Nero throws it back. 'You're right – there's nothing you can do. It's all up to the Commanders and their powers of persuasion over at Military Defence.'

The ball comes at him; this time Nero returns it with a slight spin. Just as he's getting to his feet, the interface on Rustler's desk lights up like sunrise. A stream of satellite images is projected onto the far wall.

Rustler yelps. 'Okay – we're in business at last and about bloody time.'

'I guess they've been convinced they have a mutual interest here,' Nero says, walking over to get a clearer picture of what they've finally released.

Rustler runs the image stream through his system and then goes quiet. The man just sits there shaking his head.

'What is it?' Nero asks. 'What's wrong?'

Rustler thumps the table with his fist. 'Every bloody thing they've just sent us is useless: it's all just deflected images from a completely different area of the Red Zone. No wonder the military didn't want us to see this stuff.'

Rustler's chair falls backwards as he jumps to his feet. 'What I want to know is how those bastards in the Red Zone are able to do that. They must be using the kind of cloaking technology that's really state-of-the-art. I mean, way more advanced than it ought to be.' He kicks at the prostrate chair and then winces with pain.

'In that case, that leaves us with a far bigger question,' Nero says. 'How could all that stuff have found its way past State Security into the Red Zone?'

'They must have had help,' Rustler says, hopping on one foot, 'All that stuff will have cost them an arm and several legs.'

Seventeen

She's tucked in between the abandoned buildings, merging with the shadow-line. Unnecessary, under the circumstances, but the habit is ingrained. Old advertising hoardings still flap with the last vestige of words and images torn from another era. A lone bush is sticking up through the snow; its dead branches scratch away at a door that fails to open. Every broken window has been boarded up. Someone must have been holding out for better times.

Before her, the empty valley is the wind's playground; she watches it tease and toy with the snow, driving it into wave after wave. In this half-light, those drifts could almost be sand dunes.

This is Orange Zone after all: a name that suggests a sunnier, happier region, somewhere wholesome to bring up your family. Of course, it's also a warning light instructing the inhabitants to prepare; wait when told; stop right there.

How many years has she kept watch over the people living here, observing them as they shrink back like mollusks to hide inside the crumbling shells of their homes, too scared ever to venture outside during the curfew hours?

Outsiders continue to be drawn to the seductive orange glow. Sometimes it's Free Zone big fish longing for the excitement of more dangerous waters, sometimes Red Zone small fry looking to expand their operations. This area is on its way towards reclassification. It won't be long before, like a sunset rippling over snow, it begins to take on a rosier hue. Orange might be the new peach? Yes – why not call it the Peach Zone? Roll up, roll up, get your tasty new zone here right here, so plump and ripe for the taking.

One by one, her vixens are getting closer, impatient for action. She signals for them to stay well back while she alone remains in the space between structures.

As always, her suit cocoons and separates her from the ferocity of the wind. Tonight, she's warmed by a burning hatred of their bloody zones, their bloody hands; worse still, the bloody complacency that lets others decree what is criminal whilst, in another light, the same activity is deemed legitimate. Even more than all of this, she hates herself, hates that she hadn't intervened, had allowed herself to become someone no better than the millions of silent accomplices she so despises.

Tonight, she must atone. Watching the execution of Harris, she'd vowed to become the splinter in the very heart of this state – an infiltration that works its way through everything until the damage can no longer be contained.

Despite the efficiency of the clean-up, the carbonized imprints of the dead still survive a mere stone's throw from where she's standing. Their traces persist like cave paintings fused onto concrete to bear witness to the truth of that commander's unspeakable deed.

The wind carries the sound of distant voices. In time they draw nearer. She turns her head as they grow louder. Their voices are full of confidence, paying no heed to the curfew. Are they red fish or orange ones? Could a group of these damned mollusks finally have developed a backbone?

She sees them at last – spread out against the fading light. Ten of them in total: a nice round number. Better hold off until she's sure. (The innocent must be protected, or she is no better than the rest of them.)

Ha, they're way too young – a group of silly boys and girls out looking for excitement. Well-spoken: minnows from the Free Zone daring each other on. She'll pass on these sprats.

When she opens her eyes again darkness has fallen. Looking up, she sees the sea-green tendrils of the Aurora Borealis flickering along the horizon like a restless and ghostly army gathering.

She turns away from the spectacle to the bright flashes on the horizon. There's a faint hum from something that's approaching. Definitely a hydrogen engine.

The aurora dances overhead whilst another series of blasts light up the darkness below. This time they're much closer. An odd noise: intermittent, metallic. A rattling roll followed by more blasts. Ah – target practice on a can. They must be using infrareds. Raucous laughter. High shrieks of pleasure or maybe pain? More photon fire: 0.5 ml or possibly the newer 0.8s.

The streetlights are now extinguished making it easier to spot the two of them on foot. From the way it's veering around, at least one other person is driving that vehicle.

For her amusement she'll pretend they're a troupe of travelling entertainers. No, better still, shadow puppets.

The players are closer now. Someone shouts: 'Stop acting like twats!' A man's voice – not young but not old either. 'What the fokk's the matter with you?'

Continuing to fire at the tin, the tall, gangly one shouts back: 'Lighten up, Haggerty!' (*Blast)* 'You said yourself they probably won't arrive for another hour or more.' (*Blast*) 'And there's sod all else to do out here.' *(Blast, blast.)* 'Besides, we get to practice our aim for later.' He nudges his companion. 'Don't we, Mo?'

Mo fires this time. 'Damn – I missed it that time. Fokking thing's too beat-up to roll properly. I think we may have killed it, bruv.'

Haggerty (even angrier) 'You idiots – we're not in the Red Zone now. Patrols still operate out here, you know. That blaster-fire can be seen for miles.'

The two of them lower their weapons. She creeps forward knowing the slightest sound will betray her presence.

Having got their attention, Haggerty, the driver, drops his voice. 'Besides, we don't want to frighten our new friends off, do we? If they get spooked and split, we'll have to go back empty-handed. I don't know about you two morons, but I don't want to face Lawson if we go back with nothing.'

The short one kicks at the can. 'Yeah alright, point fokking taken.'

So, this little dumb show is only the trailer – it seems there's an hour to go before others arrive and the main act can begin. With infinite care, she inches back into her hiding place. Maybe her opening line should be: '*Good evening, gentlemen.*' Or, if appropriate: '*Good evening, ladies and gentlemen.*' That should draw them all over to exactly where she wants them.

Reaching into her pocket, she caresses the contours of the small plastic object she's brought along. She's impatient for the show to begin, after all, her best work is still to come.

Eighteen

The duty officer wakes Nero from a tumbling sleep.

'Sorry to disturb you, sir.' He recognises Maxwell's voice. 'There's been another incident,' she says, 'this time in District Fourteen. Patrol just called it in. Multiple slaying, body parts scattered over some distance. Forensics already on their way.'

His naked feet hit the cold floor.

'The victims appear to have been hacked to death with a large blade of some kind and then torn apart,' she tells him. 'First report suggests signs of animal predation but this time there's some fresh graffiti adjacent to the scene.'

'Couldn't the two be unrelated?' He pulls on underpants.

'Not really – it appears to be written in blood.'

'Christ,' he says, rubbing his eyes. 'District Fourteen, you said?'

'Yes, next to a row of derelict shops, not far from the spine road.'

He grabs a clean shirt. 'I'll be there as fast as I can. Make sure they secure the whole of the surrounding area this time.'

'I'm sure they'll have already done that, sir.'

'Tell them anyway.' Nero is still wrestling with buttons. 'Spell it out. Then contact Sergeant Stefánsson. Get him to meet me there. No need to wake the rest of my team yet. I want full cover from the armoureds. You clear with all that?'

'As a bell, Inspector.'

'Oh, and Maxwell, who called it in?'

'Anonymous, sir.'

'How's that even possible?'

'Major ping-pong across global networks. They're still trying to tag it, but so far, there are too many false echoes.'

He knows the crime scene – those shops act like an Orange beacon. They'd passed close by after they dropped Harris off. He splashes water in his face and rakes more through his hair. No time to shave. If anything, he looks even worse than in the ID mug shot he fixes to his topcoat.

If he can get to the scene fast enough, he might still pick up traces of the perp. The internal lift deposits Nero only metres from the subway stop. A waiting pod has him at DSD inside four minutes.

In the locker room, he grabs his recon pack then loses a minute or two wrestling with the awkward fastenings of his body armour. At supplies, he signs out a photon and, breaching safety regulations, loads it on the hoof. He passes Maxwell in the corridor. 'Get me all available satellite coverage from last night. Call Rustler.'

'Already done, Inspector!' she shouts after him.

Nero jumps into a two-seater. It offers less protection but is much faster. In that section of the Orange Zone the tracks are still pretty good provided the snowfall out there isn't too deep.

The calculation pays off. The snow is already melted away. Nero is pleased to see two armoureds standing guard at each end. Blue and white tape encircles the line of drab buildings and a wide area out in front. It waves enthusiastically in the wind. Floodlights are illuminating the central area – like a stage without its audience.

Monitors in hand, a group of green-suited pathologists are

already combing the ground. He recognises Jue Hai amongst them.

'I didn't know you did field work,' Nero says, coming up behind him. He braces himself before he lets his gaze drop to the gory remains scattered at his feet. He hasn't seen anything remotely like this since before he took refuge in this country.

'My shift had nearly finished when this call came in,' the pathologist tells him, bending down to take a closer look at something.

'Do me a favour,' Nero says. 'I'd like you all to hold off with the bagging up until Lúter gets here and the two of us have had a proper look around.'

Jue Hai straightens up. 'There's really no need. We're recording the whole thing meticulously. Nothing will be missed.'

'Look, the two of us just need a few minutes to study the scene while it's relatively undisturbed.'

'I can't think why you still choose to work like this.' Jue Hai shakes his head. 'We'll send you holos of the whole thing without a sniff of blood or gore.'

'Give us ten minutes, tops,' Nero says. 'I don't want to pull rank, but, technically, I am in charge of this investigation.'

'You just did,' Jue Hai says. His nod of agreement is more of a bow. He goes over to tell his colleagues the bad news. Shaking their heads, they all turn towards Nero with their bloodied gloves raised before walking off to one side.

With no time to wait for Lúter, Nero prepares to walk the grid. Despite the low temperature, the smell of sweat and fetid corruption already threatening to overpower him, Nero starts at the nearest corner. The harsh light is glinting off rings and fastenings, punctuating vast swathes of frosted flesh and the dark pools of dried blood. He recognises the upright sole of a half-attached foot, a hat melded onto a head and everywhere the torn and gory remnants of outer clothing designed to shield them from the elements. Prayer seems the only sane response, but he fears all hard-pressed deities have long ago forsaken this place.

Though tempted, he can't remove his gauntlets – not with a line of hostile forensic pathologists observing his every move.

Lúter finally arrives. Nero watches him circumnavigate the corpses. Briefly, they stand together and survey the grisly tableau at their feet. They say very little as they begin a methodical sweep of the scene.

At least the remains of the victims are more complete this time – that should make identification easier. A few flies buzz, indiscriminately landing on one body part and then moving on to the next. All around him the countryside is in the grip of winter – where on earth could these have possibly emerged from?

Forcing himself to look more closely, Nero sees that the blade wounds on the victims are far more distinctive than before. The weapon used had to be heavy and sharp in order to slice through them so cleanly. A hell of a lot of photon fire had been unleashed in all directions. Not only are there extensive burn marks on all the corpses but every centimetre of the ground they're lying on has been scorched.

The decoy's previous hallmarks are certainly present. Superficially, everything suggests this was a battle between a heavily armed gang against a sword-wielding vigilante, but is he looking at the work of that same decoy or had someone else been emulating them?

He turns his attention to the boarded-up windows and the various markings sprawled across each one in what looks like blood. The words are in Icelandic. Though numerous vertical drip lines are obscuring the letters, Nero can make out the word for *walk* on one board and then *death*, then something about *fear* on another.

Lúter translates: 'And though I walk through the valley of the shadow of death, I will fear no evil.'

The accompanying symbols are less distinct. Nero turns his head this way and that but can make no sense of them. 'Does that other stuff mean anything to you, Lúter?'

The sergeant shakes his head. 'This writing, those symbols – all of it's new.'

'Yeah – someone clearly felt it was time to bring God into the equation.' Nero's monitor tells him the writer had used human blood. 'All this must have been done immediately afterwards – while their blood was still runny enough. The lab tests will tell us more about who it belonged to.'

These people were operating here in the Orange Zone; he'd put money on them being petty criminals and not major-league villains like before. Were they looking at the handiwork of the same woman or a copycat? If the latter, how many others might there be in the same damned litter? He knew Lúter was wondering the exact same thing.

The forensic squad begins to advance towards them; it seems their agreed time is up. Nero has no choice but to concede the territory. Frustration eats into him: if only he'd been able to have a minute or two alone and unobserved, he might have gotten enough to identify whoever did this.

He kicks at the kerb in frustration. Whatever their motivation, their grievance, this isn't the right way to solve anything. They have to be stopped. And yet there it is – writ large in front of him – the justification: a psalm that could have been written for all the poor decoys who patrol this wilderness, doing the city's dirty work at all hours of the day and night.

Nineteen

Leifsson arrives at his office a good two hours ahead of his normal time. On his desk, the briefing plug-ins are laid out in order of urgency. With her usual efficiency, Ami has placed a selection of brunch options on a side table along with his usual cappuccino. The room's opulence gives out a calm and orderly impression. It lies.

Sipping at his coffee, the governor paces back and forth while he waits for the progress update he asked for ten minutes ago. Barely containing his frustration, he has to suppress a strong desire to smash something. Anything. That psycho-slut decoy has been partying again and this time much closer to home. How is it possible for her to go running around like some Viking shieldmaiden wielding her sword and not get picked up by any of the patrols? She must have been tipped-off and probably by someone working inside DSD. He's already doubled the number of patrols and blown the budget to beef up the satellite coverage. What more can he do short of going out there to look for the fokking woman himself?

His stud buzzes with confirmation that the latest collection of body parts dragged into the city have all been located and removed. How long can it be before he's facing claims for P.T.S. from the civilian clean-up operators?

Relief sits him down. Avoiding the healthy options, he bites into a pain au chocolat but it's dryness sticks in his throat. His window is showcasing the rays of the sun now rising above the mountains. The backlit, silver-edged clouds would look magnificent on any other day. He tries to take in the spectacle and this minor respite.

Leifsson's stud vibrates as Ami sends through the usual summary of the morning's media coverage and, lo and bloody behold, there's yet another shit-storm for him to deal with. He wades through image after image of the carnage, each one graphically illustrating his own failure. How did those bastards get hold of this?

The dreaded black dog comes back with a vengeance; this time it feels like the beast is sitting on his chest and slowly squeezing the life out of him. It's a battle for survival now and he can't afford to piss about. First off, he has to find whoever is behind all these leaks. It's only a matter of time. When he does, he'll shove that whistle they're so fond of blowing right up their puny little arse.

The tension in Leifsson's shoulders has begun to migrate to the back of his neck. He knows it will soon give the start signal to his own, personal, migraine goblin. After that, his brain will be a plasma-ball ablaze with a million random firings.

He pops the usual pills, though these days, they're proving more and more useless. Ah yes, here it comes, right on cue – the flickering has already begun at the top of his left eye. He'd better pull the curtain against the sun and tell Ami to cancel all his meetings. At best, he'll be laid out for the rest of the morning on his black leather couch. That serpent, Hagalín, will make the most of the opportunity to be seen as the good old, dependable Deputy-in-Charge. Without seeming to be disloyal, the man will make sure there's no doubt about exactly who is to blame for this woman still being at large.

Yesterday, after the Commanders had point-blank refused to give anyone access to the decoy files, Cavallo had come in here on his charger sounding off about it. Leifsson is sorely tempted to give him the go-ahead to go marching into their HQ with his demands just to see whose career lasts the shortest.

Ami comes in with the glass of water he'd asked for. 'Deputy Hagalín has confirmed that he'll head up the two meetings you had scheduled for later this morning,' she tells him. He has to look away from the pattern on her blouse. 'He also said he was primed and ready to take your two-thirty as well, if you need him to.'

After she leaves, Leifsson takes two more tablets and lies down on his unyielding couch. When did they stop making furniture that was actually comfortable?

He shuts his eyes and tries to clear his mind. This decoy couldn't be acting alone. There was no way one lone slag could cause this much trouble all by herself. If they can uncover whoever's been briefing the media from inside DSD, they might get a lead on who's really behind everything that's happened over the last few days. He'll personally squeeze the little bastard's throat until he spills his guts.

The governor pinches the bridge of his nose and, following his therapist's advice, attempts to visualise the peace and quiet of that strip of land his family had struggled to farm over so many generations. He can see the old house with its red paint peeling. The sheep are scattered over the fields, heads down as they hunker against the wind. That stony soil stretches all the way down the slope that leads to the freezing waters of the fjord. There's no noise, nothing but the empty landscape stretching out for miles in every direction: God how he hated that fokking place.

His vision darkens; the faces of his many potential betrayers crowd in. He forces his eyes open and yet, for a moment, they're all still there in the room bearing down on him. Heart racing, he stares up at the darkened ceiling until the last of the apparitions dissolves.

Concentrating on steadying his breathing, he runs through

the steps that are supposed to calm him. How on earth is he meant to empty his mind at a time like this? They need to start by plugging this leak. When he's back on his feet, he'll assign someone he can trust to conduct an internal investigation – that's if he can think of such an individual. The situation calls for more boots on the ground. Nero Cavallo is worse than useless – the wretched man's only good for joining the procedural dots.

Twenty

The sun is now a fraction higher in the sky, melting the last remnants of snow. Nero knows they ought to be getting back but some instinct is telling him to stay. They linger at the edge of the scene as the forensic team continues to sort and label the remains. Head down, Lúter begins to kick a small pebble around. Nero blocks its path – a reflex from those childhood football games played in the streets of a far warmer place. He kicks it back.

When Lúter kicks the stone towards him, he raises a hand to stop the game. Nero's whole body grows tense. Something else happened in this place: something just as terrible.

Drawn towards the source of the emotion he can feel, Nero examines the ground. At first there's nothing except cracked concrete, but then, some distance further on, he detects evidence of scorching. He takes a torch from his pocket and shines its penetrating beam across the uneven surface in front of him and there it all is – the faded but unmistakable signature of military-strength proton blasts. The whole area is covered in them.

'What the hell have we got here?' Lúter says, following the flashlight's progress. They're looking at the signs of a full-scale battle right inside the Orange Zone. Without warning, a wave of pain engulfs Nero. Self-preservation makes him break the connection before the intensity overwhelms him. Looking up into the weak sky, he struggles to master himself.

'You alright, boss?' Lúter asks.

For now, Nero can only nod. He wills his breathing to slow down. His heartrate to return to normal.

Once he's recovered enough to speak, he says, 'We need Forensics to come and take a look at all this.' He stops Lúter with a hand to his shoulder. 'Wait. Make sure you ask Jue Hai – only him.'

Left alone, Nero takes in the full scale of the battle that must have taken place. It would have been visible for miles in every direction. There had to be a connection with these new killings. Was this evidence of some kind of turf war?

Fortunately, the armoured vehicles are quite some distance away, their occupants presumably bored and paying little attention to what Nero might or might not be doing. He takes the risk and sheds his right glove. Straight away, his naked fingers begin to tingle. Nero braces himself. Once again, he's overcome by the immensity of the suffering, has to fight to sever the connection before he can learn anything.

Given the degree of surveillance in this part of the Orange Zone, why hadn't they picked up this battle when it was happening? Nero looks over to where Lúter and Jue Hai are heads down in conversation. He's pleased to see all the other scientists remain engrossed in their work.

Lúter comes back. 'Juey says he'll take a look at this once he's finished.'

Nero continues to study the pattern of the scorch marks. He needs to double-check what he thinks he's seeing. 'Look there, Lúter,' he says. 'That bit to your left, by the big pothole.'

'Okay.' Lúter frowns. 'What about it?'

'Now cast your eyes over the section just beyond, the strip running along the edge of the kerb.'

'I see what you mean – that area is darker, sort of fresher looking.'

'Exactly.' Nero is certain now. 'The marks are more faded near the central area because they've been wiped away. Someone made sure all this was thoroughly cleaned in order to hide any trace of what happened.' Nero looks around him. 'A pretty tricky and time-consuming operation in a place like this.'

'So why would someone go to all that trouble? Why not leave it here as a warning to others? More to the point, how come this didn't show up on our radar?'

'Perhaps it did.' Nero lowers his voice. 'Perhaps what happened here was officially sanctioned.'

They stare at each other. Nero resists the urge to look over at the armoureds guarding the scene. 'We should move away,' he says, kicking another stone as if the two of them are simply out here stretching their legs.

'If this was cleaned up on someone's authority,' Lúter says, 'exactly where does that leave us?' He squints into the sun. 'I didn't join the force to turn a blind eye.'

Nero knows they ought to let this particular dog keep snoozing – give the beast an extra blanket even. 'I can handle things here,' he says. 'You should go back to the office.'

'You know, my dad still likes to go hunting in the mountains once in a while with the others,' Lúter says rubbing at his chin. 'The old men have this saying: "Sá er vinur er í vök reynist". Roughly translating it means something like: "You can't know your friends from your enemies until the ice cracks".'

Nero can sense they're being watched. 'For the moment we both need to walk right away,' he says, taking the lead.

The forensic guys are doing their work efficiently; it looks like they'll have everything done and dusted within the hour. 'Stay right here, Sergeant,' Nero says. 'And that's an order.'

He makes his way over to Jue Hai and stands there until he finally has the man's full attention. 'Make sure it's just you that examines that area Lúter pointed out,' he tells him. 'You'll need to spin some bullshit to your colleagues, maybe say something about getting comparative readings of ground conditions or that sort of thing. Give your results directly to me and no one else – d'you understand? I don't want this broadcasted.' He can see the rising alarm in Jue Hai's eyes. 'It might be nothing. Just an old battleground.'

'Leave the bullshitting to an expert – all that ground conditions crap would be a dead giveaway.' The pathologist looks at him straight. 'I'll make up some story, do the sweep alone and let you have the results before anyone else. If I think others should be told, I will do precisely that. You understand me?'

Nero smiles, admiring the man's integrity.

One of the other scientists comes over waving a plastic bag. 'Inspector, I've just found this under Doe Four over there.' She holds up her find. It's another plastic duck. 'We've run all the tests. You can take it back with you, if you like.'

The two of them walk over to the two-seater and climb onboard. 'You know, a number of my relatives still believe in elves,' Lúter says while buckling up.

Nero's eyes narrow on his sergeant. 'What's your point?'

'A lot of our traditional stories are about the Hidden People.'

'And?'

'They're supposed to lead parallel lives alongside us. Though they're invisible to most of us, they can be seen by those with a certain sensitivity. They warn them about impending dangers, that sort of thing.'

'What the hell's that got to do with anything?'

'I've noticed before that you seem to have –' Lúter breaks off, waving his hand as he searches for the right words. 'Second sight – isn't that what they call it in English?'

Nero looks away from the penetration of his gaze. 'Mykja! Isn't that your word for bullshit?' Despite the cold, his body begins to prickle with sweat. 'These long, dark nights certainly do seem to feed the imagination.'

'Okay, okay. I'm just saying, you've got some sort of *ability* and I know it's more than just intuition.'

Nero laughs out loud. 'You seriously think I talk to elves?'

'Maybe. I like to keep an open mind. Anyway, there's no need to worry, boss.' Lúter nudges him. 'Your secret's safe with me.'

Shaking his head, Nero stows the plastic duck in the front where its black eyes continue to stare at him. He notices how its shiny surface is dulled with blood, making the toy appear more red than orange.

Twenty-One

Bruno wakes to find he's curled up on the hard floor, his whole body stiff and aching. Though there's a faint, fugitive light coming in from somewhere, he has no notion of whether it might be night or day or how long he's been locked inside the room.

The woman – his captor – had called him out as a telepatico: an accusation he's been running from all his life. He'd never wanted to have these abilities: to be cursed like Midas by every touch; to know everything about anyone after the slightest brush of their bare skin against his. Over a lifetime, he's learnt to control it – to erect barriers in his mind so that his brain isn't continually inundated.

Bruno stares up at the shadows on the ceiling. If this woman can imbue the bed she sleeps on with the terrible force of her hatred, what will it be like when he's compelled to share her whole consciousness? All he can do is to gird up his loins as they used to say. Bruno wishes he didn't know that particular phrase comes from the Bible and describes the practice of binding your clothing around your genitalia ready for travelling or working hard – one of a multitude of useless things he'd learnt in his naïve attempt to cheat in that World History and Religion exam.

Old Jónsson had been making his life hell since the start

of the course, taunted him about his low grades and wasted God-given intelligence. (He hadn't specified which god had been responsible.) With only a few days to go, Bruno had decided there was nothing else for it. At the end of the final lecture, he advanced towards the man, clearing his mind and concentrating hard in readiness for the connection. He'd had to manoeuvre the book he was returning in order to "accidentally" grasp Jónsson's thin, icy fingers. The sheer weight of the man's accumulated and jealously horded knowledge caused Bruno's body to jolt so violently he'd had to grab at the desk for support. As if he'd been physically struck, he continued to stagger against the onslaught of Magnus Jónsson's knowledge of the progress and consequences of so many global conflicts. Oblivious of the enormity of the mental intrusion that had just taken place, the teacher had steadied his elbow and asked, 'Have you been drinking, boy?' Bruno had shrunk back from Magnus's touch. Along with the rest of the old man's overburdened mind, he'd had a more-than-sufficient glimpse of the dark pit occupied by his disgusting sexual fantasies.

In the end, it proved a waste of time: he possessed too much information to marshal it in order to answer questions, which seemed laughingly simplistic. He'd gained a low pass. Jónsson had said he was lucky to get that.

Bruno can hear footsteps approaching. A moment later, the door opens and the woman steps into the room. Her bone-white face seems to float in the half-darkness. 'It's time,' she announces, holding out one hand as if to help him up.

He scrambles to his feet unaided. A swift anger crosses from her face to her voice, 'I've no idea why you're being so reluctant – I'm sure you've done this many times before. Shouldn't I be the worried one?'

'Then why do it at all?'

'It's simple – I want to find out how exceptional, or otherwise, you really are.'

'I don't see how I can possibly help you.'

'Let me worry about that.' She's close enough for him to see the smirk playing on her lips. Does she think he's about to become a willing participant in whatever evil act she's intending to carry out in a sort of speeded-up Stockholm syndrome? Is she planning to keep him captive so she can use him like the ancient Greeks used soothsayers during their military expeditions? If that's the case, maybe he can persuade her he needs to examine the entrails of her tame foxes to predict the outcome of her next battle.

The situation doesn't augur well. By allowing him to become party to all her innermost thoughts and schemes, she'll seal his fate and, one way or another, once this is done, like the worst of jealous lovers, she'll guard his every move and never willingly let him go free.

'Let's take it one step at a time,' she says, closing the gap between them. Her breath is hot on his face. 'There isn't much time. I need to ascertain how useful, or otherwise, you're likely to be to us.'

'And what if I'm not, or not prepared to be?'

'I'm sure I don't need to spell it out.' She fixes him in an unblinking stare. 'Let's just say it would be better for you if our little experiment proves a success.'

She grabs at his hand before he can do anything about it. A rush of light invades his brain. It separates into strands of flickering images and distorted speech and then a cacophony of head-reeling sounds. As the connection takes hold, a deeper, darker strand emerges; her schemes and desires colonise his own thoughts like a poisonous root binding him to the core of her twisted, all enveloping loathing.

His body stiffens and his throat constricts as the power of her emotions threatens to asphyxiate him. Even while he's fighting for each breath, he uncovers again and again within her half-buried memories, a vision of her walking alone and exposed. He can trace the roots of her fierce animosity as it develops and grows into a rage that overpowers every idea, every impulse, with a burning desire for revenge.

Abruptly, it's over. She's speaking now on the outside of his head in too normal a voice for the person he now knows her to be.

Casually, she begins to massage her hand, twisting it and holding it up to the light as if she might find an imprint left there. 'You still haven't answered,' she says. 'I asked you if it worked. You're breathing strangely but, aside from that, I certainly wasn't aware of any sort of intrusion.'

Bruno can say nothing until he's more in control of himself. She sighs with impatience, her expression skeptical as if she's facing a fairground fortune-teller up to his usual tricks.

He needs to convince her and fast. 'Your earliest memory–'

'Yes?'

'Um–'

'I'm getting a little bored. Come on, Bruno, spit it out.'

'A cat jumps up onto your chest. It lies there right on top of you, its golden eyes peering directly into yours as if deciding whether to devour you or not. Your mother comes running when you scream. The cat's all innocence – ears back and those eyes now wild and frightened. "Sweetheart, what's all this fuss about?" she asks, putting her arms around you. "Don't be scared of Rufus; he's only being friendly." She caresses the damned beast. "Look how he's purring. He won't hurt you".'

Bruno inhales deeply. 'The dumb animal would have had no idea how, in just that one moment, he'd made such a formidable enemy.'

He watches her face change as she recognises the truth of his words. 'Poor Rufus – his fate was sealed, wasn't it? Would you like me to go on, Ása Sturludóttir?'

'Don't call me that. I am no one's daughter!' she hisses. Though her eyes are alive with anger, he knows the balance of power between them has just shifted.

Twenty-Two

The two-seater is quite a performer though it fails to enliven Nero's spirits on the return journey. The two of them arrive back at DSD just as the day-shift workers are streaming in. Walking down the crowded corridors beside Lúter in full body armour, Nero imagines they must look a little like cartoon heroes – the one-dimensional kind.

He checks in his weapons and then stows the rest of his bulky kit in his locker. A long shower can't expunge the sickly stench clinging to the back of his throat – the taste of corruption not confined to the physical. His actions from this point on need to be planned with the utmost care.

Nero wrestles with another conundrum. Currently, they have no genuine satellite images from inside that Double Red Zone due to the state-of-the-art cloaking protecting the whole zone. That being the case, how had Surveillance picked up the single image they have of the decoy? The two facts just don't fit together.

What next? From experience, he guesses Forensics will take a while sending through their full reports on today's Orange Zone murders. With a few hours to spare, he should question Dr Arthur, Head Psychologist at the Decoy Department. He'll take Chan along – her expertise in the field could be useful.

Back in the stuffy confines of his office, he calls Rashid and Kass in to discuss the latest developments. 'So, you and Lúter have had a busy morning,' Rashid says, a clear edge to his voice.

'I saw no point in the whole team losing sleep,' Nero tells him. He can see the man remains unconvinced. 'I want the two of you to review the overnight surveillance on that section of the Orange Zone. After that, track back to see if you can find any unusual activity out there over the last two weeks – look for anomalies of any kind.'

'We're on it,' Kass says, turning towards the door.

Rashid hesitates. 'Why both of us?'

'Because two pairs of eyes are better than one,' Nero tells him; a phrase his grandmother was fond of using.

'Okay – well you're the boss.'

'I'm going over to interview Dr Arthur and I'm taking Chan along with me.'

Rashid perks up. 'That woman is full of surprises.'

'Oh?'

'She's still a trainee but you should have seen her – she was practically ice down in the morgue. Afterwards, she opened up a bit, told me about her earliest memories. We're not talking about the usual birthday party or puppy arriving stuff. Apparently, during the Shanghai Uprising, she watched most of her family being hacked to death right in front of her.'

'Ó Guð!' Kass covers her mouth.

Nero is equally shocked. 'That was back in 'forty-four. She must have been really young – no more than three years old.'

'Hardly the sort of the thing you forget though, is it?' Rashid shakes his head.

'The poor girl,' Kass says. 'I can't imagine how you'd come to terms with something like that.'

'She told me her uncle rescued her. Later he managed to smuggle her onto a boat to Europe,' Rashid tells them. 'Eventually, he brought her up here to start a new life. Then one day he told her he was going back to China. She never heard from him again.'

'I'm surprised she revealed so much.' Nero had read her personal file, which contained no details of her life before her arrival in Eldísvík at the age of five.

'We went into the Rec at the end of our shift and she just came out with the whole story. I guess, you know, I do have a certain way –' He winks at Kass. 'I get through to women – it's a sort of animal magnetism thing, or so I've been told.'

'You do know magnets can also repulse,' Kass says, shoving his shoulder. Rashid laughs out loud – that deep chuckle they all love.

'I'll say one thing for you, Rashid,' Nero tells him, 'lack of confidence has never been one of your failings.' Like the rest of the department, he's heard of the man's legendary success with the opposite sex.

Kass is still smirking. 'I'd lay pretty good odds against that particular lady succumbing to your charms.'

'Be more than happy to take your money, lady.' Rashid holds out his hand. 'How much are–'

'Did I miss something?' Chan says from the doorway. She looks at all three of them in turn. 'What's the joke?'

'We'll get going on that right away, sir,' Kass says, hooking Rashid's arm and pulling him out of the room with her.

Nero clears his throat. 'Have you had chance to look through the intel on this morning's discovery, Constable?'

Chan nods. 'Looks like the work of the same person – and the identical duck signature object seems to prove it.'

'Although there are some obvious disparities.' Before she can say anything, he adds, 'We should get the full report through shortly. In the meantime, you and I have an appointment with the elusive Dr Arthur. I assume you remember him from the first briefing?'

'Yes, of course.'

Nero takes the opportunity to look directly into her face; the perfect symmetry of her eyes and their elegant upward tilt distract him more than he would wish.

It's a short walk. Chan easily keeps pace with him. 'I'm not sure how hands-on the good doctor is,' Nero says, his breath misting in the cold air. 'Have you met him?'

'Sort of. I attended a couple of his lectures. He was very impressive. Extremely thorough. I'd be surprised if he, personally, missed anything.'

She stops abruptly. The bitter wind is tugging her hair back from her face and making her eyes run. 'Dr Haim and his team are the ones handling my intake's psychological assessments.' She wipes a tear away. 'Sir, I'm only a month away from graduation – that's assuming this final placement goes well.'

'So far, I'd say it's going extremely well.'

'My final evaluation is coming up. It's the last hurdle before I graduate. Could me being present at this interview compromise that in any way?'

'Definitely not,' Nero says, with a conviction he hopes is not misplaced.

Dr Arthur's round, open face sits awkwardly on his thin, angular frame. Standing, he's considerably shorter than Nero and his greying temples suggest he is probably five years older – early forties or thereabouts. Like most senior personnel not working directly in Defence, his office is a large glass cube with only the thinnest steel beams supporting it. The main attraction of the room is the spectacular view it affords right across the city towards the frozen mountain ranges that encircle it. 'This is quite an outlook,' Nero says, dazzled by the intensity of the almost cloudless sky. The view is partially blocked by the stacked containers clogging up the hinterland around the harbour. Behind all the massed cranes and gantries, the glinting fjord leads his eyes away towards the open sea.

'One of the perks of seniority, Inspector.' The psychologist's handshake includes the placing of his other hand on top. The resulting sensation is far from pleasant.

Dr Arthur gestures them towards two chairs carefully arranged to one side of his substantial desk in a non-adversarial manner. The psychologist swivels his well-upholstered chair in their direction.

'I understand your work is mainly with the Decoy Programme, in particular with assessments of candidates,' Nero says.

'Yes, in partnership with Dr Magnúsdóttir's department.' *So, you begin by asking the obvious to help your subject relax a little.*

'But their role is more advisory than day to day?'

'They provide a sort of quality control service to make sure our staff are performing up to standard.'

'But isn't that also part of *your* job description, Dr Arthur?'

'It's fair to say I am the person in overall charge.'

Nero dispenses with the sugarcoating. 'As an outsider, it's hard for me to imagine how this decoy could have passed every formal assessment without you, or anyone in the department you oversee, spotting her psychosis.'

Are you hoping I'll deny responsibility? Is that what you yourself would do in the circumstances? 'No doubt the Commanders already share your implied conclusion, Inspector.'

Nero reads his resignation. 'I am not here for recrimination. My job is simply to find this rogue decoy. Have you been told about last night's murders in–'

'I'm aware of the latest killing spree.' He raises a hand. 'I wasn't surprised. What's more, I'm certain she'll continue her deadly activities until she is apprehended or killed by her own over-ambition.'

'Over-ambition?'

'Our recognition of our own fallibilities can be an asset that helps us to survive. I'm sure *you* would agree Inspector?' *It would seem you are already considerably out of your depth. I suppose I should spell it out.* 'With her continued success, and your failure to apprehend her, she may begin to believe she's invincible. This may lead her to take greater risks; pit herself against more extreme dangers until she is finally outgunned or she makes an error that leads to her downfall.'

'So, your professional assessment is that she may begin to act more rashly?'

'It's a distinct possibility, Inspector.' *Although she's shown extraordinary patience throughout her career until this point.*

'You think that now she's achieving her ambition, she'll begin to believe her media image – that she is invincible, some kind of Avenging Angel?'

'I think she probably believes that she is a force acting against evil. This may be as a result of adherence to a particular religious faith – all major belief systems ascribe similar behaviour to angels.' *The man still looks baffled, out-of-his-depth again. I could almost feel sorry for him.* 'I'm sure you are aware that angels are the superhuman intermediaries between God and mankind.'

The psychologist leans further back in his chair, comfortable in his assumption of intellectual superiority. 'The traditional Avenging Angel carries a sword and may have an ability to become invisible. It is interesting that our decoy has managed to evade all our modern technological surveillance so far.'

'Not quite all, we have the original image we captured.'

'Did you capture it, or did she release it?' Dr Arthur's smile fails to reach those pale green eyes. The decoy would cost him this job and all these fine accouterments and yet his response suggests admiration.

'Can you tell me more about your assessment procedures?' Nero asks.

'We use specialist technology to save time. Whilst regular police recruits – including Trainee Constable Chan here – are assessed by rigorous questioning, decoys are subjected to far more extensive interrogations. Their responses, together with the bio-feedback data, are then carefully assessed. I believe your officers have already subjected my staff to a similar, if somewhat cruder, procedure. Did anyone crack, Inspector?'

'So tell me – would this decoy have also been interviewed by you personally?'

A reluctance to be swayed. Tenacity may be admirable but it's hardly a substitute for intelligence. 'The results from my colleagues' in-depth assessments are passed to me for the final sign-off. I interview each decoy. It's usually very brief – I regard it as more of a formality. However, this means that I too must have failed to pick up any undesirable traits.' He stares defiantly at Nero and then looks over at Chan. 'As I've said, she must possess a remarkable ability to deceive.'

Aside from the excuses, Nero again registers the man's respectful admiration. Arthur's far too knowledgeable to betray these feelings accidentally.

'I sense your ambivalence towards the decoy, Dr Arthur?'

'Very good, Inspector – the good old policeman's snout in action. Yes, you're right in the sense of admiration for a most intriguing adversary.'

The pathologist keeps adjusting his position. He moves to balance one ankle across the opposite knee before deciding to elaborate. 'You know, as a good Jewish boy I grew up with the traditions of the Passover. I won't bore you with all of it. You may recall the background of the story is one of a series of escalating Plagues on Egypt.'

Despite his studied air of confidence, the psychologist keeps fiddling with the heel on his raised shoe as if anxious to walk away from this encounter. 'The usual locusts, rats and so forth. When the Tenth Plague grew near – the plague on the firstborns – the Jews were instructed by God to paint the doorframe as a sign to the Avenging Angel to pass over that household and leave them unharmed. The Angel then struck down all Egyptian firstborns from the Pharaoh's to the lowest born. Not even the animals were spared.'

Dr Arthur turns his chair away from the sun, muddying the cold eyes now assessing them both in turn. *You have nothing to say in response. That exquisite creature next to you looks far more pensive but* you – *you want me to spell it out.* 'The actions of the Avenging Angel struck terror into the Egyptians. They gave the Israelites great wealth in order to bribe them to leave Egypt; this led to the mass Exodus.'

'Do *you* believe the decoy is doing God's work?' Nero asks.

A smile pulls at the edges of Arthur's mouth. 'Come, come, Inspector I would hardly say so if I did. You're suggesting I might be complicit in some way. To answer your question: I don't. I simply recognise the role of an avenger to bring about change and how this may be brought on by a general climate of fear.'

'So you think her actions are likely to bring about a significant change for the better in our city?'

'I think they might make some difference, yes. Not to the likes of you and me currently enjoying every creature comfort the Free Zone has to offer.' *We who reap our rewards and go about our daily lives oblivious to the dark deeds going on elsewhere.*

'Please don't include me in that statement,' Nero tells him. 'Unlike yourself, Dr Arthur, I visited the scene in the Red Zone. And while you were enjoying your breakfast this morning, I was out in the Orange Zone looking down on last night's bloody carnage. I can still smell the flesh of the corpses she left behind. Don't tell me *she* has some kind of right to decide who will be passed over and who will die.' Nero sits back, emotion overcoming him.

Well, well. I appear to have hit quite a nerve. Interesting. Dr Arthur waits before breaking the silence. 'I see you have a passionate belief in what you do, Inspector. Despite the impression I may have given, I share your belief in the importance of the rule of law. Let us leave it at that.'

The man stands up – a signal that he wants and expects them to leave. Though more than happy to oblige, Nero defies him and remains seated.

'*Acting* Constable Chan,' Dr Arthur turns to address her directly. 'You've been silent during our discussion. Is there anything *you* wish to ask me?'

Chan clears her throat. 'Yes, Doctor. You must have looked at the intel from both scenes,' she says. 'Do you think, for certain, it's the work of the same individual, or could these murders have been carried out by two separate people?'

To the point. No hesitation. I see they were right about your potential. 'What a very good question, Chan. Sadly, it's one that I'm unable to answer. I think it unlikely that more than one decoy has gotten through our very fine net. But, not being party to all the facts available to the Homicide Department, I have, as yet, insufficient knowledge to make a full assessment.' He turns to Nero, 'I would be happy to help with this question and possibly a more detailed psychological profile. Provided I am kept fully briefed, Inspector.'

Nero gets to his feet. 'Thank you, Dr Arthur.' Speaking only to the floor he says, 'We won't take up any more of your valuable time.' Hell would become a Winter Wonderland before he'd consider asking for this man's help.

They walk back to SDS in silence. When they've reached his office, Chan speaks at last. 'You look tired, Inspector, can I get you a coffee or maybe something to eat?'

Nero comes back to the moment and realises he's both hungry and thirsty. 'Not the stuff they sell here, thanks all the same,' he says. 'I usually go round the corner to Gianni's Café on Park Street. Would you like to join me?'

'Yes, I would like that. As long as we agree to leave this case here – until we get back to DSD.'

'It's a deal,' he says, though he knows it will continue to hound his thoughts.

Twenty-Three

They walk round the corner and up the street towards the café. Nero would like to take his stud off completely, but instead he turns it to urgent only. Is it appropriate to have asked her to come with him like this? In any case it's too late for him to change his mind.

As they enter, a current of warm air sneaks around them into the street. Nero devours the smell of real coffee. Gianni greets him in a more ebullient manner than usual, looking Chan up and down with no regard for subtlety. He can't avoid the introductions.

They choose a table by the window and hang their coats across the backs of their chairs. Chan takes an age to unwind her scarf before she sits down. She continues to look everywhere but at him. Normally he's immune to Gianni's terrible musical taste, but he becomes uncomfortably aware of the perky, instrumental tune that's playing. It's a relief when it finally ends.

They begin to speak at the same time and then stop. 'You first,' he says.

'No. You go ahead, Inspector.'

'Right, well, I was just saying that it's nice to get out of DSD. It gets—'

His ears are assaulted by a sickly, sentimental ballad; Gianni

132

might as well have sent over a trio with violins. He needs to excuse it. 'I come here for the coffee and the simple food – definitely not the proprietor's excruciating taste in music.'

Chan smiles. 'I didn't think places like this existed outside of film sets. And they really do bring everything to your table? Wow.'

'Well they normally do, but your floral tea might be where Gianni draws the line.'

'It's nice in here. I like all the real wood.'

He leans forward. 'Just don't look too closely.'

Daylight is shining in through the red and green lettering on the window; it's creating a strange pattern on one side of her face. The conversation grounds. Silence occupies the third seat.

This time Chan breaks first. 'Do you live near here, Inspector?'

'Not too far. And you?'

'District Five – nearer the edge it's a bit cheaper.'

'I expect you've already worked out that you'll never be rich in the police force,' he says.

'Not even when you get to your grade?'

Nero shakes his head. 'Not even then.' He turns to look out into the street, at all the people hurrying by. The window frame cuts off their heads and feet and the lettering is staining them green and blood red. Green and red; over and over. Without heads, detached torsos and limbs carry on walking down the street. When a child walks past, he has to look away. He shuts his eyes but the carnage of earlier is still there.

When he opens them again, Chan is looking at him. 'You'll have finished growing that beard by the end of the day,' she says.

Nero forces a smile. 'The shave-mate in Clean Up is broken.'

'You could have used the one in the women's.'

'You're joking, right?'

'No, I'm serious. It's for transgender officers – mostly those still transitioning.'

'What about the other bits? I mean the legs and stuff you ladies like to shave.' He stops himself. 'That came out all wrong – please don't answer that.'

Chan goes against orders. 'They only provide a shave-mate. I guess the department doesn't feel it should fund anything more sophisticated.'

Their drinks arrive. Nero grins an apology about the tea, but Gianni serves it with a flourish for Chan's benefit, along with the umpteenth repetition of "Bellissima".

Nero sees her irritation at the man's flirtatiousness, the burden her beauty brings with it. He notices three tiny moles in a line beneath her right eye. For a moment, as she warms her hands on the cup, he tries to imagine what it would be like to be the recipient of such extravagant and unwanted attention.

He sips the too-hot coffee. The lyrics of the song take a turn for the worse; Nero fervently hopes Chan doesn't understand Italian.

Gianni returns with Nero's panini. It's impossible to eat it without making a mess. Despite his best efforts, his plate becomes strewn with torn prosciutto strips and congealing streaks of egg yolk. He wishes he hadn't noticed the rawness of the meat. Isn't he the same as any other animal consuming its prey?

Chan continues to stir the clear, golden liquid.

'Are you sure you wouldn't like something else?' He wipes his guilty mouth. 'A biscotti even?'

'I'm fine with just tea.'

All the legs outside the window are marching to the latest mortifying lyrics. He turns his attention to Chan's downturned face, her small, stirring hand. The faint aroma of flowers drifts away from her tea.

'I've been told often enough I'm no good at not talking about my work,' Nero says. 'Do you find that as soon as you try not to do something, you start to want to do it more and more?' He can feel himself blushing, for Christ's sake.

'We didn't swear not to, cross your heart and all that. If you just can't resist–'

'I don't want to even think about it – not at this precise moment anyway. What you've seen stays with you, sneaks up on you even when you're trying to think about something else.'

'I know.' She takes a few sips. Her cup resounds as she sits it back on its saucer.

'I'm sorry; I'm very poor company,' he says.

'It's okay.'

He inhales deeply. 'It's not okay.' He slaps both hands on the table. 'I know next to nothing about you. Tell me, Chan, what's your favourite colour?'

'Blue.' She gives him a long, saddening smile. 'My turn now. What's your favourite bird?'

'Peregrine Falcon – such an amazing survivor. How about your favourite tree?'

'Tree?' She frowns. 'No idea. Do people have such things?'

He tilts his head. 'Lie if you need to.'

'Okay, how about a bay tree. What's your favourite flower?'

'Hang on, bay is not a tree – it's a bush. My grandmother used to cook with it. Not allowed. Try again.'

'Wait a minute – they can get quite tall you know. There was one outside a house we stayed in when I was little. I always loved the smell. It was way too big to be called a bush.' She picks up her cup but doesn't drink. 'I'm no good with trees – they all look the same to me. Brown trunk, green leaves and you're done.' Again that smile.

'But there are hundreds of different trees in the world and they're all so amazing. You must know the oak – there's a few in the Botanical Gardens. Great, solid trunk, zigzagging leaves, acorns – the lot. Then there's the Scots pine–'

'Okay, okay,'

She touches his hand – her skin directly on his. It's a shock when he feels nothing except her warmth. 'Did you know the first settlers to this island cut down all the trees because of their need for wood?' he says, though God knows why. 'After that, all the fertile soil they were so dependent on got washed away. Most of the trees here now are less than a hundred years old.'

'Let's leave the damn trees and move on to flowers, which I do know something about,' she says. Of course, she's oblivious to what just happened or failed to happen. 'I don't suppose you know any flower names – that's why you made such a fuss about the trees.'

Her face comes closer to his, challenging him. He finds he can't remember the name of a single flower.

'Come on, Inspector – think of spring or something.'

'Cherries – cherry blossom.' He is triumphant.

'That isn't a flower – it's a tree.'

Her laugh is more of a giggle. She holds her hand in front of her mouth like someone with bad teeth does. When she sips her tea, he can see her teeth are perfect.

His stud buzzes. Kass's voice in his ear telling him they've got full satellite coverage from last night.

Chan's face is already serious. 'I better go,' she says, 'Don't want to be late for my final session at the firing range.'

Their chairs scrape on the hard floor as they rise to their feet. He touches her shoulder. 'Thank you.'

'For what?' She looks up into his eyes. 'You bought the drinks.'

'For reminding me.'

'Of what?' She's already looping her long scarf, binding it around her neck, trapping a few strands of her jet-black hair inside.

'Of how to find a separate place to go back to,' Nero says.

He waves at Gianni and then holds the door open for Chan. She hesitates before walking through.

'Old habit,' he says. 'Blame my grandmother.'

Twenty-Four

The makeshift incident room is in the lower basement. Yesterday, Nero had found it still full of surplus furniture and out-of-date equipment. Maintenance had promised to clear it by today. As instructed, they've left him only an old whiteboard on the wall and a desk. With its bare concrete floor and walls, it has all the glamour of a cell.

Kass is sitting on the desk. 'Sorry to interrupt your break, Inspector,' she says, getting up. 'I thought you needed to see this in greater detail.' She keeps adjusting the holo-pro like a nervous impresario getting ready for a show.

He stands over to one side, while Rashid and Lúter file in. With nowhere to sit, they all lean against the walls.

'The definition still isn't great on this projection,' Kass tells them. 'The tech team are working on a cleaner version, but they haven't sent it through yet.'

She extinguishes the overheads and an image springs into the central space.

'So this is the Orange SOC,' she says. The area they're seeing is dimly lit; the only thing moving is the waving scrub that surrounds it. 'Okay so we're just coming to the sequence I wanted you all to see.'

She leans in. *'Slow to point four. Now pause.'* Like a poor puppeteer, her pointing finger enters the scene. 'The first three individuals are moving in from here – two on foot, one inside a moving vehicle. The vehicle itself is unmarked – one of those monster off-roaders they used to use for tourists.' She withdraws her finger as the expo continues. They watch the two shadowy figures finally climb onboard.

Another vehicle approaches. Doors open and its five occupants step outside. Their heads all turn towards the same direction.

'Go to point ten. *Slow to real time.*' One individual begins to lash out at something. Two seconds later, the man pulls his weapon and fires. Next, a whole arsenal is unleashed – enough to floor an elephant. Nero recognises both photon and laser signatures, mostly low-grade stun-and-run.

'Concentrate on the fire-paths.' Kass is barely containing her excitement. 'See what I mean? The tech guys were so surprised they ran it through a dozen times and even tested their equipment. I'll play that bit again, shall I? *Reverse Five. Play point two.*'

Nero leans right in. The re-run confirms that each blast isn't just bouncing off the target: it's being deflected straight back at the firer.

Nero steps through the projection to view the continuing battle from the opposite angle. For a second it looks like his pants have caught fire. 'They keep changing the angle of fire,' he says. 'Their target must be moving at speed – whatever it's made from, their body armour allows an extraordinary level of agility.'

'Must be really state-of-the-art,' Rashid says, breaking the silence. 'According to Jóra Bjarnadóttir, that fragment of material we brought back from the Red Zone was made from something unknown not just to her but to the whole scientific community.'

'No one in DSD has *anything* like this, or we'd know about it.' Lúter shakes his head. 'If these suits are in production, you'd expect them to trial it with the military first.'

They all start talking at once.

'Okay, okay.' Nero raises his hand but the silence keeps him waiting. 'This stuff isn't going to be on sale in the mall. Rashid, in your report you said Dr Bjarnadóttir thought the sourcing and development of this new product material would have cost an exorbitant sum.'

'Maybe the decoy stole it from the lab that's developing it,' Rashid suggests.

Lúter raises an eyebrow. 'Or could someone have given it to her to try out? Someone high up in the military or in–'

'Hold on a second, there's more,' Kass says. '*Freeze image.*' They turn their attention back to the projection. 'As you can see, the decoy is really hard to make out – this isn't just some kind of glitch – that suit is designed to make its wearer more or less invisible.'

'*Dai!*' Nero holds up both hands. 'As if we didn't have enough to contend with.'

'The surveillance guys were really helpful,' Kass says. 'Using the disruption lines which were susceptible to computation, they've been able to quantify the negative space the wearer occupies with a fair degree of accuracy.'

Lúter frowns. 'Could we have that again in English?'

'They calculated the dimensions of the person from the mass described by the deflection points,' Nero translates. 'Very clever. So what did they conclude?'

'That this person is of slight build, around 1.7 metres tall and weighing no more than sixty kilos. From the body shape they give a 94% chance that it's a woman.'

'And did they compare those stats with the other image we have of the decoy?' Nero asks.

'No, but I got them to do that,' Kass says. She grins. 'They concluded that, although they're of a similar build, it's almost certainly *not* the same person.'

'Did they give probabilities?' Nero asks.

'No. At this stage, they don't want to be definitive.'

'So, if we are dealing with copy-cat killings,' Nero says. 'Are the two of them working together? Sharing the same suit even?'

Lúter raises his hand. 'It's quite possible the material in this suit is different from the sample Bjarnadóttir's been studying.'

'Good point,' Nero says. He turns back to the projection. 'Looks like we've got our vixens just there on the periphery.' The foxes are superimposed on his hand. 'And several more are lurking over there.'

'You're right,' Kass says. *'Run sequence at plus three.'*

Events continue to play out. The vixens move in at the same time – clearly responding to one signal. Showing little interest in the corpses, they all leave the scene within ten minutes.

'Let's speed it up,' Kass says. *'Running speed plus ten, Stop. Continue at plus two.* Here we can see the remains being scavenged by a variety of animals.'

Nero watches in silent disgust as four feral dogs arrive. Then a couple of solitary red foxes move in and a fight breaks out. Later still, a mink gets in on the act.

Nero signals to Kass. 'Thank you, Constable; I'm sure we've all seen more than enough.' He wishes he had room to pace. 'So, to summarise: this incident bears all the hallmarks of the first one including the toy duck signature, *however*, it was most likely carried out by someone else – probably another woman. This time, the vixens are only bystanders. We have proof that *this* woman is wearing a new type of defensive suit, which seems to render her more or less invincible. On the evidence so far, let's assume she's the same person who then scrawls a quote from a psalm using the fresh blood of the victims.'

'Can we even call them that?' Lúter asks. 'I mean, weren't they actually killed by their own deflected firepower?'

'Forget the finer points – we need to focus,' Nero tells him. 'Going back to what Lúter said, we can't assume the mystery material we found in the Double Red is the same substance responsible for this seeming invincibility yet, let's not forget the first decoy made sure she was seen.'

'So perhaps the suit makes the wearer invisible,' Lúter says, 'but then visible again whenever they choose.'

'Wow! You know, we could make a shed load of money if we could get our hands on a few of those things,' Rashid says. 'Imagine the customer base – just think what you could steal wearing one of those.'

'Spoken like a dedicated policeman,' Nero says.

Rashid claps him on the shoulder. 'I'm sure, when you were a kid, Inspector, you were a fan of "The Invincible Ones" just like the rest of us.'

When Lúter starts humming the theme tune, Rashid joins in.

Nero takes a step back. 'Drop all this nonsense,' he tells them. 'These deaths happened less than twelve hours ago. We need to try to capitalise on that.'

There's a chorus of *sorry, sirs*. Nero stares at Rashid who is barely stifling a grin and waits until he straightens his face. 'Listen – this is no laughing matter. We're in a grave position here,' he tells them. 'In the last few days we've had more reported killings than in the whole of last year. It has to stop. So far the dead appear to be criminals or what you might consider to be low-life. That shouldn't change our response one iota. Not only that – just imagine who the next victims might be: hapless, minor criminals we'd normally just shake down and release or even innocent bystanders in the wrong place at the wrong time.'

He stares at each of them in turn. They drop their eyes to the floor.

'We need to stop this right now.' Nero rubs at the stubble on his chin. 'Rashid – go back to Forensics. Chan is due back from weapons training; take her with you. Ask Dr Bjarnadóttir if she can tell us anything more about this mystery material.'

He turns to Kass. 'Exemplary work, Constable. Now I want you and Lúter to go over to Surveillance. They've given us nothing from the shop front angle. We're still no wiser about who daubed all that stuff in blood. What happened to those two vehicles afterwards? I'm assuming the locals were pretty quick to snaffle them – where did they end up?'

'We're on it, sir,' Lúter says.

'Get the surveillance coverage for a ten-mile radius of the scene for at least the two hours before and after this incident. We need to know this decoy's movements before and afterwards. And where did that vixen pack spring up from? Where did they retreat afterwards? Let's hope this new decoy – if she is a decoy – is less efficient at covering her tracks.'

Left alone, Nero looks up at the empty whiteboard. He picks up the marker pen and uncaps it. Normally he'd write VICTIM on one half of the board and then PERPETRATOR on the other side. Lúter had made a point. He puts the cap back on the pen and then walks out of the room.

Twenty-Five

They catch Jóra Bjarnadóttir as she's going off duty. To Rashid, she seems younger with her long hair loose. Without those baggy green coveralls, she's a perfectly pleasant looking woman; it would be hard to guess from her appearance that she spends half her working life up to her elbows in body parts.

Though she answers their questions, she remains distracted. The stench of all those chemicals begins to get to him; it's as much as he can do to stay focused. 'So really, Dr Bjarnadóttir, you can't say whether that mystery substance would give the decoy suit those properties?' Rashid wants to be certain.

'I'm sorry. Despite what that projection shows, I can't give you an answer. To do so, I'd need to subject the sample to some very sophisticated tests and we just don't have those kinds of facilities here. So far, none of the universities I sent the images to have come up with an answer.'

'Is there somewhere else you might send part of the actual sample to?' Chan asks.

'No – and I wouldn't do that unless one of the experts I've contacted agrees to help.' The woman keeps fiddling with the green stone pendant around her neck – moving it back and forth on its fine gold chain. 'It's possible the company that supplies the Decoy Department with the current exo-suits have *some* specialist testing equipment but I'm not at all certain they would be able, never mind willing, to help.'

'But there's no harm in asking, right?' Rashid says. 'Can you give us their details?'

'Sure, I'll send them through.'

He turns to leave but Chan stays put. 'Having seen that footage, what would be your best guess, Dr Bjarnadóttir?'

The woman finally lets go of her necklace. 'I'd say that a logical deduction would suggest that the two are linked. That, in all probability, given the unusual composition of the sample, it's likely that this unknown substance is what gives that exo-suit the strength to ricochet laser and even photon fire.' She shakes her head. 'Impenetrable clothing that makes the wearer more or less invisible – if I hadn't seen that projection with my own eyes, I'm not sure I'd believe it.'

Bjarnadóttir takes a silk scarf from her pocket and ties it around her neck in a jaunty fashion. 'It's no exaggeration to say it would cause a revolution,' she says, glancing up at the time display. 'Anyway, for now, if you'll excuse me, I really ought to get going. I promised to meet a dear friend more than ten minutes ago.'

Jue Hai catches up with them at the lifts. 'Back so soon?' He slaps Rashid's back in a way that's just short of annoying. 'I've just sent homicide another update. In case you haven't seen it yet, we've come up with a match on dental records for *Carlos* – the one with the head from the Double Red killings.'

'What more can you tell us?' Rashid asks.

'His name is Juan Pedro Lopez, forty-one, born in Mexico City though he spent substantial periods in Eastern Europe before partitioning. He was granted citizenship here eleven years ago. That was before his unlawful actives led to it being revoked five years later. He was, supposedly, deported back to Mexico but our bone analysis shows this must have been very short-lived and he continued to reside here.'

'An illegal,' Rashid says. 'I guess that's no real surprise.'

'There is one very surprising thing, though.' Jue Hai looks from him to Chan. 'The Intelligence team have a back door into Mexico State Records and, lo and behold, he's officially still alive and living in Mexico City. Work registration numbers, credit accounts – everything's in perfect order.'

'A false-life profile.' Chan looks shocked. 'He must have had some serious money behind him.'

'He was no lowly punk, that's for sure.' Jue Hai's gaze continues to linger on Chan. Under the pathologist's all-out stare, she eventually turns her head away. The lack of eye contact from Chan finally leads Jue Hai to look at him instead. 'You folks are keeping us busy down here. We've had to find extra storage for the latest crop. Jóra's dad's lent us one of those old-fashioned chest freezers. We had a hell of a job transforming its current and regulating it, so it doesn't freeze them solid. Would you like to see this latest batch?' He chuckles: 'We're calling them the Orange Segments.'

Rashid groans at the terrible pun. 'I don't think we need to. Nero and Lúter have already seen the corpses al fresco.'

'I'd like to take a peek.' Chan looks to Rashid for permission. 'If that's alright with you?'

'Go ahead,' he tells her, 'but I'll pass, if it's all the same.'

'Give me a few minutes to do a bit of re-assembling,' Jue Hai says before he disappears through the mortuary doors.

Rashid gives Chan a questioning look. 'I'm adopting the boss's methods,' she says. 'Getting a thorough picture of everything for myself.'

'Yes, well, I think Nero might want one of us to visit that exo-suit place. That's more my sort of thing.'

'I'm quite sure you can spare me.' She tucks a strand of her dark hair behind her ear. His eyes are drawn to the contours of her chin, the spot where her jaw curves to meet her unadorned earlobe. 'I've noticed this investigation seems to be really getting to Inspector Cavallo,' she says.

'Yeah, I guess it is. He's looking pretty rough on it.' Did

that sound a little harsh – callous even? 'Maybe I should take him out for a beer or something?' he says.

When she looks up at him, there's the hint of a smile on her lips. 'I think that would be a good idea.'

'Maybe you'd like to join us?' Rashid's careful to keep his tone casual.

She too quick to shake her head. 'I think it would be better if it was just mano a mano.'

'Seriously? No one believes in that sort of crap anymore. Besides, Nero's fond of female company – though I understand he hasn't had a lot lately.'

'Oh really – why's that?' She leans back against the bare concrete wall.

He can't help leaning in towards her. 'He was in a pretty serious relationship a while back. We thought they would, you know, settle down, have kids, all that stuff. I guess it didn't work out.'

'What about his family? He mentioned his grandmother the other day.'

So, the girl likes to gossip. 'As far as I know, they're all dead. The guy has to be what, thirty-nine? Forty even? These things happen.'

'How about you, do you have any family?' She's looking down, fiddling with the cover of her log.

'Me, I've got too much family. They drive me nuts. My mum's terrible – always saying stuff like, "You've got to come with us to your cousin Leila's birthday party". Or "It's your Uncle Sharif's wedding, get a decent suit". She's obsessed with family. Keeps on at me about being single. "When are you going to find a nice girl and settle down?" She's got two grandkids but that's not enough because her sister's got five with another on the way. I say to her, "There's no rush, Mum; I'm only thirty-one. Got to take these things slowly".'

Before Chan can respond, the mortuary door opens. 'All ready,' Jue Hai says.

'See you later,' she says. Without a backward glance, she disappears into the morgue.

He'd hoped for a parting smile. Still, in a roundabout way she'd checked if he was single and that had to mean she'd like to take things further, which was more than fine by him. A woman like that is used to being pursued; Jue Hai was practically salivating over her. He needs to bide his time, make it clear Rashid Ashram doesn't run with the pack.

In the elevator, he presses up for air. If he can get some answers about this suit it should impress the boss. Nero might be good at all the old Dan-the-Man-leading-his-gang stuff but it's hard to feel too sorry for any of these so-called victims – in truth, the city was a better place without the likes of them.

Doors open. Rashid heads towards the daylight and some fresher air. Nothing is straightforward with this case and keeping track of that shifting line between perpetrator and victim would give any man vertigo.

Twenty-Six

The Bay Club is popular with off-duty officers for no reason other than its close proximity to DSD. The main bar is underground and dimly lit. Nero can smell the earthy dampness of walls visibly in the process of rejecting the latest cheap coat of purple-grey paint.

He insists on buying the first drinks, leaving Rashid to hunt down somewhere for them to sit. It's been a frustrating day for everyone – the sort of day a few drinks might help wash away. The Shield Corporation had stonewalled Rashid, refusing to let him speak with the head of R and D about the decoy suits and denying him further access to their premises without a warrant.

The counter is lit up at the far end of the long room. He can see getting served is going to take some time. Through the gaps between the backs of other people's heads, he watches the lone bar hand struggling to serve the ever-growing queue. Her workmate has broken off his duties to chat to his friend – or lover. The woman doing all the work is very young, pretty, and flustered – a combination that's giving her a hard time with the many thirsty mouths vying for her attention.

Eventually Nero makes it to the head of the queue. The bar's equipment keeps fighting back; the girl has to enter the order code three times before the machine decides to oblige.

It gurgles into life and at last a single glass emerges from the cat's cradle of its arms.

As the woman waits for it to fill, she runs both hands down her long hair and then holds it out in bunches on either side of her neck.

Her gesture unlocks a memory: how Fede liked to hold the ends of her long plaits out like twin brushes as she balanced an open book on her lap. Rejecting every electronic alternative, his sister preferred to raid their grandmother's library for the printed versions of her favourite stories. For the first time in a long while Nero allows himself to picture exactly how Fede looked back then: sitting so still in concentration beneath that old gnarled olive tree; half-hidden by the rippling spikes of summer-dried grass. A whole afternoon could pass and she'd hardly move from the spot. His envy of that quiet absorption would send him climbing through the branches to aim a few under-ripe olives at her head. She'd ignore him for as long as she could, until he broke the spell. Her face red with annoyance, she'd aim them back at him. She never got close; she was always a rotten shot.

The room swims before him as he struggles to put Fede back with the other things he can never change. 'Anything else I can get you?' This girl's eyes aren't that same liquid brown – they're grey and flecked with green. He reads "Natalia" on her name badge and a determination on her young face that ought to get her a better job in the end.

'I didn't catch that,' she says.

He's aware of someone literally breathing down his neck. Remembering the awfulness of the beer here, he asks for a large glass of what they laughingly describe as Chianti.

Rashid is sitting in a small alcove to one side of the dance floor. 'I thought it might be a bit easier to chat in here,' he says. The cola spills as Nero lowers it onto a small, sticky table. He would have bought an overpriced bottle of wine for them to share but, of course, Rashid never touches alcohol. It shouldn't make a difference to his own drinking pleasure and yet somehow it does.

A sip tells him the wine isn't quite as bad as he feared.

'I asked Chan and Kass if they'd like to join us but they both had other plans,' Rashid says, raising his voice above the music. 'Lúter said he'd drop by later.'

The Bay Club has a certain ambiance, perhaps because each time someone opens the toilet door, a strong whiff of sewage leaks out. Restless lights are roaming the ceiling and periodically dipping down to infiltrate the various huddles of customers still in their work clothes. Nero's hopes for a relaxing evening are further stymied when an orange and red projection begins to rotate in the air around them. He follows its path to see it's announcing a live expo-mental jazz performance due to begin in an hour. He can already feel a headache developing.

'Jue Hai!' Rashid calls out, waving across the room.

The lanky pathologist comes over to join them. Balancing his half-empty pint of beer on the table, he says, 'I see you two are slumming it tonight. You must stay for the jazz. They've played here before. Great energy – they have a real intensity.'

Nero rubs at his eyes. 'I guessed as much.'

Jue Hai looks expectantly towards the door. 'Is Constable Chan planning to join you?'

Rashid shakes his head. 'No. I can't imagine this is her sort of place.'

'I take your point,' the pathologist says. 'That Chan, she is one foxy lady.'

'That's an interesting choice of expression,' Nero tells him.

Jue Hai frowns. 'Is this not right, idiomatically?'

'Oh, it's correct alright, but a little out-of-date.'

The music stops for a moment and the pathologist's face becomes serious. 'In Chinese culture, we too associate very lovely women with the fox. We call them huli jing, which means beautiful fox.' With a smirk he adds, 'Although, it can also mean something far cruder and very derogatory.'

Nero snorts and some wine goes up his nose.

'When I heard how the Decoy Programme operates,' Jue Hai says, 'it put me in mind of the stories my grandfather used to tell me.'

'Oh really?' Nero is still squeezing the bridge of his nose. 'Why's that?'

'They were often about foxes who are really spirits called "xianren" because it's bad luck to say their real names. Such stories and beliefs are unofficial, you understand.'

'A sort of folk religion?' Nero suggests.

'Yes, exactly that. Xianren come secretly into a community in the shape and appearance of different people. They're a sort of avenging spirit. They might appear to be an amiable drinking companion or a fascinating and beguiling woman.'

Nero sips his wine before asking, 'Did people seriously believe their friend or lover might really be a fox?'

Jue Hai shrugs. 'Possibly, but really these are just scary stories.' He takes a mouthful of beer and grimaces as he swallows. 'I see our murdering decoy is being described by some as a supernatural avenger.'

'Tell me a bit more about these myths,' Nero says, leaning forward.

'They're mostly about how these disguised foxes play terrible tricks on humans. In the end, the humans usually kill the fox. Occasionally, xianren go so far as actually marrying humans, though they don't have long, happy marriages – the fox either dies or disappears.'

'How can they tell who's a fox and who isn't?' Nero asks.

Rashid starts to laugh. 'Man, this is the weirdest conversation.'

'Never mind that, carry on,' Nero says.

Jue Hai scratches his head. 'Well, let me see now. A likely

xianren is a stranger who first appears alone on the streets at night. If the fox is a male, he'll seem like a clever, academic type. A female will seem like a young, innocent girl.'

A burst of loud, third-drink laughter from the group to their left interrupts the conversation. Once they can hear each other again, Nero asks, 'Do the xianren ever kill humans?'

'Not directly; it's not their way. Instead they like to use tricks or they might set fires.' A plasma light skims the tops of their heads and the pathologist's eyes follow its path for a moment while he thinks. 'I remember one story where a fox mother has sex with a human and has a child. I don't remember how a woman is made pregnant by a fox.'

'Are you lot really talking about bestiality?' Lúter asks. Nero hadn't seen him arrive. Already armed with a full pint of beer, he looks for somewhere to sit before perching on the skinny arm of Rashid's chair. 'I thought you might be talking about Jacobs and Grey. The other day, they were approached right here in the Free Zone by a guy offering to sell them porn. Not the usual variety.' He pantomimes an exaggerated wink. 'This stuff apparently involved exotic animals. They've been getting no end of stick about why he singled them out.'

'I'm guessing they seized his stock,' Rashid says. 'What's happened to it?'

'Please don't tell me if you're planning to take a look at it,' Nero says. 'And I *don't* want to find any of it on *my* stud. You got that, both of you?'

Rashid feigns outrage. 'What do you take us for, boss?'

'It's cruel how often we're maligned.' Lúter attempts to ruffle Rashid's hair. 'Anyway, I see empty glasses. Who fancies another one? You still on the sarsaparilla, Rashi? For us Catholics, alcohol is practically obligatory – it's the only way we can handle all the guilt.'

'I'm fine with this.' Rashid smiles before taking a sip of his drink.

Lúter gets up, spilling beer down his trousers. He looks

down at the dark patch above one knee and tries to wipe it with his free hand. 'What a waste of good beer! Well, beer anyway.'

'I've been telling them some Chinese stories about foxes,' Jue Hai says.

'Is that a fact?' Lúter continues to wipe at his trousers while simultaneously taking long gulps of beer. 'Here, there's a famous old story about a hunter and his obsession with shooting a fox. You must have heard it?'

They shake their heads.

Lúter laughs. 'What a bunch of ignorant foreigners you are.'

'Listen mate – without us, you'd all still be shagging your cousins,' Rashid tells him.

'Just tell us the bloody story,' Nero says.

'Okay. There's this hunter and he's a weak man – forever being bossed around by his wife and respected by no one in his village. None of his children are even his. Anyway, the man finds this already dead fox with an amazingly beautiful pelt and claims to have shot it. He's such an all-time loser no one believes him. To cut a long story short, he refuses to come clean and becomes even more of a figure of fun. In the end, his unfaithful wife and children leave him and the only thing he has left in the world is this beautiful, brown fox pelt, which he prizes above everything else. But, you see, his prized possession is actually in possession of him.' Lúter smiles. 'I think you'll agree, there's a lesson in that for us all?'

'Wise words,' Nero tells him. 'A moral I'm sure we won't fur-get.'

They all groan.

'Seriously though,' Rashid says, 'the real moral of that story is make damn sure you're the best shot in the village.'

'No, no. Lúter's story makes a good point about not over-valuing your possessions.' Jue Hai drains his glass and then holds it out. 'Whose round is it, I'm fur-sty?'

Lúter shakes his head. 'What's the point of sharing my cultural heritage with you lot when you don't give a fox.'

'Okay, okay – no more puns,' Nero tells them. He's been watching the plasma lights as they circle like wasps. 'Why don't we go somewhere else before the live music starts?'

'Excellent idea, boss,' Lúter says. 'We'll make our escape, before Satan's favourite band scrapes the wax from our ears with their blunt instruments.'

Twenty-Seven

Bruno is being held in another cold and echoing place. This time, they throw in a thin, foam mattress – the sort you might exercise on. The door is then locked and bolted. The space is slightly larger than the cupboard they locked him in last night.

They never remain in one place for long. Though individuals come and go, he's counted six of them in total. They're always shoving him into underground passages. Sometimes they're in the redundant tunnels of the expressway system; the rusting remains of the track are still there; others are parts of the drainage or sewage systems. At times, he's ankle deep in water and filth.

Whenever they're above ground, it's dark. If it's a clear night, at least he can look up at the stars and try to work out where they are. Bruno tries to fill his lungs with clear, cold air as if to store it up for later. There are great welts on his wrists from where his hands are bound behind him. This affects his balance and though he's learning to adjust his body accordingly, he often slips in the snow or the frost-hardened ground.

With the Northern Lights flickering overhead, they could be rats running inside a plasma globe. Whenever they're about to make a move, they ask him if they'll meet with any opposition. 'They'll attack us all. You won't be spared,' the big, blunt-headed one likes to remind him. 'It'll be far safer for you if we can avoid them.'

He has to keep reminding them that he's not a surveillance lens, that his ability to predict is more random – that he can't flick some kind of mental switch and see the future. They're disappointed by his limitations and it's clear that disappointment is beginning to foster a seething resentment.

Today, there were four of them – two in front and two behind. They were inside a narrow service tunnel and the air smelt rank but at least it was dry underfoot. After a few hundred metres, they'd reached a junction where the tunnel diverged.

'Wait. Not that way,' he'd hissed. 'We need to go left. There are ten of them, maybe more, heading straight for us.'

For a moment, they'd hesitated, eying him with deepest suspicion. He'd raised his voice as much as he dared. 'Come on – we need to hurry.'

Finally, they took his word for it and went down the left-hand vent. He could see they were tempted to hide in order to check the truth of what he'd told them but in the end they'd decided to press on.

They'd encountered no opposition. He'd heard them muttering up ahead. The truth is, none of them knew what the consequences of turning right would have been. There's no way to prove what would have happened on the route they didn't take: a brush with one of the more obvious paradoxes that had them all shaking their heads.

The incident did little to dispel their collective scepticism about his usefulness. The woman is the one exception – though she's absent most of the time, she keeps the faith.

He's thankful for the small skylight set into this ceiling. The air in the room is heavy with dampness and something fouler. There's a bucket in the corner – the usual crude sanitary arrangement. Bruno can hear scratching and scurrying just behind the crumbling wall plaster. To begin with he'd been frightened by the rats and other vermin they'd encountered but now he welcomes any small diversion.

Though he can't see the sky, he's aware that the daylight hours are beginning to increase. Other things have improved – he's occasionally allowed water to wash with and given a change of underclothes. They bring him more recognisable food although he still has only water to drink.

Left alone, he keeps thinking about Krista. Every time he remembers the accident, he feels a new contraction in his stomach. How long has it been since she had her operation? Would she have recovered by now? So many questions remain unanswered. And then there's always the big one: why hadn't he been able to foresee the accident?

In these empty hours, he likes to conjure up cozy pictures of Krista all rosy-cheeked again and going home to her solidly functional family to be spoilt rotten. Sometimes, he pretends these are genuine visions – that he's watching her regain every aspect of the carefree existence she'd enjoyed before having the misfortune to get involved with him. That she's out there somewhere regaining the life he'd so nearly stolen from her in that one stupid moment. Even if he finds a way out of all this, he'll never again have the opportunity to get close to her. Perhaps it's just as well. She should keep her distance if she knows what's good for her.

There's a sound behind the door, and then a metallic note as it's unlocked. This time it's the taller, broader one who comes in alone carrying a tray. This would be the perfect opportunity to try to overpower him, if only that were remotely feasible. Above the grey scarf pulled up around his mouth and nose, the man's dark eyes continue to glower their suspicion. Again, Bruno spots the tattoo of a salamander on the man's exposed forearm and, once again, he gets the impression of a false clue being placed too conspicuously before him.

Such contact between Bruno and his guards is always kept to a minimum. Each time one of them appears, he tries to make conversation – the odd joke on a good day. He's never succeeded in raising a laugh but perhaps they smile beneath their masks.

The man puts the tray down on the floor next to the door. They're always careful to keep this physical distance – afraid of his knowing touch; scared he might spring on them and glean some fresh, uncensored information.

An odd relationship is developing between them. Jónsson, his old History teacher, had known a worrying amount about the infamous Stockholm Syndrome – how the term had originated from a six-day bank siege in that city in 1973. The hostages had rapidly come to experience a child-like, utter dependency on their captors, which, when their living conditions began to improve, caused them to feel gratitude that led to an extraordinary empathetic bond with their abductors.

From the smell, he can tell the man's brought him some kind of fish stew. There's no distinction between what they feed him for breakfast or for dinner but the cooking has got better. They must be trying to elicit his gratitude. Brainwash him – ah the irony of that word – they hope to turn him from captive to committed activist like a modern-day Patty Hearst.

Thanks to Jónsson, he knows it's not a one-way street: the same process begins to make it harder to kill the people – or person – you're holding captive when you've come to know them.

Before the man can disappear, Bruno springs up. Pointing at the bowl of food he asks, 'Did you hear about the baby octopus that was held to ransom?' he waits a beat. 'Yeah – they reckon it was squidnappers.'

This time he thinks he hears a brief exhale as if the guard might be groaning or smirking. It's a tough call though – these lame jokes might just make him easier to kill. The man leaves without saying a word.

In the long hours after that, Bruno lies on his back staring at the darkened skylight. Funnily enough, if Ása Sturludóttir and her band of less-than-merry men had tried reasoned argument he'd be more sympathetic to their cause. Through her understanding, he's aware of how corrupt the governance of the Eldísvík really is. Her evidence is undeniable. However, armed with his stolen understanding of historical consequences, he knows any attempt to replace the current administration by force might unleash something far worse. Though Ása isn't the rebel movement's only leader, it's hard to imagine how such an overpowering, malign influence wouldn't corrupt its nobler aims.

Right now he needs to concentrate on his own fate and that has to start with him getting out of here. Acting's never been his thing so it's unlikely he can pull off pretending some kind of Damascene conversion. No, he'll need to take things slowly. When Ása finally reappears, he'll begin a dialogue that ends with him revealing a few of the things he's certain she'll want to hear.

Lying there in the darkness, Bruno takes comfort in the fact that he already knows what his final means of escape will be.

Twenty-Eight

Lúter knocks on the open door before walking in. Looking up, Nero watches him move the metal coat-rack in order to firmly shut the door. The current of displaced air causes the whole thing to waver beyond his outstretched hand before crashing to the floor. The resulting noise causes every head in the outer offices to turn in their direction.

Though the glass door is unbroken; the racket reawakens Nero's hangover. 'Subtly done,' he tells him, none-the-less intrigued.

Lúter stoops to pick up the fallen stand and its contents. 'Sorry about that, boss,' he says, his heightened colour so at odds with his white-blond hair. 'I thought we should have some privacy to discuss what we found in the Orange Zone.' He holds up a hand in defence. 'I know you said you wanted to handle that part of the investigation, but just now I happened to be in Surveillance and so I asked them for anything they still had on Orange Fourteen over the last month. Told 'em I was being thorough.'

Nero isn't pleased but he lets him continue.

'Reeves told me straight out it wasn't available. Said everything gets automatically wiped after two days, unless it's flagged as significant. He gave me some bullshit about how they've had to set new limits on Orange Zone data storage due to a temporary problem with retrieval; claimed it had something to do with budgets, the age of the system, oh, and giving preference to the Free Zone.'

Nero frowns. 'You've got to be kidding me. That's the first I've heard of it. When we checked the movements of those GRSK dealers in Orange Twelve last week, how far back did we go?'

'Must have been at least three weeks.' Lúter looks worried. 'They've sent me what they claim is all they have.' He shrugs. 'There was no unusual activity. You can take a look if you like.'

Nero waves away the suggestion. 'No point.' He stands up. 'Exactly how are we supposed to do our jobs without adequate surveillance? I'm going to take it up with Leifsson once I've seen Jue Hai's report on that site.'

Lúter produces a sheet of printed material. 'It's right here.'

'He gave it to you? I told him only me.'

'He knows we're looking into this together.' He points at a particular sentence. 'It's all in the dot in that exclamation mark right there.'

'A micro-dot. You're joking? He must have been watching old spy movies.' Nero takes the paper and peers hard at the ! to see if there's anything distinctive about the dot. There isn't. Lúter's still peering over his shoulder. 'Look, I appreciate your efforts,' he tells him, 'but from now on you need to leave this side of the investigation to me. Understood?'

He waits for assent and it comes as a nod. The man needs distracting. 'I've got Jue Hai's other report on the Orange victims, but I haven't received an update on their IDs. If we can identify them, we need to trace and inform next of kin asap. Can you go and see what's holding things up?'

'Okay, understood.' Lúter opens the door to silent speculation. Watching him walk away, a deep unease steals across the back of Nero's neck.

A half hour later, Chan comes in balancing two coffees. 'These are from the café you took me to,' she says. 'Double espresso, black no sugar – that's how you like it, right?'

Nero takes a sip. 'Perfect.' He tries to enjoy the pungent taste and the welcome hit of the caffeine but instead worries about the degree of intimacy her gesture might be suggesting. Better to concentrate on the business in hand. 'You and I are off to see Professor Zhender at the university,' he says, standing up a little too close to her.

She doesn't step back. 'I've heard of him,' she says. 'He's profiled in an article I read. Specialises in understanding and treating serial murderers. Apparently, he's both a psychologist and psychotherapist.'

Brushing past her to retrieve his coat, he detects a slight citrus note. 'I'm not sure I care about the exact distinction between the two,' he says. From her intake of breath, he can tell she's tempted to enlighten him about the difference between the two disciplines but then thinks better of it. He buttons up his coat. 'I thought the professor might help us work out how these two crimes might be connected,' he tells her.

The subway is busy; they're pressed up close in the overcrowded pod. He feels the light touch of her hand alongside his on the grab-rail; the contact with her bare skin gives him a jolt – though not the usual kind. He quickly moves his hand away but is left feeling oddly disquieted.

Swaying together as the pod shoots through the tube, he continues to breathe in the sweet-sharp aroma of her hair. Alone for the last three stops, they move only slightly apart. She keeps looking at him quizzically. 'Tell me, Inspector,' she finally says, 'isn't Dr Arthur similarly qualified. Wouldn't it have been far easier to consult him instead?'

'Under the circumstances, I prefer to get an outside opinion.' Nero's already rehearsed this excuse in case Leifsson asks.

'That makes sense,' she tells him, though her expression remains less than convinced.

At the university's main gate, they confront a massive banner. Daubed in crude red paint:

TOGETHER WE CAN HEAL
OUR DIVIDED STATE.
HEAR THE VIXEN'S CALL!

Nero looks in vain for those responsible in the throng of students heading for their next lectures. '*Image capture,*' he says, before blinking twice. '*Send to Zeitgeist Department. Copy to DSD intel.*'

'I've just seen that two more of these have appeared in the City Centre,' Chan says. 'They're being pulled down as we speak.'

'So much for freedom of speech,' Nero mutters.

The entrance to the main block is crowded with students. Chan could easily be mistaken for one of them. She's wearing a beige coat, which, to his mind, isn't nearly thick enough for such a cold day.

They're directed to the sixth floor where the professor's stout, female assistant shows them into his empty office. The view is even more spectacular than the one from Dr Arthur's room. From here, it's far easier to grasp how the two mountain ranges almost encircle the city. Sunlight is staining the snow-covered peaks a pale pink. Down below, students are still milling around the grounds. With only the tops of their heads visible, they look like randomly colliding particles.

Hearing a noise behind him, he turns. Professor Zhender has arrived looking flustered. In his mid-forties, he's wearing jeans and a blue shirt beneath a formal jacket. 'Sorry to keep you,' he says, enthusiastically shaking hands with them both. From the brief connection, Nero instantly picks up the man's restless curiosity.

The professor moves the chair from behind his desk so that the three of them are sitting in a wide curve and not in opposition. Seated, Zhender's long limbs jut out at sharp angles. He keeps brushing back the fringe of dark hair, which has a tendency to flop across one eye.

'Right – well, I'm sure we're all busy people, so let's get down to it. How can I be of help?' The professor takes care to make equal eye contact with both of them.

Nero begins. 'I'm sure you've already seen the media reports about the two multiple murders.'

'It would be hard *not* to be aware of them. I'd be delighted to assist if I can. I'm assume that's your next question?'

'Yes. We'd welcome your input.'

'Would this be in addition to that of your colleague, Dr Arthur?' *I hope this consultation doesn't put me into an awkward position. Arthur's a bit of a strange fish but I wouldn't willingly upset the man.*

'Yes, of course.'

'I imagine your main concern, Inspector Cavallo, is to prevent any further bloodshed.' *The woman is quite mesmerising: such extraordinary poise. A most unlikely police officer.* 'These murders have caused some heated discussions on campus. Many of our students seem to feel that they call into question the way our city is so strictly divided into its zones. Such protests and unrest seem rather apt – it being the centenary of the famous student protest movements in Paris and America. To quote Larkin: "Sex was invented in 1963, between the Chatterley trial and the Beatles' first LP."' *Damn, did she just catch me staring at her breasts?*

The professor leans back on his chair. 'But we mustn't get distracted. If you send me the reports, I'll certainly study them and give you my conclusions.'

'As you can imagine, Professor, there's a fair degree of urgency.'

'Understood.' He drags his attention away from Chan. 'Perhaps you could give me some information about the two crime scenes?'

Nero describes what he'd seen with his own eyes and then a brief summary of the forensic reports. 'This is the one image we have of the woman we believe to be the perpetrator,' he says, handing the professor a printed copy.

Zhender rubs his right temple as he studies the image. 'Such a slight figure to have caused all this extraordinary upheaval,' he says. *So here she is then, this supposed decoy. Not much to go on.* He continues to stare at the photograph as Nero describes the psalm and symbols written, as they now know, in a cocktail of the victims' blood. 'At both SOCs we found one of these,' he says, handing the professor the two bagged, plastic ducks.

The professor turns the bag this way and that to get a better view of the objects. 'A signature – and such an appropriate one. I see one is far more bloodied than the other.'

Nero makes a point of turning to Chan. 'Did I miss anything, Constable?'

'You didn't mention the behaviour of the vixens, Inspector. They took an active part in the dismemberment of the bodies in the Red Zone,' she says, looking uncomfortable under the professor's gaze. 'But the pack did next to nothing to the Orange victims – their bodies were scavenged but this time by various wild animals.'

'Mmm.' The professor rakes his hair back again. 'Neither of the acts you describe appears to fall neatly into what we'd expect of a mass murderer or alternatively a serial killer.'

'I agree,' Nero says. 'As you know, a typical serial killer murders at different locations. It usually has little to do with material gain. In both these cases, there's no obvious sexual motive, no discernable torture of the victims before they were killed.'

The professor's finger rubs away at his temple. 'With your typical mass murderer, there will be more than one victim at the same location. They kill to draw attention to themselves and their deep-seated anger and hostility.'

Chan interjects. 'Yes, but the *dissimilarity* here is the degree of premeditation. Leaving those ducks, for instance.'

'A typical mass murderer shows disregard for their capture and punishment,' Nero adds. 'They're prepared to go out in a blaze of glory.'

'That is the classic profile, yes.' Professor Zhender steeples his fingers for a moment and then puts them behind his head. Perspiration circles decorate the underarms of his blue shirt. 'From what you've told me, it's clear the Red Zone murders show evidence of longer-term planning whereas the Orange Zone killings suggest much less. The vixens had to be re-trained in order to participate in the first, but in the second murders they didn't. Preliminary profiles suggest the victims were more carefully selected in the first incident.'

He swivels his chair towards Nero. 'You said the Orange Zone victims were lesser criminals. They might just have been unlucky to be present at the wrong time. If we add the psalm written in blood, we see the perpetrator has far less self-control – undoubtedly, it was an emotional act. Yes, in both cases, the perpetrator is bitter and angry, but in the first the anger is more controlled allowing a greater degree of organisation and planning.'

'I'd agree with all that,' Nero says. He notices Chan has taken out her log and is making supplemental notes.

The professor stands up. 'I think we can safely conclude that we're dealing with two separate killers. The original and a copycat – but someone who knew enough to leave the exact same signature duck.' He begins to pace. 'Next, we need to ask ourselves – what exactly is the relationship between these two killers? How does the first one feel about having her work emulated? Has it made her angry or was she complicit? Mmm.'

'Before we get onto that,' Nero says. 'Can you give me your initial conclusions on profiles?'

Zhender sits back down. 'At this stage, it's difficult for me to add anything to what you already know. You say there's evidence both these murderers are female – that's really most unusual. As I'm sure you both know, women commit only about one per cent of such killings and are more likely to kill those close to them: husbands, lovers, et cetera. Usually, it's family members or co-workers. Though we can't be certain, here, that seems unlikely to be true in either case.'

He picks up a pencil, of all things, and begins transferring it from one hand to another then abruptly he turns to stare at Nero. 'Inspector, you'll be familiar with the main phases of a typical serial killer's behaviour. In the Aura Phase, the perpetrator withdraws from everyday reality and this is often accompanied by a heightening of their senses.'

He leans forward. 'The decoys' role in law enforcement means that they're habitually in that position. What must it be like to be virtual outcasts from the society you serve?' *I can't begin to imagine their sense of isolation.* 'It must be a small step from there to creating a sustained fantasy you decide to act out.'

The professor swivels his chair round to gaze out of the window. Nero waits.

'Their line of work would make it easier to move on un-detected to the second or "trolling" phase where they identify and stalk their victims.'

'What phase do you think each decoy is at right now?' Nero asks.

The pencil makes a couple more transfers and then comes to rest in the professor's right hand. He turns to point it at Nero. 'It's possible that our Red Zone killer – let's call her Killer A – has moved on to the "totem" phase. She may be collecting the information and speculation in the media.' He's waving the pencil like a wand. 'In the past, this would have been newspaper clippings; nowadays it's normally holo images.'

'So, she'll be pretty pleased about her new celebrity status,' Nero says.

'Or, more specifically, the power that it represents. They're calling her an Avenging Angel; that's bound to help justify her future actions.'

'As I recall, the final phase is "depression",' Chan says, still with her head down writing. 'Might either of them have reached that phase already?'

'Yes, it's quite probable,' Zhender replies. *Very good, Constable. Not just a pretty face.* 'I'm guessing these particular victims were not the precise target of their individual anger and so they can no longer represent the real victim, or victims, they would like to strike back at. Killer A, in particular, will be feeling dissatisfied that her fantasy is incomplete. She'll have a strong desire, an urgent need, to perpetrate further acts.'

'Can you give us any idea who her next target is likely to be?' Nero is, quite literally, on the edge of his seat.

The professor turns his gaze back to the window. He begins to slowly shake his head. 'I'm afraid that's an impossible question to answer with any accuracy. It all depends on the origin of her initial sense of injustice. Assuming both these women are actually decoys, as relatively powerless cogs in the DSD wheel, their grievances may well be generalised against the whole organisation; possibly against what the naive like to call *The System* – the status quo that appears to exploit the vulnerable to protect the powerful. If I'm right, both these women may target their former employers – heads of departments, even Governor Leifsson himself. Equally as likely, one or both of them may turn their ire against the cartel heads who operate with apparent impunity within the Red Zone.' He holds up his hands. 'Why not both?'

'Our two killers must have displayed some of the classic signs of antisocial personality disorder,' Nero says. 'Wouldn't those signs have been apparent to an expert?'

The professor stands up. 'I believe I've already speculated enough for one morning.' *It's clear where your question is leading. I won't be drawn into criticising Dr Arthur.* He looks from Chan to Nero. 'Anyone can be fooled by a clever sociopath or psychopath. We professionals are no exception. They can dazzle us with their superficial charm and all the while tell us elaborate lies. They can make us believe we've successfully rehabilitated them whilst their underlying personality traits remain doggedly unaltered.'

He gives Nero a rueful smile. 'In everyday life, they may show us what we think is genuine affection, become the friends, or even lovers we long for. All the time, they're hiding the shallowness of their emotions, their lack of shame or remorse and ah – ' He turns to address Chan. 'A grandiose sense of self, which makes them feel deserving or entitled to whatever they desire as their absolute right.'

'But not all psychopaths are criminals,' she reminds him.

'You're right. Some are able to lead apparently normal lives. But we must beware of them.' He looks at Nero. 'We must know our own vulnerabilities. Psychopaths tempt us by offering us what we haven't been able to achieve ourselves.'

For a moment, Zhender remains quite still.

'And now you'll have to excuse me, Inspector. Constable Chan. For the moment, there's nothing more I can add. I've got a lecture in a few minutes and really must check my presentation material.'

'Thank you for giving us your time,' Nero says, rising. 'Feel free to contact me as soon as you've finished studying our reports. I'd welcome any further thoughts you might have.'

Zhender shakes their hands with conviction and then opens the door. 'I'll do that. Pleasure to meet you both. Do give my regards to Dr Arthur.'

In the lift, Nero's stud buzzes. 'I see Leifsson's just issued a statement to us all.'

Chan laughs. 'I must say I quite like that bit where he

says he's "confident the scholarly traditions of hedonism and apathy will prevent any lasting student action".'

The jocularity of her mood disarms him. For a moment an invitation seems to flicker across her dark eyes. The next minute, he's less certain.

'In my experience,' he says, 'it's easy to miscalculate the strength of other people's feelings.'

Twenty-Nine

Nero contemplates the exclamation mark for some considerable time. Where in the hell had the Jue Hai found the equipment needed to produce a microdot? More to the point, how is he expected to read the damned thing? His stud won't do it – the available magnification isn't sufficient. Unlike Jue Hai, he doesn't have daily access to powerful microscopes.

In desperation, Nero decides to borrow a hand-held monitor from Supplies. The place is staffed by guys who never look you in the face, but greet the equipment you return with parental enthusiasm. He submits the relevant application. If they bother to review it, the request might raise suspicions; his hopes are pinned on their usual lack of curiosity about their fellow human beings.

Once Nero's collected the device, he takes it back to his apartment. He struggles to adjust the scanner's range, has to repeatedly override the machine's insistence on the more usual band of magnifications. It's a tedious battle of wills, but finally the report is projected onto a blank area of his bedroom wall.

It makes chilling reading. No wonder Jue Hai had shown such caution. The signatures of the photons are definitely and unmistakably that of their own military. The central target had been human, but the others were not. Jue Hai speculates that the carbonised "negatives" he'd seen are those of a large number of dog-size creatures – most probably foxes.

The rest of the picture is undeniably bleak. It's obvious a decoy, along with his or her pack, had been subject to execution right there in the Orange Zone. Jue Hai confirms the site had subsequently been cleaned with precision using military grade decontamination fluids. However, some tiny residues remained in the cracks around the margins. From his analysis of these, the pathologist concludes that the executions had taken place "quite recently".

Nero frowns at the uncharacteristic vagueness of Jue Hai's estimation. Was he too nervous to be precise? What is clear is that at least one of the Commanders, with the assistance of a military unit, had annihilated an individual decoy and vixen pack. Given the proximity to the point where they had dropped Harris off, could it have been him? Surely the military wouldn't contemplate such senseless brutality.

Slumping onto the bed with his head in his hands, he tries to imagine an alternative scenario. Maybe the Commanders, using the satellite information which the military had refused to hand over to his department, had gone ahead and apprehended the first decoy and then, in order to avoid the ramifications of a trial, they had simply wiped her and her pack from the face of the earth.

The latest massacre, right next to where it happened, was no coincidence. Most likely, it was an impassioned, retaliatory act, possibly perpetrated by someone close to the murdered decoy. In which case, were those killings the work of a fully psychopathic personality?

He goes to get a glass of iced water, while his mind reconfigures the dots. He'd prefer a glass of wine but needs to stay sharp.

His stud buzzes with a communication from Kass with the results from backtracking the vixens present during the Orange Zone killings. After that, a course of action suggests itself.

Hunger is gnawing at his stomach. Nero opens the cryo-unit and finds a new container has arrived. He inputs the receipt code for the new order. The pack's ingredients offer a number of possibilities but, like always, he returns to a favourite.

The Re-Gen flickers across his chosen line-up, and then returns to boil the pasta. Nero switches the machine off, preferring to finish the pungent, squid-ink sauce himself. He stirs the mixture then adjusts the seasoning until a spoonful tells him it's perfect.

Mixing the cooked prawns into the pasta, he finds he's already decided. Fokk it – why not open that Nobile di Montepulciano he's been hoarding. If this is to be his last supper, he wants to enjoy it. If he's lucky, he'll live to regret it.

Thirty

The restlessness of the pack is all that's necessary to wake her. She leaves the shelter to get a better look at what could be stirring them. The black tips of their ears all move in unison towards a sound that's inaudible to her. Her stud confirms there's another six hours before daybreak.

The vixens rise as one. The balletic synchronicity of their movements always astounds her, as if an invisible thread joins them; a thread of common understanding and loyalty that humans can never hope to possess. It's humbling that they never question her leadership.

Cloud moves to obscure the first quarter moon, deepening the darkness. She waits. Like most of her colleagues, she seldom uses infrareds. At first she'd felt blind without them. Harris had been the one who explained, had shown her what a handicap such devices can be, how, without them, her sight would improve along with all her other senses.

On such a still night, the sound of footfall travels a vast distance across open ground. She signals for her vixens to bide their time; she prefers to wait for visual confirmation. The slight breeze means the thin cloud will eventually clear away and there should just be enough moonlight to see this interloper.

The animals continue to rotate their ears as they strain to listen, their tails held aloft in readiness for an attack. Now she too can hear what's spooking them: a solitary person is walking along the centre of the old rail track incautiously avoiding the soft verge that would have deadened the sound of their approach. They're either an idiot or someone too brazenly sure of themselves.

The vixens are quivering with anticipation. With the re-emergence of the moon, she can see how the ridges of their hackles have risen. They wait, eager and ready for her signal.

Whoever it is, they're moving at a steady pace. The dilapidated station buildings obscure her view. She scans the scarred rooflines and peers at the clearing on the other side. A moment passes before a figure is revealed, moving against that row of small huts – the unmistakable outline of man.

She follows his progress. He crosses the small valley directly in front of her then leaves the track. Breathing heavily, he clambers up the steep, frost-hardened ground towards the ridge. She waits for him to gain the high ground.

Hands on hips, he simply stands there surveying the sweep of the empty landscape. Once he's regained his breath, he sits down on the stump – the same place she often sits to watch the vixens as they enjoy their supper.

She's quite certain this invasion isn't accidental; this man is going nowhere else tonight.

They move towards him in a wide, outward arc. The vixens' soft pads ensure their approach is silent. As always, *she* is the fallible one who might step on a twig or rattle the bare branches of a bush.

Once they're on top of the ridge, they sweep in from behind overpowering him with swift and disappointing ease.

The man lies quite still, inert, pinned to the ground at her feet where he offers no resistance. The weight of her vixens presses down on him, their open mouths so close to his face that he must breathe in what they exhale. Although he won't be able to see her face, she deploys the hood as a precaution.

With practiced ease she searches his pockets. 'You'd better

talk fast,' she tells him, the software in the microphone reconstructing her words. 'What are you doing here?'

Her gloved hand is able to extract nothing except a police ID badge. 'What have we here?' Her visor's lens zooms in. 'Inspector N. Cavallo of the City Police Department. Such a long way out of your comfort zone, I imagine. N. Cavallo. I wonder what the N stands for? Neanderthal? Nut-job? Or how about: needs-a-check-up-from-the-neck-up?'

She increases her boot's pressure, 'Let's just cut to the après chase. You have thirty seconds to persuade me not to snap your neck.'

'As you can see, I came here, alone and unarmed. I simply wanted to talk to you before –'

She's learnt not to ease up, even though he's having difficulty speaking.

'My name is Nero. I'm investigating the murders two nights ago in the Orange Zone.'

'Are you now?' She increases the pressure on his windpipe.

'I'm also… looking into the illegal killing of a decoy… and a vixen pack.'

She decides to let him spit it out.

'I believe the decoy's murder happened in the same vicinity a few days before. It seems likely that the two are–' He spits out a small clump of grass or possibly fur. 'In some way connected.'

She eases back just enough to hear him more clearly. 'I believe that murder was also unlawful and I thought you might be able to, ah, help me with my enquiries.'

She laughs, knowing the distortion will make her sound deranged. 'You want me to help the police department with their enquiries? Isn't that a pretty unrealistic suggestion under the present circumstances, Mr Cavallo?'

'Maybe – but I believe we share a mutual interest in exposing the murderer of this decoy.'

'And what about the other incident you are investigating, Inspector? The one that seems to have slipped your mind.'

'I suggest we put that to one side for the time being.'

This time, she's genuinely amused. Her laugh could be a hyena's. 'I see. So we just ignore all that do we, Nero? Well, that seems a bit – how should I put it – a bit unrealistic that we should ignore the elephant not in the room but with its boot on your fokking windpipe.'

She ups the pain another notch.

'Let's just consider this a temporary truce. Aah –' He tries to cough. He tries to move his body to ease the pressure on his throat but fails. 'Until the end of tonight's – aaah – discussion.'

Not wanting to kill him yet, she eases off. He takes the chance: 'After that – I promise I will walk away and leave you in peace for the rest of the night.' In a hoarse voice he adds, 'Assuming, that is, you remain peaceful tonight.'

'You are hardly in a position to dictate terms, Inspector.'

'Look – I came here alone to simply talk to you about the murder of the decoy and their pack. It wasn't my only option – as I'm sure you'll agree. You might well be in custody now if I'd acted differently. Let's just say I got your message. Isn't that what you wanted?'

'And what could you, a mere police inspector, hope to do about it in any case?' She trusts her scorn is electronically translated.

'I can't promise anything, but I will fully document my findings. If there's enough evidence for a prosecution I will insist on one. If I'm blocked, I'm prepared to approach the media with the evidence.'

She lets him raise his head from the ground. 'I promise I'll relentlessly pursue those responsible for the killing and put them on trial. It's my job and I plan to do it.'

'You'll be wasting your time. Despite all these oh-so-noble assurances, D I Cavallo, can you begin to contemplate, never mind stand against, the opposition you'd face?'

'I'll give it my best shot. You never know, I might just succeed. Got to be worth a punt, wouldn't you say?' He waits a few breaths. 'Just as, from tomorrow morning, I'll be doing my best to arrest you and prevent you from taking the law into your own hands.'

She laughs at the man, at his sheer naivety. 'Why, Inspector – surely that's exactly what they pay me to do.'

At her side, one of the vixens emits a low, throaty gekkering sound. The others are showing signs of increasing restlessness. The man tries to say more but she prevents any further contribution from him while she considers his proposition.

Was it worth taking the risk? In truth, she's more than a little annoyed that he's discovered this feeding area, but if she kills him, then no doubt others in his department would come here too. She's made a mistake, left a trail of some kind. In any event, she'll have to concede ground here and relocate this feeding area.

She releases his neck, hears him gulp down long mouthfuls of air. 'Okay, Inspector, I accept your terms. I'll tell you what you need to know. We'll call pax, as they say in the playground, until tomorrow morning. If I see you here again, or anywhere else for that matter, without the slightest hesitation I'll kill you.'

'Me too, if you resist arrest.'

This time they both laugh.

'One other thing,' he croaks. 'Could you get these bloody vixens out of my face? Their breath is a pretty lethal weapon.'

She signals the release. 'Now lie very, very still Inspector or they'll be on you again in a flash.'

This isn't strictly necessary. This man will have to fight every instinct to maintain this position of complete and abject surrender. At her feet, corpse-like and breathing in the pungent dampness of the earth, at least she'll be getting his undivided attention.

Sparing no detail, she begins to describe exactly how the Commanders executed her best friend.

Thirty-One

Nero's balaclava is a leftover from last year's "Cops and Robbers" Christmas party. It's a struggle to get it over the infrareds and he smarts as he pulls it down over the bruising on his left cheek.

Everything he now sees is framed by the jagged edges of the eyeholes, offering a new perspective on the world as it appears from inside the Orange Zone.

Thanks to DSD's own schematic, he's fairly confident he'll be able to avoid the surveillance points. On the way in, he'd decided that being spotted by a criminal gang would be more dangerous than by his own patrolmen, now, on his return journey, he's not so sure.

He breaks into a steady jog – not fast or slow enough to attract additional suspicion. At this hour, thanks to the curfew, the streets and alleyways are all deserted. If he can keep up this pace, he ought to make it home in time to change and leave for work around the normal time.

After half an hour or so, he's beginning to flag. He stops, bending over, hands on his knees. His stud confirms that he's now on the threshold of the Free Zone.

Stretching out in front of him is a lava field. It appears to be unguarded – probably because no one in their right mind would cross this treacherous ground at night. He can see the narrowest of tracks – probably made by animals – running through it. If he strays just a little from the path, he could easily fall into one of a thousand craters and crevasses that pepper these places, breaking a leg or worse.

Nero pulls a thin backpack from his thigh pocket and stows the hood along with the infrareds inside. He waits for the minute or two it takes his eyesight to adjust. The wind has picked up – must be what's causing the low, wailing sounds he can hear. He'd read somewhere that in the old days the locals believed the Little People haunted these places, lurking in the deepest of these holes in order to hide from the full-sized humans they didn't trust. Who could blame them?

Nero picks his way across the terrain. His progress is slow but steady.

Finally, he reaches the edge of a moon-silvered lake – the last hurdle. There's nothing for it but to wade chest deep into the icy water. The shock of the cold makes it hard for him to breathe. There's a saying in this country that there's no such thing as bad weather only bad clothing. At least his doesn't let him down; he makes it to the other side a little wet around the edges but otherwise dry.

Nero's stud confirms he's crossed the zone boundary. His teeth are chattering and he's shivering like someone's shaking him.

In front of him, the ground rises up. To warm himself, he tries to break into a run but only partially succeeds. Once he's cleared a small copse he's at last able to survey the glowing expanse of the city below. After where he's just been, it looks like the Promised Land.

Nero's soon within the grid of quiet residential streets. He tries to walk with confidence past the blocks of orderly apartments, although smelling of lake water and dressed from head to foot in black, he's every inch the outsider – an interloper to be feared. A little further on, the buildings become grander, huddling down behind high security fences. He's careful to avoid their gated entrances. Once or twice he glimpses a dozing or distracted security guard.

With his walk-on-the-wild-side over, Nero begins to fret about what had transpired. Did he make the right call not arresting the woman when he had the chance? Possibly. Despite having her boot on his windpipe, he'd believed every word of what she told him. From this moment, his priority is to hunt down and arrest every one of those responsible for such a barbaric act. If humanity had learnt anything from history, it was that following orders is never an excuse for killing a defenceless man – in this case someone who'd spent his career risking his personal safety to safeguard law and order.

Anger is raising his body temperature. That damn moon seems to be shining only on him. If he'd played it by the book and succeeded in arresting the woman, bringing murder charges against her would be difficult. Her defence lawyer would argue she hadn't actually killed those men – she'd simply stood there deflecting their own fire, which had been aimed at her. Self-defence had never been a crime in this city. Cutting up dead bodies for anything other than an autopsy is an offense contrary to Section Six of the Religious Tolerance and Desecration Act only if the deceased's friends or families can convince the Commanders' Court that a violation of the person's sincere religious beliefs, or cultural practices, had occurred. The maximum permitted jail sentence was three years unless she was considered a danger to the public. Mmm.

The expressway with its surveillance-analysis isn't an option. Aware of the time, Nero starts to jog. To a bystander, he might be a crazed, keep-fit fanatic. He keeps to a rapid but not suspicious pace and sticks for the most part to minor pathways and alleys until he finally reaches the city centre.

He makes it back to his apartment block only ten minutes after his morning alarm would normally be activated. The lobby's Secure-a-Beam scans his handprint and left retina.

There's just time for a shower and to snatch something for breakfast. Shaving helps to give his face what he'd hoped would be his normal appearance in about five years' time. He vigorously brushes the memory of the vixens' breath from inside his mouth. No wonder those dog foxes don't stick around.

He needs time to plan his next move but there is none. The crucial thing right now is to show up at work on time and try to put in a routine day.

Thirty-Two

Chan comes into Nero's office ostensibly to give him an update on the identification of the bodies. She must know he's aware of all the latest analysis. Is she trying to impress him with how hard she's working or simply wanting to talk it all through with someone more senior? Part of his job, after all, is to mentor younger officers. It unsettles him that when their hands had accidentally touched in the subway he'd been unable read even her most superficial thoughts. Right now, he has no idea what she might want from him.

Nero offers her a seat. 'Wow, that's quite a bruise,' she says, frowning at him.

Instinctively, he rubs the offending area of his cheek. Thankfully his shirt is hiding the marks on his neck. 'Long story,' he says. 'I won't bore you.'

Her face looks so fresh, her skin remarkably unblemished though she wears no discernable make-up.

They discuss the dead. It's clear they are a class apart. In life, the Double Red corpses had managed to impressively evade every method used by the city to keep tabs on its citizens. Juan Lopez is still the only definite match. By contrast, each of the Orange Zone dead now has a name – in most cases more than one – linked to an exhaustive rap sheet. The cause of death for all has been officially confirmed as deflected photon or laser fire. Jue Hai has ascertained that, in every instance, the blade wounds on their bodies were administered post-mortem.

'Do you think they'll ever identify those Red Zone bodies?' she asks.

'Unlikely – by now, we must have exhausted every avenue.' He can hear the note of despondency in his own voice.

She hands him some papers – the C87D certificates from Jue Hai – and his hand momentarily brushes against hers; again, he feels nothing but how cold her fingers are.

Now that he's the most senior police officer, Nero's counter-signature is necessary to release the Orange Zone bodies for burial. He signs each certificate with an increasing weariness, his name good for nothing except putting an official end to these shadowy lives.

Chan picks up the documents and leans forward to tap them into alignment on the surface of his desk.

He gives her a brief smile of thanks.

She gets to her feet but remains standing in front of him. Has she forgotten something? He glances away – back to the report he'd been reading – and waits for her to speak.

'Do you like Chinese food?' Her face gives him no clues.

'Yes, as a matter of fact I'm very fond of it,' he says. 'But then there's not much I don't like – to eat, that is. I hate kidneys. Oh, and Brussels sprouts – those nasty mini cabbage things.' He's gabbling now. 'Does that make me sound really greedy?'

'I think it just makes you open-minded.' Still hugging the documents to her chest, her smile does that clever trick on his defence mechanisms. 'Besides, you look like you're in pretty good shape.'

A deep blush spreads across her cheeks like a rash. He wants to run his hand over those three moles on her cheek. 'Sorry – that was far too personal,' she says. 'An inappropriate comment to make to a senior officer.'

He waves her concerns away. 'I'd be offended if it wasn't a compliment.'

Her expression softens. 'It's just that, well, I was wondering if you would like to come over to my apartment tonight for a bite to eat? I'm planning to cook something my aunt showed me how to make many years ago: niang pi zi. My kitchen's very basic but, when I have time, I like to make things from scratch. The recipe's too complicated to bother just for one person.'

He stares into her extraordinary eyes looking for further evidence.

'I suppose you'd describe it as a sort of pasta,' she says, 'with a rather special Chinese sauce. I usually serve it with strips of chicken-style. I'm sure you'd really like it.'

'Yes, I'm sure I would. That – it – sounds delightful. I–'

'Eight o'clock, then. You already know where I live.'

She's out the door before he can finish what he was about to say. Without bothering to check, he's certain going to a junior officer's flat alone must go against DSD's personnel guidelines. Last night he'd snatched only a couple of hours rest before his trip to the Orange Zone. He'd been planning to catch up on his sleep as soon as his shift was over. Common sense tells him the whole idea of having dinner with her is unwise.

Nero's more than tempted to go after Chan and, as politely as he can, make an excuse to decline her invitation. Instead, he tries to turn his attention back to the report in front of him – a demonstration that's being interpreted as a sinister threat. In the past, such peaceful protests might have been seen as a sign of a healthy democracy in action. Nero suggests a downgrade of the threat level being assigned to it.

After that, he tries to focus on the rest of his work but it's no good – his concentration is shot to bits.

'Hello, Inspector.' As always, Jóra Bjarnadóttir gives him a no-nonsense flirtatious grin. Her fingers like to play with the smooth surface of the jade pendant at her throat. 'It's nice to

185

see you in the flesh,' she tells him, leans in close; so close he feels the pressure of her breast against his chest. Jóra lightly touches the bruising on his face. 'Ouch! Looks like you've had quite a run-in with someone.'

She takes hold of his chin to turn his face this way and that like he's one of her cadavers. 'Would you like me to rub something on it?' Jóra's desires have always been obvious enough without needing to read her mind. Perhaps it's true what they say about the proximity to death raising a person's libido.

'You should see the other fella,' Nero says, taking several steps back. He hopes her practiced eye won't have spotted the impression of the decoy's boot. 'We've seen quite a bit of Constable Rashid recently, and your trainee, Chan, has been down here several times asking Juey questions. Not that he minds. I guess her being young, beautiful *and* interested in forensics is ticking all of his boxes.'

'Talking of Jue Hai,' he says, 'I wanted a quick word with him. Is he around?'

'Just got back from a suicide in district eight.'

'Ah yes. I sent Lúter and Kass over to take a look. I understand there were no signs of foul play. They found it hard though – both being parents themselves.'

'She was only fourteen-years-old, Juey said. Such a sad waste of a young life.'

After a moment, her solemn look mutates into a smirk. 'We've noticed jumpers are popular in the winter.' She gives a loud, snorting laugh.

Out of politeness, Nero attempts a smile.

'He's just gone to change his scrubs,' she says, nodding towards the clean-up area.

Jue Hai emerges on cue. 'Nero, what brings you to our humble crypt?'

'I just wanted some clarification on a report.'

'I'm surprised you didn't send the lovely Chan to do that,' Jóra interjects from behind his back.

'Jóra thinks I've found my destiny with your trainee.' Jue Hai smirks. 'I can't deny a certain interest – I'd say there's more than a touch of chemistry between us. She's a remarkable young woman, that Chan, though somewhat enigmatic.'

'Yes, I know what you mean.'

Jue Hai nudges him. 'So you find us Chinese inscrutable, eh?'

Nero laughs out loud. 'Not you; you're about as scrutable as they come – if there is such a word. I'm afraid you, my friend, are pretty much an open book.'

'I'm not sure I shouldn't take offence.' Jue Hai's smile drops. 'And I'm not the only one you've offended recently, judging by the size of that bruise.'

Nero holds up his hands. 'I tripped on some ice.'

The pathologist looks more than skeptical. 'Anyway, as I was saying, Constable Chan is particularly interested in forensics. Yesterday, she asked me about algor mortis calculations. She was so keen to learn more, I even let her take a few body temperatures.'

Nero frowns. 'Temperature loss after death – I'm surprised she hasn't fully covered all that in her training. Perhaps she was just being thorough.'

He turns to check Jóra has gone then clears his throat. 'I wanted to ask you a few questions about your other report.'

'What report would that be?' Jue Hai gives him a hard and meaningful stare.

Nero hadn't imagined the Forensics Department would have listen-ins, but he realises Jue Hai must think so.

'I just wanted to be certain that your Orange Zone report is one hundred per cent accurate,' he improvises. 'We may need to rely on your evidence in court.'

'I doubt that particular report will ever be needed in a court of law.' For their unseen audience, the pathologist adds, 'I expect you're really here to arrange that pool game we talked about. This time we should make it winner takes all.'

Thirty-Three

Bruno has spent so many hours in darkness with nothing to do, he knows it's beginning to take its toll on him both physically and mentally. He's been trying to keep himself fit, though with so little food to fuel his strength, today he could barely manage ten press-ups before collapsing onto the cold concrete.

His under-occupied mind is always crowded with images, as if random scenes from too many movies are all running at the same time. These competing visions are so vivid and so numerous they begin to threaten his sanity.

When he was much younger, all he wanted was to be like other kids. He'd gone so far as to smash his head repeatedly against the wall trying to damage whatever part of his brain might be responsible. He should have tried harder.

How long has he been in this particular room? The space is barely two paces by three. He'd have another go at banging his head right now if he thought it would help him get out of this place. It won't.

Sometimes he sees himself free at last and the vision lifts his spirits; at other times, he fears it's all just wishful thinking. He just needs to stick to his plan – the way out he's foreseen.

Starved of stimulus and conversation, Bruno's genuinely thrilled whenever anyone comes into the room. And he's little short of delighted if they talk to him. It's not difficult to demonstrate his gratitude for that extra blanket to calm his shivering or a hot drink to warm his half-empty belly. Each time he shows them how his will has weakened; how, like a broken-in horse, he's now ready to acquiesce to their demands. Once they no longer regard him as a threat, they'll ascribe him a role in their little conspiracy and that will finally lead to his release.

The door opens and a man comes in with food. It's the same bloke as usual, an ungainly giant – around two metres, twenty – with the sour odour of someone who seldom washes. His unkempt hair would be a lot blonder if it were ever clean. He always carries the same tray in with his bare hands and so, from that object alone, Bruno's discovered his name is Erik Ármannsson though he sometimes calls himself Gunter *Einarsson* or Jon Ólafsso. A scarf hides his mouth and nose. The skin on his upper face is ruddy and pockmarked. Despite their frequent contact, there's never any sign of recognition or empathy in Ármannsson's dark eyes. The man's habitually irritated by this whole turn of events, itching for an excuse to rid himself of the nuisance Bruno has become.

Like you might feed a dog, Ármannsson nudges the tray towards him with his foot.

Bruno pounces on the food. His mouth full of stale bread, he gulps down water to soften it. It's fair to say his table manners are not what they were.

The big man always watches him with a look of disgust in his eyes. He's been studying the giant's mind, which is extraordinary in its simplicity. Bruno's seldom encountered such single-mindedness, such binary certainty about what he likes and dislikes; what interests or bores him; what he believes or doesn't. Erik Ármannsson is a born subordinate – provided his leader's aims and ambitions align with his own.

Bruno likes to play a thought-guessing game at these times; his success rate has been rising with every encounter.

He's begun to anticipate exactly where Erik's thoughts are going next – even before the man himself knows. Today, for some reason, Bruno's having less success.

He's only halfway through his meal when the door opens again and two more men walk in; this time without their masks. This might be a very good or very bad sign.

The size of the room means they're soon upon him. Bruno looks up expecting the usual glowering expressions but the act of removing their disguises seems to have softened their faces.

Ármannsson now pulls down his own scarf. The only surprise is that his nose is more refined than the rest of his face had suggested. The big man's hand grabs at the front of Bruno's jacket, pulling him roughly to his feet and then up onto his tiptoes until he's staring right into that ugly, pitted face. The stench of the giant's unwashed body makes him gag.

'I had a dog called Bruno once.' Ármannsson turns to include the others in his harsh laughter. 'A brute, he was – made a good guard dog. Always hated the bastard, but at least he had balls.'

He drops Bruno like an object discarded. 'Well now, Mister Mastriano, I'm sure you'll be pleased to hear that we're all about to go walkies together. He gestures to the other two men.

The muscle-bound one steps forward. His full beard means his unmasked appearance is little changed. He produces a set of plastic cuffs and, in a single movement, secures one end around Bruno's right wrist before slapping the other around his own. Ármannsson nods his approval. 'Kleiner here will be your sweetheart – he'll be holding your hand all the way.'

Kleiner yanks his arm to demonstrate that the leash is secure. Bruno looks towards the other man. Ármannsson leans further into his face. 'I don't need to tell you what will happen if you pull any funny stuff.'

'Where are you taking me?'

Ármannsson gives a mirthless chuckle. 'You seem to be

losing your psychic powers, boy. I should have thought you'd already know.'

'We're going into the Free Zone,' Bruno says. 'You want me to make contact with someone.'

The three men slowly applaud, Kleiner's hand jerking his own back and forth like a puppet's.

Thirty-Four

Nero's stud is buzzing with so much intel he's forced to remove it. He'd scheduled this meeting with Jacobs and Grey – the team leaders of the drug squad – some time ago. It's obvious their two departments would benefit from working more closely together.

The men sitting opposite him seem to have grown more alike over the last couple of years. Both are a little younger than him – mid to late thirties. Their well-worn clothes are in a range of colours that runs from grey to black. Both men are showing the classic signs of male pattern hair loss and also have impressively large noses along with thick stubble on their chins. Medium everything else means they're pretty well-suited to undercover work.

Their office is a replica of his own though marginally bigger. Framed photos are proudly displayed on their respective desktops. The back wall is a mass of mug shots arranged in descending order to form criminal family trees.

'So you've seen a marked increase in the supply side, of late,' Nero says.

Jacobs leans forward. 'To the point where it's getting bloody silly.'

'The cartels are using ever-younger children for their street-level activities,' Grey says. 'I've got kids myself.' He cups his curled fist. 'Those bastards don't give a shit who they exploit.'

'They'll be setting their stalls up outside the kindergartens next.' Reddened skin is spreading up Jacob's neck like a rash.

Grey takes up their mantra for the afternoon, 'We need more feet on the ground – it's as simple as that.'

Nero sighs. 'I'm afraid there's nothing much I can do to help. Right now, with this decoy thing hanging over us all, Leifsson has finally assigned a few more personnel to the patrol but still short of the numbers we need. Frankly, we too are stretched to the limit.'

Grey continues to shake his head. 'Narcotics operations fund all the cartels – it's their life blood.' His fist slams into his hand. 'Hit them there, where it hurts, and the rest of their activities will suffer.' He holds up both hands then lets them fall to slap his sides.

Nero echoes his gesture. 'I'd be the first to agree with you on that but convincing Leifsson to open his wallet is another matter.'

Grey jumps up, his chair scraping the floor. 'Our glorious leader has never been receptive to this department's needs. It makes you wonder.' He tilts his head to suggest more.

The man's frustration is understandable but this meeting has gone on longer than scheduled and there's little more to be said on either side.

Nero gets to his feet. 'Let's not fight amongst ourselves – on a day-to-day level we're all starved of resources. If we can agree to work more closely together, at least it's a start. I have a feeling this current state of unrest will prove the point.'

The other two nod their silent assent. He has to squeeze past the still-seated Jacobs on his way to the door.

Back in his own office, Nero slumps into his chair. He notes Jacobs' and Grey's remarks on his report and gives it a double arrow to Leifsson.

He closes his eyes. His drooping head startles him back to consciousness and he slaps at his cheeks in an attempt to stay focused. Desperation sends him to the machine in the corridor for what is laughingly described as coffee.

Nero winces at the drink's blandness and yet it still gives a bitter aftertaste. He checks the latest incomings and sees the ongoing demonstrations around the city have raised the threat level up to category six. If it reaches eight, they'll send in the armoureds. His next thoughts are of Harris's fate. Nero shudders.

The caffeine in the ersatz coffee does at least do its job. He reviews the criteria for his task list and it's instantly re-prioritised. As always, he begins at the top.

When he finally checks the time, it's a little after seven-thirty. Chan's expecting him at eight. He should cancel and continue with his work here. Alternatively, there's just enough time for a shower in Clean Up. He chooses the second option.

In the subway pod on the way over, he sees the worry etched on faces. The woman opposite is constantly looking about her, the old man beside him keeps a good grip on his bag.

He half expects Chan to open the door dressed in something flimsy. Instead she's wearing a simple pink blouse and grey trousers. Her long, dark hair is tied back and fully under control.

Inside her apartment, there's no softness to the lighting, no smooth music is playing. He's got this wrong. His disheveled appearance had simply led her to take pity on him. This meal is merely a homely gesture of friendship, which is probably just as well.

'I have some vino,' she tells him. 'Would you like a glass?'

The wine is cheap and full-bodied and he swallows it far too quickly. She sits down in the opposite chair, her feet curled up beneath her.

'Can I get you a top-up, Inspector?' With an elegance of movement, she brings the bottle over and pours the golden liquid into his offered glass. Up close, she smells of something floral and wholesome.

The wine eats into his control. He studies the way she moves when she gets up and crosses the room to add more spice into the dish she's cooking. Heady aromas entice him as she stirs it, dipping in and sucking its taste from her finger. She bends to take something from the oven; desire wraps itself around him and restricts his breathing.

He puts down his glass. Hadn't he known all along this was a mistake? In any case, it's his alone. There's no way on earth she'd be tempted to act out the fantasy playing in his mind. He needs to maintain his self-control.

She assaults him with that slow smile. 'Should be ready in a minute.' Her expression drops. 'You look a little uncomfortable, Inspector. I apologise for the surroundings. This place may not be smart but it's cheap enough.'

He looks around the small room, the paintings, the holographs, the artful bright covers on the budget furniture. 'You've made it your own,' he says, knowing how difficult it will be to leave.

Thirty-Five

'You're using secure functions?'

'Of course – you're not dealing with an amateur.'

'I've been hearing things about the Homicide department. Information that has – how can I put it? – disturbed me more than a little.'

'Don't worry, the situation's in hand. There's no threat there.'

'I need more than simple reassurance.'

'Believe me, you won't have to wait long. It's best I don't go into specifics, as I'm sure you understand. I anticipate certain developments, which I'm sure you'll approve of.'

'Don't let me down. There's no backward gear on this.'

'You've got my personal assurance.'

'Are you kidding me?'

'Like I said, it'll be a short wait.'

'Good. See that it is. I look forward to hearing more.'

Thirty-Six

Pulling his arms. Lifting him above the surface. Oh, God! Down under icy water. Can't breathe. Can't break their fokking grip. Going to die. No knife. Can't –

'Inspector!'

Something else then? A rock–

'It's okay. Nero!'

Another world overlays the glowing disc in front of him before the darker shapes dissolve. Daylight burns into his retinas. Where is this?

'Nero?'

He's staring into a light pipe. Nero turns towards the voice. God it's her! She's still holding his upper arm.

'Are you alright?' she asks. 'Must have been some dream.'

The sweat runs hot all over his body. 'Thank Christ.' His breathing is slowing.

Has he conjured her up from his unconscious? He rubs his eyes awake. Runs a hand through his hair, trying to take in his surroundings and how he might have got there.

'You fell asleep. I hope you weren't too cramped.'

His bent limbs confirm what she's just said. His feet and half his legs are protruding from the scarlet covering she must have laid over him. The sofa's arm is still rationing the blood supply to his feet. As he raises his head, the pressure from the other arm is heavy on the back of his neck.

Nero's mouth is a dustbowl, his dull head overloaded. The twisted sleeves of his open shirt restrict his arm movement so much he shakes the whole thing off. It's a struggle to sit up, to begin stretching his body back into its normal shape.

Chan appears. She walks over to the kitchen area. Red, silk wrap, slim legs bare to the thigh, hair swinging loose at her waist. He wonders if she's fully naked underneath that robe. An embroidered dragon snarls at him from her back.

She comes over with steaming coffee. The cup is china. As she bends, a lock of hair falls to obscure her face. He notices the raised scratch across one of her shins. She straightens up, tucking the escaped hair behind her ear. He looks up into her face and her extraordinary beauty strikes him anew. Has to be way out of his league.

A dishevelled blanket is spread out over the couch and he thinks of drawing it around himself. He's disorientated; doesn't trust himself to move yet and so he remains as he is.

The coffee she hands him tastes good, its steamy tendrils curling up into the chilly air. 'I didn't want to wake you,' she says.

His body welcomes the jolt of caffeine. As he sips at it, he half convinces himself this is normal. He rubs at his eyelids with his free hand. 'I must have been dog tired.'

'I've not heard that English expression before,' she says. 'With a name like Cavallo, shouldn't you be horse-tired?'

He gives her a weak smile. 'I'm sorry for my lapse of manners. However we describe it, I must have been seriously exhausted to practically pass out on you like that.'

'Don't worry; I took it as compliment that you felt you could relax.'

He gets unsteadily to his feet, still gripping the drink's lifeline. Something snags in his brain. 'Bit of a strange compliment,' he tells her. 'Not one I would have expected to pay you.'

'The bathroom's just there.' She touches his bare arm and once again nothing comes with the connection – at least not in the regular way. He can't read what she's thinking and it's both a relief and a worry. 'I'm afraid it's only just big enough for a stand-under and the air-dry unit's packed up. I put a clean towel on the rail.'

'Thank you, um, Chan.' He walks over to the washroom door. 'This – it's all very kind of you.'

Pipes groan and wheeze when he presses the controls. The water is a long time coming and then changes from tepid to hot with nothing in between. He readjusts and it settles on something less than blood heat.

While he's showering, he remembers the way her food had reacquainted him with the exotic spices he'd last tasted in his youth – a time before travelling had lost its freedom. It's surprising she can still get all those things. The wine had worked well with it – too well.

The small towel is another lost familiarity. He struggles to dry himself. Yes, now he can remember her sitting beside him on the cramped sofa, handing him a delicate glass full of a sweet liqueur that had tasted of nothing and everything.

Steam is hiding his reflection in the mirror; maybe it's just as well. He puts on his underwear and trousers, has to step back into the damp bit before he can open the door to leave the room.

She's changed into her work clothes and has loosely tied her hair back. Nero goes over to retrieve his crumpled shirt from the couch, shaking it out before pushing his still-damp arms into it. He plans to change into the clean one he keeps in the office for all-nighters. His wet hair smells of her shampoo.

'I used your mouthwash,' he tells her, remembering the vixens' breath. 'Hope that was alright.'

'No, you'll have to spit it out.' That unexpected giggle again.

While he's struggling with buttons, she comes over to where he's standing. 'You mustn't forget your stud, Inspector.'

He doesn't remember removing the device. Perhaps those details, along with the many other blanks, will come back to him in a minute or two.

Her expression is more than amused. 'I know the word stud has another meaning altogether.' She's still holding the device. Before he can take it from her, her fingers go up to his ear and she fixes it in position over the implant.

Nero can't read this scene from her angle; can't make any of the usual judgments about what's happening here. 'I can only apologise again,' he says. 'Thanks for everything. I'll sort myself out when I get to work. At least they've finally fixed the shave-mate.'

With no warning, her hand is on his face caressing his stubble. 'I think a beard rather suits you, Inspector.'

He almost holds his breath while her fingers trace a path around his jawline and then travel on past his earlobe to the back of his neck. Her hand plunges deep into his hair.

Nero's frozen, under her control as he feels her exert a gentle pressure that is unequivocally drawing his head down towards hers, blurring her exquisite face. A soft lick along his upper lip and then her small tongue pushes itself slowly and firmly between his lips and on into his mouth.

Lust grips his body; every rational thought is annihilated. He reaches down to cradle her head. Their tongues meet in wetness and heat.

He runs a hand over the slick material of her blouse and finds her breast. His ear buzzes: 'We have a state of undress. Code red, Inspector.' Rustler's voice is in his head. Insistent.

Nero gasps for air.

'Your stud has been inactive. I repeat, we have a state of unrest, code red, D I Cavallo. Large demonstration, getting out of control in Section Nine. Please acknowledge.'

'What?' Was he fokking hallucinating?

Chan's mouth is withdrawn.

'Leifsson's ordered all section heads to convene in Room 507,' Rustler tells him.

'Acknowledged. I'll be there as soon as I can.'

Nero tears himself free. His raised arms appeal to her for clemency.

She steps back, turns right away, 'I think you'd better go now, sir.' There is no warmth left in her voice.

Thirty-Seven

The journey back to the Free Zone is long and circuitous. Near the border, they blindfolded Bruno in an attempt to hide the precise location of the tunnels leading into the expressway. They fail to understand how easy it is to glean this information from their thoughts.

They finally uncuff him in an alleyway behind the seedy club that he knew all along was their destination. As he rubs his sore wrist, the men surround him like a pack. 'Remember – we'll be right there watching every move you make.' There's no mistaking the threat in Ármannsson's tone.

He signals for the other two men to go ahead and they soon disappear around the side of the building.

With the big man right on his heels, Bruno follows their lead. He already knows there will be no opportunity for him to escape or get help.

The streets are deserted except for a locked-together couple barely concealed in a doorway. Heavy dumpsters block the emergency exit right next to them. In case he's mistaken, Bruno still checks along the shabby flanks of the building for a window or opening but, of course, there are none.

They turn the corner and approach the entrance, Ármannsson's echoing footsteps are right on his heels.

The incessant bass of the music begins to infiltrate his body.

A flickering neon sign is attempting to spell out the name of the place. The two L's in Jolly aren't working. Is this down to poor maintenance or had some vandal preferred the name: The Joy Roger.

One after the other, they sidestep a pool of orange vomit. There's no doorman to question anyone's suitability to enter this establishment.

Inside it's packed out, dark and sweaty. His eyes quickly adjust. It's not difficult to spot Kleiner leaning on the bar; the brute has taken off his jacket and his bodybuilder's muscles are clearly defined underneath the lights.

He looks round to see Bresson, the third member of the trio, over on the far side of the room, his gangly body propped up against the wall of a shadowy alcove.

Bruno is all too aware of his instructions. He examines the clientele. Some are drinking, some are deep in conversation; a handful of men and one rather beautiful woman are moving in time to the music, their eyes peculiarly disengaged.

The stares of several lone men fall upon Bruno as he approaches the bar. Inside his pocket, he feels the edge of the cred-log they'd given him to allay suspicion. His new identity is contained within it. He's been reborn: recreated as Salvatore Machelotti or Salvo to his friends.

The very first thing Salvo intends to do is buy himself a large beer.

Above the bar, a projection plays pornography. Bruno's eyes are drawn upwards to the extraordinary close-up landscape of writhing bodies, images so magnified he could be watching some odyssey over a barren, flesh-coloured landscape. Despite his many hours of incarceration, he finds nothing arousing in all that mechanistic coupling.

'So, what I get you?' the fair-haired bar worker asks in an accent that could only be Russian.

'A beer,' he says. 'A very, very large one, please.'

His courtesy surprises her. Her eyes begin a reappraisal.

When she leans towards him, her ample bosom is thrust nearer his face. Bruno, as Salvo, can do nothing but stare at her truly magnificent breasts.

'If I ask what nice boy like you is doing in place like this,' she says, 'you will say is none of my business.'

'You'd be right.' Bruno is trying to control his nerves. 'But it's nice of you to ask.'

He worries that the drinks machine might flash up a rejection of his false credit log.

'Are you sure you really want this?' she asks. Once again, it's a struggle to raise his gaze from her chest. She nods toward the machine. 'Is no problem. I can give you refund if you prefer to go find nicer place down street and turn to right at junction.'

A man comes to stand alongside him, knocking his arm and so spilling his own drink. 'Eh – watch it,' he growls. 'You've gone and wasted half my beer. Reckon you owe me another drink.'

'I don't think so,' he tells him.

'Katrina, I'll have the usual at this whipper-snapper's expense.'

'No.' She plants her hands on her ample hips. 'Is such a stupid trick this man like to play because he have no more brains than the dumbest ox.'

The pair continue to trade insults. Bruno has his orders and they most certainly don't include getting embroiled in an altercation that was now attracting some attention.

An older, well-dressed man steps forward. 'What say I settle the matter by buying both you chaps a drink?' he says in a voice too cultivated for such a dive.

Reluctantly, Katerina backs down and then gives the machine its orders.

The smart man turns his attention to Bruno. 'I'm David by the way,' he says, extending one manicured hand. 'If pushed, I answer to Dave.'

Bruno tries his alias for the first time, 'Salvatore Machelotti,' he says, controlling the quiver in his voice. He shakes the man's hand. 'My friends call me Salvo.'

'Do they now.' David raises one eyebrow. 'Salvo – mmm, I would make a joke about simultaneous firing, but I don't want to shock you.'

Thirty-Eight

Leifsson holds the section heads meeting in the emergency control centre in order to concentrate minds on the worsening situation. In addition, live links from each of the disturbances are running onto the curved walls that surround them.

He looks around the conference table. Hagalín, Davison and Rustler already occupy the seats on either side of him. He'd also asked Eivin, his speechwriter, to join them. At the sharper end of the oval, two undercover officers from the university team nervously take their seats. The link with the Committee of all the Commanders goes live; their scaled-up images fill the far wall.

For a moment Leifsson is reminded of being inside of a diving bell – one that might leak at any minute.

One seat is empty. Trust bloody Cavallo to be late; the man seems to be losing focus faster than a dodgy hand-held.

At his signal, the sound is reduced and all discernable speech is transposed into subtitles. Behind the assembled section heads, protesters continue to throw bricks, stones and makeshift missiles at police lines. Two placards, at crazy angles, have jostled their way to the front of the crowd. "WE WILL NO LONGER BE DIVIDED!" he reads. "RE-UNITE OUR CITY NOW!" another declares.

Various individuals begin taking aim at the surveillance

equipment. Rustler automatically ducks when a missile appears to be heading straight at him.

To Leifsson's left a group of massively out-numbered counter-demonstrators are being squeezed out of the picture. They're still trying to hold aloft a banner that proclaims: "THE TRUE GOD NEEDS NO AVENGING ANGEL."

Leifsson clears his throat. 'You can see for yourselves why I felt this meeting was necessary.' He waves his hand at the images and, as if on cue, a female patrol officer is hit by a missile. She slumps. Leifsson wonders if she's going to be trampled underfoot. Fortunately, another officer grabs her arm and pulls her back to her feet.

They all start talking at once. Leifsson raises his voice above them. Looking directly at the Commanders he says, 'I think it's clear to everyone here that we need military assistance to reestablish order.'

'Are you suggesting armoured patrols out on the streets of the Free Zone?' Rustler asks, 'because, in my opinion, that would just inflame the situation.'

Commander Rockingham's classically handsome face looms over the meeting, his right hand raised in the time-honoured manner of a peacemaker. 'Of course, I fully take your point, Governor Leifsson.' His mouth breaks into a wry smile. 'I think I speak for the other commanders – we are more than happy to provide additional security on the streets. It might be best not to declare a state of emergency, as such.'

'I agree,' Commander Grímsson adds. Leifsson can't help but notice the way the light shining on the man's bare scalp makes it look like the top of his head is missing. 'Such an announcement would be too provocative and, frankly, rather meaningless.' His fellow commanders nod their agreement.

Hagalín's quick to make his play. 'A wise decision, gentlemen. Current estimates of crowd size are in the high hundreds but those numbers could easily swell. Even students have to drag themselves out of bed sometime.' Sitting back in his chair, the man basks in the general laughter this provokes before continuing. 'Distraction can only be a short-term policy to allow us to identify the ringleaders.' He pauses to wipe a hand theatrically across his brow. 'I'd like to draw your attention to the longer-term strategy I've suggested in my report.'

Not for the first time, Leifsson suspects his deputy has had coaching to control the natural whine in his voice – Hagalín's current tone is almost statesman-like. He might have guessed the man could always be relied on to make the most of this opportunity to ingratiate himself.

'We are all ears, Deputy Hagalín,' Commander Avraham says, his voice mellifluent with authority.

The door opens to admit Nero. All eyes turn towards the intrusion.

The man looks a mess, hasn't even bothered to shave. 'Good of you to join us, Inspector,' Leifsson says, turning to allow his smile and its implications to sweep across the assembled Commanders.

'Many apologises.' Cavallo's open hands appeal to the room. 'My wretched stud is malfunctioning – I didn't receive the governor's message until fifteen minutes ago.'

He receives only hard looks. The room is all out of slack.

'Well, D I Cavallo, let us hope you're up to speed now.' Leifsson grins at the others. 'You can see from our surveillance links – ' He gestures to the surging crowds. 'The situation is getting rapidly out of control particularly around the university area. It's currently at Level Seven and rising. Deputy Hagalín here was about to suggest a short-term distraction of some kind, whilst we all consider our longer-term strategy.'

Nero continues to look bemused. 'Tell me, Inspector,' Leifsson says, 'what action would *you personally* recommend in this ongoing situation?'

The long silence that follows is almost painful. Nero looks around the room like a drowning man. His gaze lingers on row of projected faces dwarfing all the other participants.

Addressing the Commanders directly, he finally says, 'Why don't you start by listening to them?'

Leifsson tries to disguise his delight. 'So, as head of Homicide, your recommended tactic is to simply give in to mob rule. One wouldn't expect – '

'Brilliant!' Commander Rockingham interjects. 'Yes, we should offer to set up a Student Representatives Council.' The man's smooth grey hair is perfectly matched to the authority in his voice. 'Explain to them that once these individuals are democratically elected – a matter that may take some time – they will be invited to face to face meetings with the City Governance Committee.'

Cavallo frowns. 'Is there such a body?'

'Such cynicism, Inspector, of course there is,' Commander Grímsson says. His giant mouth breaks into a smile. 'We just have to find where we've hidden it.'

A chorus of chortles from the Commanders sets off an imitating echo around the room. As his own forced laughter fades, Leifsson turns back to Cavallo.

The expression on Nero's face is close to a rictus of revulsion.

Thirty-Nine

Bruno gulps his beer. He stops just short of draining the glass. 'I was thirsty,' he says, wiping his mouth with the back of his hand.

'So I see,' David says, chuckling. Behind his back, multi-coloured lights continue to circle the dance floor in a forlorn effort to get the cliental more energized. Although Bruno's grateful for the drink, this man is not the person he's supposed to make contact with. If he's to convince that witch Ása of his loyalty, he needs to carry out his orders to the letter.

David sips at his drink – some kind of green cocktail with a slice of lemon in it. In between sips, he continues to grin as if secretly amused by something.

A quick glance to Bruno's right confirms that Kleiner is lurking four drinkers along and is looking far from pleased at this development.

The volume of the music has been ratcheted up and, though a few people are now dancing, it's all pretty lacklustre and solitary. Double-checking the sea of faces around him, Bruno can see no one remotely resembling the target. It must be morning by now and it looks like they've got their stupid plan all wrong and this person won't show at all. Across the room, Ármannsson is in the far corner while Bresson is hanging around to the left of the main exit.

David coughs to get his attention and leans further forward. 'So, Salvatore – it's really none of my business but, if you don't mind me asking, what on earth made those marks on your wrists?'

Instinctively, Bruno curls his fists. 'Just an accident,' he half-shouts back. He pulls at his sleeves to hide the worst of the livid marks. 'A daft game I was playing with my mates.' He shrugs his shoulders to indicate how little he's bothered.

David coughs again in a not-too-convinced sort of way. 'I see.' Though he continues to look skeptical, he nods his head.

The man is handsome for an old guy – in that silver-fox sort of way. From the quality of his clothes it's clear he's got a healthy cred log and must be doing more than alright for himself. What the hell's he doing hanging about in a cesspool like this? It seems unlikely he's simply after a taste of the wild-side. He's grateful the man hasn't asked more questions about his injuries.

David leans right into his ear again. He can smell his expensive cologne. 'I can't say I've seen you in here before – is this your first ever – um – visit?'

'Yup.' Bruno can't help a smile. 'This is, in fact, the first occasion I've visited this fine and distinctive establishment.'

Head back, David laughs out loud. It's a kind and generous laugh. 'Well then, no offence, but possibly it ought to be your last.'

'Oh, I don't know, there's a certain honest charm about the place.'

Bruno doesn't want to lead the guy on, but the beer is already relaxing him a bit and, after all that's happened of late, it's nice to talk to someone normal, even for just a few minutes.

Shaking his head again, David leans in to say, 'Sadly, I don't think there's much honesty in this particular establishment.'

They say nothing more for a while and then the older man's face grows serious. 'I know this may sound unlikely, but I'm actually a doctor – a surgeon – and I think you may need to get further treatment to those gashes: it looks to me like they're rather badly infected.'

'Oh shit!'

'Hey,' David holds a hand out to calm him down. 'No need to panic. I could be wrong – believe it or not it has been known. It's really hard to see for sure in this god-awful light.' He gives Bruno the sort of reassuring smile they probably get you to practice in med school. 'Look this really isn't a line, but would you mind showing me your hands again, Salvo?'

Though he's reluctant to initiate the connection, Bruno's worried enough to hold out both hands. It makes him feels like a supplicant – or a maybe beggar.

He's surprised when the surgeon takes hold of his fingers and draws his hands towards better light.

At first touch he only registers the man's genuine concern for his welfare but then, as the surgeon slowly turns over one hand and then the other, he has it all – this man's whole life.

The shock nearly unbalances him. Bruno tries to hold himself together knowing he needs to concentrate on seeming normal. David gently touches his wrist – but it's only to take his pulse. 'Your heartbeat's a little raised,' he pronounces. 'I'd like to think I'm the cause of that effect, though I'm guessing I'm not.'

Not wishing to offend, Bruno can only reply with another shrug. 'What can I say – it's not your fault, it's mine.'

Again the surgeon throws back his head as he laughs. The man's already clocked his soiled clothes and concluded he has the desperate manner of someone down on their luck. He hasn't guessed how far down or how far out he is.

Even before he says it out loud, he knows the surgeon is about to make him an offer he will not refuse.

'I was thinking,' David begins. 'My partner and I need some help in our yard – grounds I should say. It's quite a big area to deal with and the old guy that tends it really could use a younger assistant.' He waits to see if Bruno seems open to the idea. 'I reckon we could even throw in a small bedroom next to the pool house.'

'You have a pool?' Bruno says, feigning surprise.

He wrinkles his nose. 'There's even a bit of a spa area next to it.'

Bruno's so busy recalculating, he almost forgets to give the guy an answer. 'If you're sure, then that would be amazing. Really fantastic.'

The surgeon's face becomes serious again. 'We'd pay you a fair wage for the hours you worked. There really are no strings attached to this offer, I assure you.'

'Yes, I know. I mean – I trust you, you being a medical man and all that.' He takes another swig of his beer to calm himself. 'This is so kind of you. I can't thank you enough.'

'Good, that's all settled then.' He looks at the old-fashioned clock hanging over the bar. 'It'll be light soon. What say we finish our drinks and take our leave of this fine establishment?'

Bruno downs the last dregs of the beer. 'I just need a piss before we go.' He nods towards the toilets.

Before he can even unzip, Ármannsson and Bresson burst in. They stand on either side of the urinal. A hapless customer stumbles in. Thankfully, the man immediately reads the situation and leaves the three of them to it.

'What in the fokk are you playing at, pretty boy?' Ármannsson demands. 'We haven't brought you here so you can hook up with some sugar daddy.'

'Too right.' Bresson repeatedly jabs one dirty finger towards Bruno's face to demonstrate how much he'd like to poke Bruno's eye should the opportunity arise. 'You need to lose that poncey idiot,' he jabs. 'You got that?'

Bruno's in a dilemma: part of him wants to protect the surgeon from all this; on the other hand, their chance meeting has altered everything. If he can seize control of this new situation, he'll be able to call the shots and they might both get out of this alive.

He turns to direct his next remark at Ármannsson – the unacknowledged leader of this band of three. 'I don't think you'll say that when you hear what I've got to tell you about that so-called ponce.'

The big man grabs the back of Bruno's neck. 'You've got thirty seconds to convince us before Kleiner goes out there and makes sure he won't be bothering you, or anyone else, again.'

Bruno rolls his head in an effort to loosen the man's grip but this only makes him tighten it. 'I wouldn't do that, if I were you.' He looks the brute square in the face. 'Ása really won't be pleased if you waste this opportunity.' Damn, he didn't mean to say that bloody woman's name out loud.

Ármannsson begins to look less sure of himself. 'What fokking opportunity would that be?'

'You Neanderthals need to listen to me. That man I've been talking to isn't who he claims to be.'

'So what,' Ármannsson grunts, 'you could say that about half the bastards in here.'

'Yes, but then none of the others are likely to be someone as important to Ása as this guy could be. If you don't give me the chance to explain, she'll do more than kick your arses when she finds out – and you know what she gets like when she's angry.'

Bruno looks from one sour face to the other. 'An extraordinary opportunity has fallen into our laps. At least have the wit to listen to what I'm suggesting.'

The big ape finally lets go of him. 'Okay, pretty boy, you'd better spit it out and fast.'

Forty

Nero unwraps his spare shirt. A trace of Chan's perfume still clings to his chest as he slips his arms into the stiff, new fabric. The blades of the repaired shave-mate scrape at his chin. In front of him, the mirror shows the crosshatched red lines it's leaving along his jawline. Those bruises from the decoy's boot are still a livid reminder of their encounter. All in all, he doesn't make a pretty picture.

Origami folds dissect the front of his brand new shirt. He tries to smooth it down while his empty stomach growls back at him.

Allowing hunger to overcome his better judgment, he stops to buy a coffee-calz-combo at the dispensary's hatch.

A faulty light continues to flicker off and on as he walks the long corridor leading to his office. Once inside, Nero puts down the cup and bites into the calzone. Its super-heated filling scalds his lips causing him to almost drop the whole thing. He reattaches his stud and it beeps to draw his attention to an unacknowledged request. It seems that unspecified "evaluation exercises" require Chan's immediate attendance.

A stack of "eyes-only" plug-ins sits on his desk, each one vying for attention. He loads them onto the monitor while sipping at the grey-brown, tasteless liquid.

Next to the monitor, a sheet of paper is propped up.

Inspector Cavallo

Please note my final training requirements as per official request. The assessment process lasts two days.

Sergeant Kass has kindly authorized my absence from the department.

Constable Chan.

Her formality is a punch to the gut. In any case, he could have offered no sensible objection to this request. After what happened a few hours ago he should welcome this chance to put some distance between the two of them. Even so, he's tempted to make some excuse to go over there and speak to Chan directly.

Nero takes another bite into the warm dough and wills himself to compartmentalise – wasn't that meant to be a man's default setting? He needs to concentrate on arresting the first decoy; for now the copycat killer poses less of a threat.

For the good citizens of the Free Zone, what goes on in the outer zones has been largely a matter of out-of-sight-out-of-mind until now. If the actions of one woman can cause so much unrest, what will happen if – or more accurately when – she strikes again?

He sits down, his mouth full of synthetic puree and rapidly solidifying cheese. As a homicide officer, he's learnt enough about what goes on in the Red Zone – the frequent slayings resulting from bitter disputes between rival cartel members. He's had to deal with the unidentified corpses that from time to time wash up on the shores around the fjord. For want of any leads, the investigations they've carried out have never led to arrests. Once they close the file, the bodies are simply kept for the statutory six months before official disposal. The execution of Harris suggests that at least one member of the Committee of Commanders is capable of behaving in an equally ruthless manner.

His thoughts begin to curdle like acid dropped into milk. This morning's meeting has given him further insight into the way the Commanders operate. If either decoy is picked up by the military, it's more than likely the Commanders will try to avoid a trial at all costs. If he doesn't get to them first anything is possible. However, if his team makes the arrest, he can make sure the prisoner doesn't just disappear.

As things stand, any serious escalation of the situation will provide the Commanders with new opportunities. More slayings by either decoy are likely to trigger responses and counter-responses that could lead who-knows-where.

Nero tries to work his way through the plug-ins – for the most part unsubstantiated speculations and rumours. He gives up. Sitting back in his chair, he aims the remains of the calzone and bulls-eyes the recycle bin. The mess it makes isn't pretty to look at.

Nero's hand continues to worry at the rawness of his chin. *Monitor on. Show University Sector.*

His console springs to life, automatically cutting between the various surveillance feeds around the university. He can see that the crowd controllers have been ordered to adopt non-con postures – shields down, visors pushed back to reveal their human faces.

Arm-banded negotiators are now filing through their ranks towards the arrowhead of students apposing them. Across the base of the projection, a banner subtext shows the threat level classification at 6.5 – a small reduction at least.

It's clear they're taking the conciliatory approach he himself suggested only a couple of hours ago. Regardless of the motivation behind it, for the time being at least, this development has to be better than the alternatives.

Democracy in this city has always been a pale and sickly thing. He's reminded of a cartoon he once saw, which showed the slight and nervous figure labelled ELECTED DEMOCRACY teetering on the rim of a volcano. Down below, a fiery death awaits if this scrawny-legged figure should overbalance. Right behind him, a towering and sinister creature in military uniform is already on the path to the summit.

Mid-afternoon, Nero receives a personal message from Jacobs saying that he and Grey are on their way. They claim to have new information that might be of considerable interest.

The teams squeeze into the incident room and line its walls. All eyes avoid the gruesome images Kass has fixed to that old whiteboard.

Anticipation is using up most of the air. The two sergeants are both dressed down for the street. Their clothing has a damp-dog sourness that begins to engulf the small room.

'Early this morning I shook down a little weasel of a dealer named Nathan Sams.' Like a genuine junky, Jacobs has a habit of leaning in too close when he speaks. 'Half a kilo of GRSK – third time we've charged the little rat. He's looking at a stretch well into middle age. Once he's been processed, we get a message that he wants to see us with some information he wants to trade for a dumbing-down of his charges.'

'He claimed to have heard something about the woman responsible for the Double Red murders,' Grey tells them. 'The man was very specific about that – like he already knew she wasn't responsible for those Orange Zone murders.'

'He tried to demand a formal offer on the table before he'd cough it up,' Jacobs shakes his head in disgust.

'But you agreed?' Nero asks.

'No. We told him we couldn't make any promise unless he gave us more.' Jacobs' fists are tightly coiled. Not for the first time, Nero wonders about the man's usual methods of extracting information. 'It took us a while to make the guy spill the beans. He said a friend of his told him the decoy we were looking for had a base of some kind in district sixteen.'

Grey takes over. 'He claims it's in a boarded-up bank right on the border.'

Kass snorts. 'A person will say anything if they're desperate enough. What makes you believe this brundþróis is telling the truth?'

'Instinct. The way he told it,' Grey says. 'My friend here thought the exact same.'

Nero looks towards Jacobs who nods his agreement. 'We pushed him for more.' Jacobs scratches his bald patch. 'He claims to have sussed it out from across the street. Described the building – said it had those ornate grills over the exits and a couple of stone pillars still standing either side of the main door. I punched up Sixteen and immediately found it on Lime Street, right on the corner.'

'We cross-referenced it with reported incidents. And – ' Grey waits for their undivided attention. 'It's slap bang in the centre of a dark patch.'

'Do you mean nothing at all, or just the odd incident?' Nero asks.

'Almost nothing. A couple of street level cautions; just enough to keep it ticking over. Unlike the rest of that sector, where they come thick and fast.'

Bending a little, Jacobs beckons them further in. 'I thought you might like to see the latest aerials.' Once he's made a few adjustments to Nero's monitor, an image is projected onto the opposite wall.

Nero walks over to get a better view. The bank is only a few hundred metres from the Red Zone and less than 1,500 metres from the Double Red boundary. He can see multiple routes in and out. The accompanying intel lists no residential properties in its vicinity.

Nero buzzes Surveillance and asks them to send the raw stuff, whatever they have on Lime Street, from the last few months. Five minutes later the team receive a stream of images but none more than a week old thanks to that so-called "temporary data storage limit".

'This looks promising,' he tells the two sergeants. 'We really appreciate your help on this.'

Rashid slaps Jacobs on the back. 'First decent lead we've had.'

'We'll need to take a closer look at the intel,' Nero says, 'before we can be absolutely certain it's worth pursuing.'

'Make sure you keep us in the loop if you decide to check it out.'

At the door, Jacobs turns. 'Oh, and l thought I should pass on a message from Sams.'

Jacobs looks along the line of homicide officers. 'The man said, and I quote: "Don't you blame me if she burns their arses!" Thought you'd appreciate the sentiment.'

Forty-One

Nero makes sure they review every available image of the bank and the surrounding 300 metres. Together, his team goes through the surveillance material from the whole of sector sixteen, viewing what little they have from every conceivable angle.

What they're not seeing impresses Nero. It's clear the area around the building is actively avoided both day and night. Of course this might be explained by the circulating rumour Sams had picked up on. Alternatively, the locals might have learnt to avoid the area because of a genuine threat.

Either way, it's clear to Nero that the next step has to be another recon mission. If he makes too much of this tip-off, Leifsson will want them to send in an army. The last thing Nero desires is the military's over-enthusiasm. The governor will no doubt give the armoureds leave to blast at everything in sight.

On the other hand, going in under-manned means putting his team at considerable risk.

Nero draws them together in order to spell out his reasoning. He tries to be frank about the situation they're facing though only up to a point. For their own protection, he says nothing about what happened to Harris. He wishes Lúter hadn't been with him when he discovered the site where the poor man was murdered – after all, the man has a growing family.

'What if we have to go up against this woman?' Lúter asks him. 'What do we do if she's in that invincibility suit?'

Kass snorts. 'We sure as hell don't return her fire.'

'Look, at this stage, our aim is merely to get the lie of the land,' Nero tells them. 'We need to find out if she's using that bank as a base and, if so, how she's able to come and go from it. To me, it seems highly likely there are others helping her.'

Rashid's undisguised excitement is a further worry. 'We have the element of surprise on our side,' he says, flexing his shoulders as if he's about to enter the ring. 'The woman will be off her guard. We might even find her in her jim-jams.'

Kass scoffs. 'Spoken like a true misogynist.'

Nero holds up a steadying hand. 'Look, I've no intention of deliberately provoking any kind of confrontation. This woman is an assassin – remember that. I won't deny it, this is a risky mission. You all have loved ones to think about. Just like before, I'm giving each of you an opt out – no questions asked and no recriminations.'

All three remain solidly committed. Though Nero is impressed by their professionalism, as the person calling the shots, he's only too aware that his prime responsibility is to bring them home safely.

To source the equipment they need, he will have to get Leifsson to officially sanction the mission. Ami, the boss's Executive Assistant, relays the message that if it's of genuine operational necessity the governor can squeeze him in at 16:20.

Nero knows he'll have ten minutes, at best, to get what he needs.

'Glad to see you've smartened yourself up, Inspector,' Leifsson says, barely glancing up. 'So, what's all this about?'

'We've had a tip-off about a possible sighting of the first

decoy – although the source is unreliable at best.' His shrug has a careful nonchalance. 'To be on the safe side, I'm going to need a vehicle and all the usual for a recon. Our destination is inside the Orange – Sector Sixteen. I think we should go in tomorrow afternoon just as it's getting dark.' He'd rather be going in right now but if he makes the whole thing seem urgent it's bound to raise the man's suspicions.

'You seem to have developed a fondness for these little recces, Nero. Perhaps you should forget the photons and tote a shotgun instead.'

'Very droll, sir.' He laughs along. 'Like I said, Governor, there's no real evidence to back this up. I'd be the first to admit it's likely to be a complete wild goose chase.'

Leifsson is still chuckling to himself. 'If by some miracle you find this bitch, you have my permission to fire before you enquire, as they say. What's that other one?'

'Terminate before you speculate,' Nero tells him.

'Yes, exactly. Glad you take my drift, Cavallo.' He attempts a wink but can't seem to sustain it properly.

Nero doubts that Leifsson's high can be a natural one. He looks into the man's eyes. The state of his pupils suggests the governor should be way more careful with the dosage. 'So I take it I have your permission to requisition a four-man armoured along with the necessary wrist-monitors and photon weapons and so forth?'

'Yes, yes. Permission granted, Inspector.'

Leifsson waves him away in a gesture more appropriate to an annoying wasp or a mosquito. 'Go knock yourself out.'

Unseen in the corridor, Nero salutes his boss with a time-honoured hand gesture.

Forty-Two

Like the others, Nero is restless, impatient to get going, but there's no point in setting out too early – they need to take full advantage of the coming darkness. It's his responsibility to make sure they're all fully prepared for this mission.

For no good reason, he's reminded of when they used to cruise around in that battered old Fiat Hy-G, all squashed together in the back with Marco's older brother, Alessandro, at the wheel. This one time, they left the village and went all the way down to the coast. Tiring of the unrelenting sun, they'd loitered in some old Roman ruins near the shore kicking a can back and forth. Night had come too soon. On the way home, they'd leant out to jeer at the men stopping to do business with the many desperate prostitutes emerging from the shadows along the roadside. He can't have been more than thirteen at the time. Nonna had given him hell for weeks afterwards.

Nero shakes his head – that was more than twenty years and a whole other world ago.

He goes from Kass to Rashid and then Lúter making damned sure all their wrist-monitors are fully synchronised and working correctly.

The bulk and weight of their body armour slows their progress around Munitions. With departure time now approaching, he gets them to triple-check every function on their weapons.

'Chan will be sorry to have missed this,' Lúter says.

Nero doesn't respond. In truth, it's a relief not to have to decide whether to take her along. If he'd been able to find an excuse to exclude her, her protests would have been loud and clear for all to hear.

'Yeah, it sure is,' Kass says, looking at each of them in turn through her weapon's sights. 'Bad luck her being called away like that.' Flouting regulations, she straps a large hunting knife to her ankle. Kass looks over at him and winks. 'Belt and braces, sir.'

It's time. The four of them squeeze into one lift and drop several floors down to the hangar area. An old but serviceable E20 Nordic Warrior has been made ready for them; it's lighter and quieter than any of the newer models. Up close, it smells of warm metal and lubricants.

He asks Kass to take the controls, notices how Rashid can't quite shrug away his disappointment.

Once strapped in, they leave the shelter of the building and head out into the failing afternoon light. Nero takes a deep breath, holds it steady and then slowly exhales.

They've reached District Fifteen – the ugly twin of the Free Zone's inner suburb. Outside temperatures are dropping fast. Though the ground is still clear, snowflakes are being blown around in the wind. He looks out at all the dull-faced pedestrians. Not one of them meets his eye, unwilling to give even a curious turn of the head as the Warrior passes.

Curfew is waiting in the wings for the weakening sun to exit another short day. In the few shops, cafes and bars that are still open they're already pulling down heavy metal grids. It's a wonder any of these businesses remain viable enough to provide employment for those who can't, or won't, make the daily commute into the Free Zone.

'You know, I don't get it: why in hell's name don't these people leave this god-awful place?'

Lúter's question remains unanswered.

They turn a corner. When he'd first joined the city police, Nero had spent a few months on patrol in this sector and the neighbouring one. Before the nightly curfew was imposed, the pimps, prostitutes, dealers and punters would emerge at this hour to play out the night in the spilled light along this strip of bars. As a new constable, much of Eldísvík's Orange Zone had both shocked and excited him. Almost fondly, he recalls the casual but deadly violence and every-gender sex that went on in that fusion of fast food and competing soundtracks. These days, only the furtive and the joyless have been left behind.

At least somebody here must be doing alright from the sale of the composite board and nails.

The armoured pitches then levels out as it crosses a sprawling intersection. Out here, even the mag-tracks tend to deviate from the straight and narrow.

'Onboard monitor shows a patrol vehicle – a Viking 55 – approaching from our left,' Kass tells them. 'Anybody got a visual on that?'

'Yep, there it is,' Rashid shouts back.

'They've just acknowledged us,' Kass confirms. 'Looks like they're going right down Ellington and Fitzgerald.' The vibration from the Viking penetrates the cabin for a moment.

The Warrior moves on. They pass several bricked-up expressway entrances; improbably, their ornate arches are all still intact. Jacobs had warned them about the illegal new access points being blasted into these disused tunnels. As soon as the military seal one up again, another appears. According to Jacobs, the continuing existence of these rat-runs means the security patrols are becoming little more than window-dressing. It seems these parallel pathways continue to flow like magma out of the Double Red Zone and will soon colonise every kilometre of the other exclusion zones. It's not a pretty picture.

Nero checks in with Rustler to be sure there are no breaches in surveillance.

'Control, approaching District Sixteen.' The people and buildings become a lot sparser.

'Control to Warrior 8. All systems are fully functional. We'll stream anything of interest to your wrist-monitors,' Rustler says. 'Don't worry – one way or another we'll be following your every move until you're inside the building.'

'What then?'

'Your individual trackers will take over at that point and, before you ask, all four are fully linked. We'll be able to keep an exact fix on everyone's positions using the architect's schematic.' He coughs. 'Thermal images all blue – whole place is a morgue. No heat signatures detected inside the building – looks empty but we can't be 100 per cent certain on that.'

'What d'you mean – you're not 100 per cent sure, for Christ's sake?'

'The place was a bank, Cavallo. Walls real thick, lots of multi-layered glass and lead-lined vaults in the basement.'

'Shit.'

'On the positive side – we'll get infrared of any hostiles approaching. H Patrol are about ten minutes out from the target. We'll keep them circling at that distance in case you need backup.'

They are about as close as it's safe to get and the sky is still too light. 'Park up near that overgrown hedge,' he tells Kass.

A thick bank of cloud is moving in from the north-east. 'We'll wait here a few more minutes before we move in,' he tells Rustler. 'Warrior 8 out.'

'Understood. We'll keep checking your backs,' Rustler adds unnecessarily.

They wait in silence.

'As we have a few spare minutes, I wanted a chat about that stud of yours, Cavallo,' Rustler says, not utilising the privacy option. 'You remember – the faulty one you replaced because it made you late for yesterday's Section Head's meeting.'

'What of it?'

'Odd thing is – the tech guys couldn't find a thing wrong with it. They told us its backup tracker system shows you slept over in District Five.'

'Like I said, the damned thing was malfunctioning,'

Rustler whistles. 'That's one hell of a glitch. It seems to have somehow projected your image to the street monitors in the East Krókeyri district. Over.'

'It's none of your damn business where I go, and what I do, when I'm off-duty. For Christ's sake man, this is hardly the time–'

'I thought, just to pass the time, we could try to figure out what happened. I'm sending what we have to all of you.' Behind the man's voice, he hears jeering. 'We seem to have caught you coming and going not long before and after another officer on your team.'

Kass and Lúter are not very successfully suppressing their amusement.

'Knock it off!' Rage tightens Nero's throat. 'Sei un fottuto pezzo di merda, Rustler.' He takes a deep breath. 'This is hardly the time –'

'Just calling round to give *Trainee* Constable Chan an update, were you?' Rustler asks. 'Or maybe you were showing her your log?' His ear is full of their raucous laughter.

'That's enough!' Rashid shouts. 'This behaviour is totally unprofessional.'

Nero's grateful for his impassioned loyalty.

'Okay. Subject dropped. But I must say it's a bit rich accusing *us* of being unprofessional.' Rustler's voice is now petulant. 'Over and out, for now.'

Nero's fury keeps the rest of them quiet. The darkness seems to bind them together and yet keep them apart. A nearby streetlight wakes up, its thin light stops short of the Warrior.

The moon's light disappears behind cloud as the snowfall

thickens. It soon begins to settle on the ground. If they leave it much longer, they will show up against its whiteness.

Into the stillness a lone fox strides past, looks at the vehicle as if assessing it and then crosses the street. Their hands all instinctively go to their weapons.

'It's okay, I can see it's a dog-fox,' Nero assures them. 'You can tell from its size.'

'I expect he's just visiting his lady.' Kass snorts. 'In another district.'

Lúter's hand remains on his photon. 'Let's just hope he's not here to check on her night out with the girls.'

Forty-Three

She's standing just inside the ornate entrance looking out into the half-darkness, enjoying the absolute stillness – such a rare commodity these days.

Far off, a lone dog begins to bark.

It had been right to wait but she's glad the waiting is almost over.

Once inside the building, she looks up at the central atrium with its ornate ceilings hidden in shadow. Turning her head, she hears the faintest of creaks from above, probably just old timbers settling down for the night. Through the tall windows she can see nothing appears to be moving outside.

The wide marble staircase turns a corner before sweeping her up to the second floor and its vantage point. Clouds part and moonlight shines in through the window; she has time to admire the striped pattern the handrail's spindles are casting. Outside the temperature is dropping. Snowflakes are circulating. Perhaps, in the morning, a hoar frost will be sparkling the hedges and bowing down the emasculated trees out there.

All is clear as she crosses the landing and begins to check each of the rooms in turn.

The air inside the Warrior is close and stifling. Rashid's fury is so uncontained he's thankful for the shadows and the silence. Cavallo is opposite him, their knees are almost touching. He'd feigned anger but right now Nero is probably revelling in his little triumph. A snort of derision almost escapes Rashid. Underneath all that body-armour, he can still detect the smell of the man.

Rashid had refused to look at the images Rustler had sent but now he pictures them anyway – the clandestine "lovers". Chan runs outside after Cavallo. She's still in a flimsy wrap. He stoops to kiss her goodbye right there in the early morning street for all to see. Maybe his hand infiltrates her robe, his thick fingers all over her small breast. The inspector then turns towards that all-seeing eye with a look of self-satisfaction on his face. Swinging his coat over his shoulder despite the cold, he shows that sweat-stained, crumpled shirt. The same shirt Rashid had watched him discard in the clean-up area.

Nero's superior rank must have been the draw. From his sisters, Rashid knows all about how girls can fixate on their teachers. Yes, that must be it. She had admired him like a schoolgirl mooning over her instructor. Cavallo had recognised her extraordinary beauty – who wouldn't – and been determined to have her first.

Despite himself, Rashid pictures the two of them screwing – the crude grunts Cavallo emits as he comes inside her, leaving his sperm to colonise her body. He shrivels fast, pulls out of her to flop naked onto the bed; his stain, his mark, left there on her sheets; he lies there in all the cloying stench of possession.

'We'll go in five,' that same fokking man is ordering him now. 'It's a warren of a building so, once we're inside, it may get confusing. Stick close; remember to cover each other. The whole place may be empty but then again it might not be. Use the utmost caution. If she is in there, and wearing that exosuit, our fire will come straight back at us – let's not become our own assassins.'

Stating the obvious – was that how you got to be an Inspector? Inspect her. 'Okay, boss,' Lúter answers for all of them.

The gullible might believe his decoy woman is some sort of jinn but in reality she's just some crazy, screwed-up bitch. If she's unarmed, he could easily overpower her with his bare hands. The weapon he's carrying could blast her to Jahannam and back.

'So, we're not aiming to arrest her at all costs?' Kass asks.

'Definitely not at the cost of any one of your lives,' Cavallo tells her. 'There are four of us; with the element of surprise on our side, we'll be able to overpower her physically. But if she's not alone, or it's clear she's armed, we'll withdraw and call for backup. Everybody got that?'

Rashid drags himself back to the present. 'Yes, sir,' he confirms a little later than the others.

Cavallo's eyes are now on him. 'Rushing straight in there from this distance is way too risky. We'll try a slightly subtler approach.' Maybe he'd like to try using his charm on this woman like a gnarled old Gujarati with a cobra.

'Rashid – you're with me. We'll be going in from the front.'

Is that so? Well he's damned if he's going to risk his life for this asshole's greater glory. A caustic mix of emotions is rising in his chest.

'Lúter – you go right; check the side and then the rear. Kass – you do the same from the left. We know the back entrance has been bricked up. The two of you need to check the grills on the windows – are they properly screwed down? If you're satisfied she can't escape from the rear, carry on round and in behind us at the front. Everybody got that?'

'Yes, sir,' he says, this time in unison with the others.

'It may be an odd thing for your C.O. to say, but I don't want any heroics.' Cavallo looks at each of them in turn. 'Okay, now let's go get this woman before she can do any more harm.'

Rashid slides from his seat and out of the vehicle into

freezing air and the inadequate shadow of the hedge. Behind them, the Warrior has already sealed up its doors.

Forty-Four

Nero steps into the sickly illumination of the streetlight then waits a full minute before signalling to the others.

Together, they begin their approach. The roads around them are all unnaturally empty, their ringing footsteps the loudest thing for miles. They turn a corner to enter the long approach road; high walls on either side will offer no cover until they reach the pillars of the portico.

Above them, the laden clouds part to reveal the moon. They're less than thirty metres away. He signals for Lúter to peel off to the right, Kass goes left.

Cursing the moon's light, he advances step by step toward the bank's front entrance with Rashid just behind him. They duck down below the two ancient CCTV cameras. It's impossible to tell if the damned things are still operational or not.

'Wait here,' he tells Rashid as he moves on through the two stone pillars to approach the tombstone of a door. Unfortunately, he can see no sign of rot; the whole thing seems as solid and secure as it was in its heyday. The oversized handle glints softly but refuses to turn. Nero removes his gauntlet to place a bare hand on the wood but can gain no further clues about how he might open this beast.

So be it. With considerable care, he extracts the first tube from his pocket and runs a line of gel around the frame near the handle and then on down the opposite side, giving particular attention to where the hinges are likely to be situated.

'Okay. Rashid – fall back. Here we go.'

Sotto voce, he begins the steady countdown for the rest of the team.

'Three.' The ignition gel begins its chain reaction.

'Two.' He retreats at speed.

'One.' Hand firmly on holster.

'Zero.'

A half-beat of silence.

The explosion fells the mighty door and simultaneously bulges the glass behind the grills blowing it into thousands of lethal shards.

The air around him stops and then recoils.

Nero runs straight into the acrid cloud. One, two and he's over the supine door. His boots scatter the gravelled glass strewn inside the smoke-filled body of the building. In turn, he scans each of the four corners of the lobby along the barrel of his photon. Light shines down through the high arches illuminating the churning clouds of dust and debris.

He sees no movement. No figures emerging.

Nero turns. No Rashid behind him.

He backs up, is about to check what might have happened to the man when Kass and Lúter run in with Rashid just behind them. All three give him the thumbs-up.

With a raised finger, he signals them into a rough parallelogram. They switch to infrared overlay – the best of both worlds – and methodically comb the rest of the empty lobby for the heat signatures of life or cooling death. Nothing.

Metre by metre they advance towards the offices that are some way back from the lobby. Each door only requires a turn of the handle to open. Nero almost expects a frightened clerk to emerge from beneath every counter or desk.

Like ancient portcullises, all the internal grids are still there in their raised position. They check all down the east and west wings before returning to the lobby. At the far end of the main corridor, the upper vault's massive doors are wide open, its steel and brass interior reflecting nothing but past glories.

Switching his stud to a wider range, Nero whispers, 'Ground floor, east west and central blocks are all clear.'

'Aside from slight residuals from that blast, infrared shows no heat in the upper building,' Rustler's voice assures them. 'Outside's all clear. No sign of hostiles approaching.'

With the external fire escapes long removed, the schematic shows only two routes to the other floor: an ancient lift and the grand staircase dating from the height of the building's grandeur.

The upper floors seem a safer place to start.

They mount the stairs, advance in pairs thirty metres or so apart. He's out in front – this time with Lúter just behind him. Their four shadows grow larger than life as they near the first-floor landing.

Tired old floorboards stir to creak their arrival to the circle of doors surrounding them. He signals to Lúter that he'll take the first one. Its handle offers no opposition. Nero walks inside behind his raised photon. The door creaks as it closes behind him. He's inside a large, empty room – the sort they might once have used for conferences or board meetings. The air is stale and smells of damp. At the far end, two large reinforced windows offer a view to the outside; one of them has been part-crazed by a stone. The cupboard between them is empty. Nero peers through dark glass. Outside it's all shadows.

All clear. He turns to leave.

His infrareds blind him. The flash rips the door from its hinges taking him with it. Caustic air invades his throat and sears into his lungs. Sprawled half underneath its weight he crawls out, his gun raised in defence. Grey powder is falling everywhere like snow. There's an acrid, barbecue stench.

Another flash and he's flying like a toy, smashing into the far wall head-first He hears the snapping of his own bones.

Pain clamps itself around his chest, then his whole body. His vision blurs; feeble, mutinous fingers lose their grip on the weapon. He hears it clatter uselessly to the floor.

The dust is already sealing up his eyes and mouth. Is there someone standing over him? Can't move his hands in any case.

They'd chanted that silly rhyme together. Sitting on her lap, playing the game where she hits you with your own floppy hand.

Mano mano morta.

How did the rest of it go?

Ah, yes. He remembers.

Dio che ti comporta.

God holds you up.

Forty-Five

Leifsson hasn't been sleeping well of late. Marty keeps complaining about his restlessness and how it's affecting his own sleep and subsequently his performance in the operating theatre. Talk about a guilt trip.

Under the current circumstances, he'd hoped Margaret might have stuck around to help. She's always been popular with the electorate – her approval ratings consistently a good percentage higher than his own. For whatever reason, she'd taken the kids off to stay with her mother on the other side of town. She's still a class act. He knows for sure she has some fella waiting in the wings for his public life to be over and she'll no longer be needed to grace his arm. For Margaret, his political demise can't come soon enough. Still, in their different ways, they're both loyal to a relationship that had started in their fumbling teens before he took public office and his first same-sex lover.

As he was leaving the house earlier, Marty told him that, if he came back at all, he'd be sleeping downstairs. Long ago, they'd talked it through and decided they wouldn't keep tabs on each other. Some mornings, despite the ridiculous number of bedrooms in this mansion, he finds Marty sprawled out on some couch downstairs. At other times, he goes AWOL (or should that be AWL) for a day or more. Leifsson suspects his partner has a penchant for cute young hustlers from what they used to be able to describe as the wrong side of the tracks.

As far as he knows, he's alone in the house tonight – aside from his security officers.

This mansion came as part and parcel of his elevation. It's never been any kind of home. When they'd moved in here, they heard so many strange noises he'd called in security and then, later on, overpriced structural engineers who'd assured him the old house was sound enough, even though everything rattled and stirred in the slightest of winds.

Something's woken him up. He gets up without switching on the lights. Various sensors wake up; their tiny red beams begin to follow him around. Once he's taken a piss, he wanders downstairs and heads towards the kitchen.

This whole mansion is nothing but an empty showcase: a nonsense of faggoty marble and brass the state-appointed decorators had judged befitting. He wasn't really given a say in any of it.

Rosita's clear distain for the place had told him the truth where no one else had dared. Day to day, she mutters her many criticisms, preferring to cook their supper in her small flat and then reheat whatever it is on the vast stove that supposedly complemented the Italian wall tiles so perfectly.

The only thing Leifsson ever does in this cavernous room is to make himself a drink. Coffee is what he really wants right now, though it won't help as much as the herbal tea Margaret recommended.

It takes him several attempts to find the right drawer and a simple mug. The dried chamomile smells of all-too-brief summers.

A strap is digging into Nero's forehead, he can feel another one across his chin. His eyelids are weights.

Something blue is flapping against his cheek. Fingers prising at his face, shining a light that's too bright; saying a name; it might be his. Over and over.

All too loud.

Whine of an induction drive – has to be a Kestrel nothing else makes … Yes – they're flying. If he could just sit up …

Doors, lots of doors; lights above his head; red then white, snaking on and on like station stops ignored. Speeding up. Someone keeps shouting at him to stay awake.

Mouths opening. Horseshoes of upside down teeth – so funny with their tongues moving up and down in and out like snakes.

Nostrils overhead – three pairs. A chemical smell; he knows it – it'll come in a minute. Those mouths are moving again. Where's the sound gone? Miming – must be some sort of joke.

It's no good – his body is no longer taking orders.

Is this it? Is it all over? His eyes are hot streams. Much better to close them.

Mano mano morta,

Che batte sulla porta.

Buum!

She'd make your floppy hand hit your own head once, twice, three times – until you fought back.

Leifsson is out of breath after climbing the stairs. He walks the length of the landing corridor passing those empty bedrooms on the way.

Something is trilling at him from somewhere – two matching notes and then another higher one. He retreats a few steps. The landing contains a number of fancy European chairs and a narrow, marble-topped table. He locates the source of the noise on this.

He'd all but forgotten this backup device. Remembers now that it needs the imprint of his thumb and the password Birta – his mother's name – before it can be activated.

'Governor Leifsson, we've been trying to contact you – your stud's not receiving.' It's a woman's voice.

He puts down his mug. 'In the middle of the goddamn night?'

'Sorry, sir. Rustler – I mean Inspector Le Ruste – thought you should be informed immediately.'

'Who is this I'm speaking to?'

'Constable Maxwell, sir. Night Communications Officer.'

'Well, Maxwell, why did *you* think whatever it is needed my urgent attention?'

'We have officers down in District Sixteen, sir. Inspector Cavallo's team.' Ah yes – he remembered Nero putting in a request for an armoured. 'You better give me the details, Maxwell.'

'Looks like they walked straight into an ambush. There's not that much hard information, as yet. Reports of multiple explosions and extensive damage to the premises of a former bank. Debris is scattered everywhere. Hrafnkelsson's patrol was first on the scene. He says it looks like a war zone. They've set up a half-kilometre cordon. Medics are still at the scene.'

'Did they catch the damned decoy?'

'Negative, sir.'

'Helvítis fokking fokk.' Of course they didn't. They'd wasted this opportunity. 'Did they get sight of her? Are we any further forward identifying the woman?'

'Negative again, sir; at least, as far as I'm aware.'

'Where the hell was their backup?'

'It was all over when patrol officers arrived.'

'So, Cavallo went blundering in and achieved nothing?'

'Without further information, I couldn't possibly comment, sir.'

There will be repercussions. He's bound to face a load of flak, explain why he let the man go blundering in there like some John Mc-fokking-Clane. He needs to contain the situation and fast. 'How many people know about this, Maxwell?'

'Just yourself and the officers and medics at the scene. Oh, and Inspector Le Ruste and myself, of course.'

'Make sure it stays that way. We need a complete communication blackout on this. Understand?'

'What about Deputy Hagalín, sir? Should I inform him?'

'No. Let's keep him out of this – at least for the time being.'

'Understood, sir. I'll check the log for all those with knowledge and make sure they're issued with a non-disclosure order.'

'Is there anything else, Maxwell?'

She hesitates. 'Perhaps you'd like more details about the casualties, sir.'

'Oh yes, of course.'

'I'm afraid one of them has passed away. A second officer is currently on the critical list and might not make it. The other two officers have sustained serious but non-life-threatening injuries.'

'Which one bought it?'

'Sergeant Lúter Stefánsson, sir.'

Leifsson remembered the man's affable manners and ready smile. A solid, dependable officer. The man had kids too. They will have to be seen to give him a proper send-off at the appropriate time. This was not it. A memorial ceremony once this is all over – more dignified than some over-emotional funeral.

'Which one's on the critical list?' he asks.

'Inspector Cavallo, sir. Suspected fractured skull, high probability of some kind of spinal injury, burns, cracked ribs. I could go on.'

'And the prognosis?'

'They're not sure he'll live. If he does, he could be facing total paralysis from the neck down.'

'The poor bastard.' Leifsson rubs at his forehead. He feels

genuinely sorry for the guy, though the fokking idiot had more or less done this to himself. When he was in his twenties, he'd faced the prospect of paralysis himself following a rugby injury; he wouldn't wish that on his worst enemy. Nero didn't qualify in that respect.

'So Kass and Rashid are the walking wounded. Are they likely to be fit for duty soon?'

'The full medical report hasn't reached us yet.'

'Okay Maxwell, well I'm now going back to bed. I'll deal with all matters arising in the morning. Don't disturb me for anything short of an uprising until seven a.m.'

'Okay, sir, Goodnight. Sleep well.' Did he detect a note of derision in her voice? So what?

Leifsson picks up the cooling tea and heads back to his bedroom.

'Lights – level two.' Like a boat in dry dock, the vast, oak bed dominates the room. No amount of covers or pillows can turn it into a luxurious private retreat. Marty often jokes that he's sleeping in his own coffin. He straightens the covers out before turning his attention to that malfunctioning stud.

On his bedside table, precisely where his stud ought to be, sits a small plastic duck; its orange surface flecked with red. Sprayed in red paint right across the ornate marquetry surface he reads the words: YOU ARE NEXT.

He grabs the marble shaft of the bedside light and holds it out in front of him. Heart thumping, he scans every inch of the room, his other fist curled in readiness. Nothing has been moved, not one thing looks at all out of the ordinary.

Should he search the bathroom, the dressing area? No. Why be a fokking hero? Others are paid to put their lives on the line to protect him. For the first time ever, he says, '*Panic button. Bedroom.*'

It's a long time – far too long – before he hears their hurried steps approaching.

Forty-Six

Leifsson is finding it hard to concentrate. It takes him some considerable time to draft the statement; he's all too aware that he needs to be in full control of the narrative. He reads and re-reads the final draft.

It is with great sadness that I announce the death of Homicide Officer Lúter Stefánsson. In pursuit of the perpetrator of recent unlawful executions, Sergeant Stefánsson, was killed by assailants in District Sixteen. He was an exemplary officer who had served this city for more than ten years. Three more police officers were seriously injured in the line of duty – one of them is sadly fighting for his life in hospital.

Our thoughts and prayers are with the family of Lúter Stefánsson, a native born citizen of Eldísvík, a loving husband and a proud father of two. We pray also for the friends and family of all those who were injured in this cowardly attack. Let me assure you all that, along with every officer of the DSD, I will leave no stone unturned in the pursuance of these murderous criminals and ensure that they are swiftly brought to justice.

Governor Leifsson

They jump on the story in seconds. POLICEMAN KILLED BY ROGUE DECOY one announces. DECOY'S UNPROVOKED MURDER OF POLICE OFFICER is swiftly followed by: SO-CALLED "AVENGING ANGEL" DECOY IS NOW KILLING INNOCENT POLICE OFFICERS. GOVERNOR VOWS REVENGE.

Not bad. He gets up. Despite the hour, he goes over to make himself a drink. Why not celebrate a little – the tide may already be turning in his favour.

By lunchtime, Leifsson really needs to stretch his legs. He leaves his office, taking the stairs instead of the lift, makes his way down four floors. As he approaches Surveillance, he hears raised voices. One of the speakers is Rustler – he doesn't recognise the other.

Leifsson stands to one side of the open door, hidden from their sight as he listens.

'So far they've counted more than eight of them dumped in the central fountain – another couple left here and there. Trails of blood stretch right back to the main entrance.'

'For fokk sake – are these morons planning to shoot every fox in Eldísvík? And why would any target a shopping mall in district three?' Rustler asks.

'It's a busy place – I guess they want to make a show of fighting back. By the way, the manager's demanding we remove the carcasses. Their own cleaning staff are refusing to handle them.'

'Guess it's not in their job descriptions. You better tell Vasiliev to get it sorted.'

'The clean-up teams are really struggling, sir. They've already got a load of dead animals waiting to be incinerated.'

'Well they'd better get used to it – I'd say the open season has well and truly started,' Rustler says.

Leifsson retreats a few steps, makes sure to cough loudly before he walks in.

Rustler jumps to his feet. 'Governor – I'm glad to see you're all right, sir.' He gestures towards his own seat. 'Please –'

'I'm not fokking ill, Inspector.' Behind him, the long streak of a constable has already retreated out into the corridor. 'Although, I must say, it's no thanks to your department or my so-called bodyguards.'

He bangs his fist on the man's desk, tries not to wince at the pain in his hand. 'I demand to know right now why, with all that state-of-the-art hardware littering the place, you haven't got one single image of this decoy either going into or coming out of my house?'

Rustler's raised hands make a plea for clemency. 'I'm really sorry, sir, but, as far as we're able to tell, every monitor was working correctly.'

'Skítur! Don't give me that!'

'I had my whole team on it before dawn, sir.' The wretched man's hand is shaking as he points to his desk monitors. 'We have the complete and uninterrupted stream from last night.' He meets his gaze at last. 'I'm really sorry, sir, but it showed nothing but the usual coming and goings.'

'That mansion is bristling with more spikes than a goddam porcupine.' Leifsson can feel his heart racing too fast. 'How could this little hóra come and go without being picked up?'

A voice behind him says: 'Sorry, sir, but it looks like it might have been an inside job.' The constable is still there after all.

'What the hell do you mean?' he barks at the scrawny, red-faced lad.

'We think it might have been one of your security personal, sir. Or possibly one of your own domestic staff – a person who could come and go and without arousing suspicion.'

'This fokking decoy is running the show.' Leifsson is tempted to grab Rustler by his collar. 'Do you expect me to believe she's just a humble cleaner by day and a killer by night? Is that your big theory?'

He's not sure he'd be able to identify many individuals out of the various men and women who busy themselves with all the primping that goes on in that mansion. Leifsson leans all the way forward to address the man eye to eye. 'I want every last one of my staff not just questioned but *interrogated* – you understand me, Le Ruste? As the department is a team down, Dr Arthur's lot can pitch in.'

As he turns away, Rustler clears his throat, 'Sir, I was just wondering what you plan to do about the Homicide Team. I myself have a lot of – '

'You let me worry about that, Inspector. You have your orders – get to it, man.'

Forty-Seven

'I assume you're up to speed about last night's – umm – developments.'

'Yes. I have been kept fully informed.'

'I trust you approve?'

'I'd say, on the whole it's a pleasing advance. The outcome is less conclusive than one might have liked.'

'It's enough. As you might imagine, there was a certain time pressure. No point in overdoing things at this stage.'

'Mmm. A fair point.'

'So now I assume we move on to the next phase?'

'Be sure to wait for my orders. Wouldn't want you to go off half-cocked now, would we?'

'You know where to find me.'

'Oh – indeed I do. As always.'

———————

Rashid stares out at his own reflection. A deep cut is almost closing his left eye. He turns his head to follow the path of the suturing; they extend for about a centimetre or so around the side of his face. Fully dressed again, there's no outward sign of the purple bruises that cover his upper body and run down both his shins – wounds sustained not in combat but from the fall on the stairs; the fall that ended his pursuance of that fleeing perpetrator. Not for the first time, he wonders why whoever it was hadn't stuck around to finish the job.

He turns from the window to the man in the bed. Nero's bruised and blooded face is at least recognisable. A breathing tube is snaking into the side of his mouth. With the exception of his left arm and hand, the man's whole body is swathed in various braces. Another tube is feeding drugs into his body. He has no idea what story is coming from the stream of data lighting up the monitors. As he looks down at the broken man who was meant to be his friend and colleague a wave of self-loathing encompasses him like a body cast.

He's been waiting all night and half a day for more news and every time he looks at Cavallo he's tormented afresh.

The door behind him opens. It's Jue Hai. He nods at Rashid and then spends the next few minutes checking all the information.

'Nero's in a medically induced coma,' he says, shaking his head.

'So is that why he looks like he's already dead?'

'Yes. They needed to steady his breathing and heartbeat. They're also attempting to prevent any permanent damage to his brain by giving him various drugs that reduce the metabolic rate of his brain tissue along with the flow of cerebral blood.'

'I see,' Rashid says, though he's not sure he does.

Jue Hai gives Nero the briefest of looks. 'Listen, I'm going to have a word with the doctors. I'll be back shortly.'

Left alone, he keeps watch over Nero's chest, follows each rise and fall as if it might be the man's last. He's not sure he wants Jue Hai to return with the doctors' judgment; to hear the final verdict that will seal the inspector's fate.

In the centre of it all, the man sleeps on in oblivion.

Others were less blind. He'd done nothing but look on while Kass had been the one to act. She'd been Nero's saviour

– dragging him outside that door before the whole thing went up in flames. She'd tried to keep him conscious, talking to him, holding or shaking his one good hand for those long, terrible minutes before the Kestrel had finally arrived.

Kass herself had needed a mid-flight transfusion. The woman has a line of stitches like a seam running the whole length of one arm.

With only superficial injuries, he'd been allowed to stay there at the scene, stumbled over to witness the zip on the body bag being drawn up over Lúter's melted face. It had always been so easy to love Lúter for his stories and that slow, angled smile of his. With the heel of his hand Rashid brushes away the tears running away from his eyes like fake stigmata.

There was no way he could stay here.

The door opens and, this time it's Chan who walks in. He can hardly look at her. In any event, she ignores him as she approaches the bed and squeezes into the gap between the monitors on the other side.

Without a word to him, or any sign of recognition, she sits down, the monitors' light reflected in the tears on her face. Her small hand finds Nero's undamaged one and she begins to stroke it rhythmically, whilst whispering something in a Chinese language that could have been anything, but sounded like a declaration of unconditional love.

Rashid leaves the room, relinquishes any right he ever had to be there.

Forty-Eight

Chan Jie Ning looks up as a female medic enters. Jue Hai is just behind her.

Her name badge reads Dr Rishi. She stands to one side while the doctor checks various readouts. Once she's finished recording the results, she retreats to the foot of the bed and clears her throat to speak. A hem of green silk shimmers like a secret beneath her overall.

'We've now completed our full evaluation of Mr Cavallo's condition,' she tells them. 'From this evening, we'll begin to reduce his medication, which should bring him back to full consciousness within a matter of hours. With that will come some discomfort and stress, of course, although we'll obviously do our best to control both.'

'Perhaps you could talk us through your assessment of his injuries?' Jue Hai is eager to hear the finer details.

'There are three areas of continuing concern. Firstly, he has a fracture to the skull. Fortunately, it's a linear break, which doesn't extend to the base of the skull, as we'd first feared. Luckily, no bone fragments have penetrated the brain tissue.'

'So will he need an operation?' Chan asks.

'No. Provided he rests, we're hopeful that it will cause no further problems.'

'I understand you were worried about internal damage

from his cracked ribs. What are your findings?' Jue Hai's face is all concentration.

'When Mr Cavallo came in, our scans revealed a pneumothorax which we were able to release under anesthetic. An area of surgical emphysema also caused us some concern, but I'm pleased to say that's beginning to clear up. Much of the swelling from the photon damage has gone down and we can detect no injuries to any of his internal organs.'

Chan is still waiting for the "but". 'What about his burns?'

'We've been able to use Mr Cavallo's own healthy cells to create a type of biological bandage.' Her hands attempt to mime the procedure. 'These create an extraordinary restorative power in the tissue underneath, causing it to rapidly regenerate – literally to heal itself.'

'Will there be any lasting paralysis?' the pathologist asks.

'Not as far as we can tell.' She looks at them in turn, as if waiting for applause.

Chan smiles for the first time. 'So he's going to be alright?'

'Let's say the general prognosis is optimistic – provided Mr Cavallo is patient.' The doctor grins back at them both. 'Not something that comes easily to a police officer.'

Forty-Nine

Leifsson asks Ami to come in. Today the woman looks all of her forty-seven years; the redness around her eyes suggests a surprising sensitivity about what happened to the homicide team.

'Look, Ami, it's four-thirty now. I've been waiting since early this morning for that new stud. I could go down the street and buy one quicker. Get onto supplies and find out what's holding things up.'

'I'm sorry, sir. I actually went down there earlier to ask them again. They're waiting for one of those new ones. They were promised it by midday but there's been some kind of hold up.'

'What's wrong with the regular sort?'

'Inspector Davison insists you're issued one of those new AVR models.'

'AVR?'

'He told me it stands for advanced something-or-other.' Her worried expression looks down on him. 'As I was leaving, I overheard him discussing what would happen if the wrong people get their hands on your stolen stud; that they might be able to bypass the encryption system and gain access to who-knows-what. They're worried all of DSD's intel, including all personal data, could be what he called compromised. Putting two and two together, I reckon–'

'For God's sake, Ami, do you think I don't know all that? You shouldn't have been over there eavesdropping in the first place.'

'I'd hardly call it that, sir. After all, I've got the highest security clearance. It's not like I'm some–'

'For fokk sake woman, get back to your desk and put me through to Dr Arthur on a secure connection. Then chase up this AVR or whatever this new piece of crap is called. If it isn't here by the end of the day, heads will be rolling like snowballs.'

Red in the face, Ami goes to say something else and then literally bites her lip. The wretched woman would be utterly useless under interrogation if it ever came to it.

Ami's disembodied voice tells him, 'I've got Dr Arthur for you.' Could her sudden insubordination be the result of an undercurrent of criticism here or in DSD? Are they trying to blame him for what happened to Stefánsson and Cavallo?

'Governor? You wanted to talk to me?'

'Hi there, Kevin, how's the family?'

'All fine, Governor; thank you. I expect you're still more than a little shaken by last night's visitation – I know I would be.'

Leifsson refuses to be drawn. He waits.

'Anyway, Governor, how can I be of assistance?'

'I'd like to borrow a couple of your interrogation specialists for a day or so. We need to question all my personal staff along with my security detail. As you must have heard, DSD is currently stretched to capacity.'

There's a brief pause. 'If it's only for a couple of days, I should be able to spare the two senior members of my team – Dr Mark Davis and Dr Silas Young. I'll send them over sometime tomorrow, if that suits.'

'I'm afraid to say, Kevin, the situation we're facing is rather more urgent than that.' Perhaps he should ask the decoy if she minds having a couple of days off whilst they patch up the homicide team and they all got some sleep? This bloody man has no idea – needs to get out and deal with the real world instead of all that theoretical shit.

'We need their help right now. Today.'

'It won't be easy to spare them just like that.'

'Well, maybe you could send one of them over shortly to begin the interviews and the other could join him this evening.'

There's a long pause before Dr Arthur says, 'If that's what you need, Governor, I'll arrange it.'

'Good man.'

Leifsson remembers his other problems. 'One other thing, Dr Arthur, have you finished the final evaluation of the current batch of trainees?'

'We're just putting the finishing touches to their records.' The man sounds puzzled.

'As you know, Trainee Constable Chan has been doing an impressive job with the homicide team,' he tells him. 'She was very fortunate not to get caught up in what happened in District Sixteen.'

'Yes. From her point of view it was a lucky coincidence that she was needed to be here at the time.'

'Exactly. Anyway, moving on, I'd like to appoint her to the homicide team on a permanent basis, provided you're all happy with her final assessments, that is.'

'Hold on; I'll just check.' He can hear the man's breathing. 'Chan: Jie Ning. Yes indeed. Exceptional scores throughout. Slight question mark over deference shown to senior officers, but we've found that's often an indicator of future potential. I'm happy to sign her off as a full Constable right now. I'm sure she'd like a day's leave to attend the official graduation ceremony in three weeks' time.'

Leifsson can't resist. 'Wouldn't want her missing out such an occasion to pursue a cop-killer, would we?'

He knows full well Arthur will have bridled at that. Perhaps it shouldn't antagonise the man too much. 'Many thanks, Kevin. I appreciate your help on this.'

'More than happy to help, Governor. I'll go and have a word with Davis and Young right now.'

Leifsson gets up to pace the room. Though they've diverted a military patrol to guard the mansion, he's not prepared to go back there until they've caught whoever put that duck by his bedside. That hard-as-a-hora's-tits leather couch in the corner isn't ideal even for a brief lie-down never mind a full night's sleep. But, as things stand, he can't afford to be finicky: no hotel can offer this building's level of security and that has to take priority over his comfort.

He'll announce that he's staying right here ready to take charge of the situation as it develops.

Fifty

Someone laughing – a long way off. A whole load of ugly clanking, then a low hum. Voices going away. Good.

Whoosh of a heavy door opening. Rustling. 'Mister Cavallo?'

He opens his eyes then shuts them against the attack of light.

'Mister Cavallo?' He can smell jasmine. Gelsomino, oppure? oppure rosa. Warm roses. A cold hand on his forehead. 'Sei tu Nonna?'

'Mr Cavallo; Nero. You need to wake up now.'

She's wrong. 'Sento. Leave me alone.'

'Do you feel any pain?'

'Non lo so. Incerto, chi sa?' What did he feel?

'I'm sorry, but I need to look in your eyes.'

'Okay – okay. Basta! I can do it myself. Stop shining that fokking light right in my eye.' The light moves across to the other eye. He tries to push it away but his arm won't move. Why can't he move his fokking arm?

'It's okay, Nero. You're in hospital. Just calm down or you'll damage yourself. Try not to struggle. Relax.'

A hand on his head again. 'I'm Dr Thorvaldsen. You're restrained because we need you to lie quite still for a short while.'

His concerned face hovers above Nero. 'You're going to be

fine but you really *do* need to lie still. Do you understand, Mr Cavallo?'

He can't breathe. Really painful now. 'Something's on my chest?'

'You've broken a few ribs. I can give you more pain inhibitors if you need them.' A blond moustache obscures his mouth. 'Please try to relax.'

'Christ that hurts. Go away – damn you.'

'So you felt that?'

'I feel a hell of a lot of things. Which particular area of fokking pain d'you have in mind?'

'Concentrate on your feet, Mr Cavallo.'

'You're squeezing my big toe.'

'Very good. Now here?'

'Arm, the right one. Left upper thigh. Nice of you, doc, but not sure I'm in the mood right now.'

'Okay, that all seems satisfactory. I'll leave you to rest.'

'How am I supposed to rest in this much pain?'

'I've just upped your meds a little. You'll drift off again in a minute.'

'Look, I'd sooner sleep right through this part – wake me up when I'm better.'

'I'm sorry, Mr Cavallo. The pain will begin to ease in a minute.'

'Just hope I can get back to winning the downhill slalom.'

'You're a skier then?'

'No, hate the cold but it helps to numb the pain.'

Nero's shaken awake. The bed creaks. His mouth is parched like it's never known water. A darting pain as he lifts his eyelids and then they're running like an egg yolk pierced. When he can focus, he's looking at a blank wall.

'Only a tremor,' a woman's voice tells him. 'Nothing to worry about.'

He turns his head just a fraction and it triggers a stabbing sensation all over his body. By tiny increments he turns his head all the way to the left.

He sees a network of tubes and two large, faintly humming monitors. There's another dark shape further away, he just needs to focus on it. It moves now in a way that he half recognises. 'Ho bisogno di acqua,' he says. 'Acqua – some water.'

He hears it being poured. A green beaker appears in front of his face. His head is lifted up. A feeding cup like you'd use for a child; he sucks greedily at its spout and water trickles into his mouth, though he needs more, much more.

'Take it slowly,' a voice instructs him in accented English. 'Let that go down for a minute and then I'll give you some more.'

He cries out when the cup's pulled from his lips.

Shock rips into his body as he remembers the blast that knocked him off his feet. Other memories return, each new one worse than the last until he wants to scream.

No tears – his eyes are too dry still. Nonna lying utterly still and broken. Fede screaming, sobbing 'Nero, Il mio pied! Mio piede davvero male, Nero! Nero!' Twisting and turning until he got his legs free at last. So close, so near. But no – she's so heavy. 'Fede! I can't –.' He shouldn't have rested. The explosion sent him flying through the air. Angry flames envelop the door.

'Nero, it's okay, Nero. You're in hospital remember. Try to relax, you're going to be fine.'

Kass's voice. He knows Kass, knows all at once that he's no longer a boy. He feels again the searing blast and then whole sections of what happened in the bank drop into place until he has it all – a life that almost seems like his.

He focuses on her face. She's right there at his side – her usual self, except. 'What's the matter with your arm?'

'Bit of a cut – well more of a gash if we're being precise.' She tries a grin though her eyes remain resolutely sad. 'It's nothing. I'm okay. Try not to worry about all that right now,' she tells him. 'You need to concentrate on getting better. You're lucky to be alive; the doctors have worked miracles.'

'Can I have some more water?' He already hates being so dependent.

'They've reduced your meds and taken you off saline so you do need to start drinking again. Too much at once and you might be sick.'

The beaker returns. She lifts his head up and he feels her hand make contact with the bare skin of his neck. This time, instead of the usual tingle, the connection is more like a burning sensation. 'Only a few sips, they gave me strict instructions about that,' she says.

He can't swallow, even when she tilts the spout to his lips again. Nausea takes over, burning the back of his throat as it rises. With infinite care, she withdraws the beaker and lowers his head back down to the pillow.

'I'm really sorry, but I have to tell you something,' she says. 'I wish I didn't have – ' The words catch in her throat.

'I already know.'

'About Lúter?'

'Yes.' It comes out as a whisper. He begins to retch.

'Here,' Kass holds out a bowl just in time to catch the water he's just drunk re-emerge almost as clear. He retches again and again until his stomach is utterly emptied. Exhausted, his head flops back onto the pillows.

The woman, one of the doctors he half remembers from before, is back now.

'It's okay, Mr Cavallo,' she says. 'Leave it a few minutes and then you can have another go.'

'I don't want to try again,' he tells her. 'Just give me something for the pain. I need a whole fokking armful.'

Fifty-One

The ground beneath Bruno is rocking gently; all the water on the surface of the swimming pool is vibrating. Several tiles slide off the pool house roof and shatter at his feet. He looks up into the pale sky, but it remains cloudless.

Then it stops.

A minor tremor – some volcano flexing its muscles or the North American and Eurasian plates showing puny mortals how restless they are to go their separate ways.

When he arrived here, the old gardener that showed him around, proudly explained how this pool and the smaller one are fed by an underground geyser and have to be cooled down to blood heat. The surplus heat kept the rest of the buildings, including his precious glasshouse, a constant temperature even in the depths of winter.

Bruno would love to put more than his hand in the water but the whole place is under constant surveillance. He isn't being paid to swim.

When it's dark and everyone else has left except the security detail, he likes to come out here and look up at the stars, breathing in the trace of sulphur in the silent garden around him. Bruno especially likes to watch the steam escaping from the surface of pool, caught in the light for a moment before it rises up and disappears into the night air.

When he first arrived, they'd all been pretty friendly. Now, no one wants to chat or risk an unguarded remark to someone they hardly know. They keep their heads down as they go about their usual chores. When forced to speak, their eyes are full of suspicion. Being the new guy, naturally, they distrust him more than anyone.

He fetches a broom and begins to sweep the pieces of tile into a pile. Looking up from his task, he sees one of the security guards walking towards him with purpose. Bruno recognises Frank by his height and girth. He's got to know this man a little, which is good since he's the person calling the shots. Frank calls out to him. 'Salvatore, you're wanted in the office.'

'What right now?' Sweeping his hair back from his face, Bruno manages to dislodge his stud. Before Frank reaches him, he lets it drop into the pile of tile pieces. He brushes a few more pieces on top of it.

'Stop what you're doing.' A meaty hand comes towards him but only to ruffle his hair. 'No need to look so worried, Salvo.' Frank's face looks all wrong when he smiles. 'Not unless you got something to hide, son.'

He grins back, shrugs his shoulders for good measure. Frank walks alongside him into the building and up the back stairs to the main office. A tall, dark-haired man in shirtsleeves stands up to greet him with his hand outstretched. Grasping it firmly, Bruno instantly learns that the man is a scientist and a professor – unfortunately one who specialises in interrogation techniques.

'My name is Mr Young.' He holds his hand out in the direction of a chair. 'Please.' *So – a good-looking young man; bit of eye-candy for the governor to have around.*

Young waits until Bruno complies before sitting down himself. 'I'm helping to investigate the recent break-in, which I'm sure you're fully aware of.'

Bruno nods.

'As you can imagine, Governor Leifsson is eager to find out

who broke into the mansion.' He holds out a calming hand. 'Don't worry, young man, you're most certainly not being singled out. I'll be having a bit of a chat with every one of the staff working here. I'm obliged to tell you our conversation is being recorded – my memory's not what it was.' *Hands trembling though not overly so.* 'Try to relax. There's really nothing to fear.'

He smiles back. 'Okay.'

'I'd prefer to keep things informal; is it alright if I call you Salvatore?'

'Sure.' Bruno throws in another shrug.

'Good. And please call me Silas.' He sits forward in his chair. 'I'm sure you have work to get back to, young man, so let's get started, shall we?'

He opens the top of a small case and the side of it drops down to reveal a bio-feedback machine. So much for that bit-of-a-chat line; Bruno almost laughs out loud.

Once he's all wired up to the equipment, Silas starts with all the obvious questions. Bruno worries he might detect something not quite right in his bio-readouts but the prof continues to be reasonably satisfied with his responses. He takes care to answer as fully as he can; understanding just how crucial it is to stick to the truth where possible.

Heartbeat markedly raised though not to an alarming degree. 'So now, Salvatore, you must have felt you'd fallen on your feet when you managed to get a job like this?' *It fokking beggars belief that a drifter like this could be employed at the home of our head of state with no previous experience and no references.*

'I wouldn't have stood a chance if I hadn't met Marty – Governor Leifsson's friend.'

'And exactly how did you make the acquaintance of Marty?' *This I have to hear.*

'I was in The Jolly Roger club one night. He was at the bar and we got chatting and, you know, we got on well and so, after a bit, he asks me if I'd like to come and work here as a pool boy. To begin with, Marty told me his name was something different. I guess he didn't want the type of people in there knowing his real name and – well, you know – who he really is.'

Silas dips his head to stare directly at him. His eyes home in on Bruno's face then flick across to the machine and back. 'Let's just pause there for a moment shall we, Salvatore?' *He seems to be telling the truth alright.* 'This place – the Jolly Roger – what sort of a club is it?'

Young tries to hide his excitement but, of course, he's dying to hear the salacious details. The prof is getting turned on. Bruno ladles it on a bit – repeatedly mentioning the various drugs, drunkenness and casual sex on offer at the club. Call-me-Silas loses interest in anything else Salvo might have to say.

Young leans back in his chair with a half-hidden look of satisfaction on his face. 'Thank you for your honesty, Salvatore.' *Shit – is that the time? Better press on.* 'Tell me, have you ever been inside the mansion itself?' *He doesn't have the required security clearance but Marty would clearly be capable of flouting that.*

'Never.' He holds up the security pass pinned to his jacket. 'I'm allowed inside the grounds and some of the outbuildings but that's it.'

'Yes, I see.' *No surveillance evidence to suggest otherwise.* 'In that case Salvatore – thank you for your time, you can go.' The prof looks away, doesn't stand up, doesn't shake his hand.

He turns to go.

'Oh, one more thing,' Young says. 'I notice you're not wearing a stud.'

He's prepared for this. 'I was pruning a tree earlier and one of the branches sprang back and sort of scraped my ear. It must have fallen into the flowerbed.'

'And?'

'Its locator unit is back in my room.' He points a finger over his shoulder. 'I was just planning to go and get it when Frank came to fetch me.'

'Well, once you've managed to find it, I'd like you to hand it in at the front desk so we can take a look at it. Don't worry, young man, we're not in the least bit interested in how you keep yourself *entertained* in the evenings. We just need to check its location log.'

A guard escorts Bruno to the outside door. He walks back to his brush and that pile of broken tiles. At least his false ID had stood up to that level of scrutiny. Bruno has a growing fear about exactly what might have befallen the real Salvatore Machelotti. He's tempted to go and visit the guy's home – the address he's had to memorise. He won't though – it's far too risky. In any case, the Machelotti family must have already lost a son, a brother even; no point in putting them in any more danger.

Fifty-Two

The nurse – a well-built, black man – walks her to the door, tells her she can only stay for a few minutes. 'The man needs his rest,' he reminds her. Not too subtly, he checks out her arse as he walks away.

The room is dimly lit. Nero is, in any case, fast asleep. He looks better than he did; those bald patches on his scalp are already sprouting dark stubble. They've removed most of the bandages from his head and shoulders and much of the livid bruising on his chest has faded to various shades of violet and red, yellowing around the edges. Here and there on his bare torso there are pink patch-bandages and large areas of pale, hairless skin have already replaced his more superficial burns. The man is a veritable rainbow.

Looking up, she's surprised by his open eyes. How long had he been lying there watching her? She can't read the expression on his face. 'Welcome to the Twilight Zone.' He smiles at last, looks down at his chest. 'An interesting look, don't you think? Puts me in mind of one of those old-fashioned camouflage suits.'

'You're a chameleon.' She forces lightness into her voice. 'Who knows what other hues you'll be when they take the rest of the bandages off.'

'Well now thanks for that, full Constable Chan.'

'You heard.'

'Congratulations seem to be in order. Well done.' He rubs his eyes. 'By the way, I think I'd rather be compared to a cuttle-fish or a seahorse.' He chuckles then winces from the pain of it. 'In any case, I'm not sure I want to be some kind of walking work of art.'

She takes hold of his good hand. 'I could say you are already but that would be a bit corny. They tell me you're making extraordinary progress; it seems you're something of a medical miracle.'

'I hate just lying here like this – there's way too much time to think.' His smile fails to mask a deeper despondency.

'But isn't that quite a luxury in a way?' she says. 'You can contemplate the universe or, you could watch some old movies, listen to music – all that kind of stuff.'

'I've asked the department for a new stud. I said it was so I can stay in touch with my friends. In actual fact, I want to keep track of what's going on out there.'

'It sounds like you don't trust us; you don't think we'll get anywhere without you.'

He looks plain annoyed now. 'It's not like that. I simply want to follow your progress.'

'Is that all?'

'Look, the department's short staffed; it's possible something could get overlooked. Anyway, I've literally got nothing else to do.'

She frowns at him. 'I think that's a really, really, bad idea. Why don't you just take things easy? Concentrate on getting better.'

His face reddens; a vein in his forehead rises to the surface. 'You expect me to just fokking lie here watching some crappy film when Lúter's killer is still running around out there?'

'You need to calm down,' she tells him.

He pulls his hand away. Raising his forearm causes him to wince. A sensor responds and the bed rises slowly until he's in a sitting position.

'Anyway, I came to share some good news with you,' she says. 'We've had quite a breakthrough – the Commanders are finally going to hand over the personal records of the decoys. Should make it a whole lot easier to identify the ones we're looking for.'

Instead of being pleased, he frowns. 'Just like that – the Commanders have simply thrown up their hands and said you can have everything?'

'Something like that.' His forehead remains furrowed. 'They refuse to send it through in the usual way,' she tells him. 'They insist two armed officers are to go over to the secretariat, sign for the plug-in, and then escort it back to Homicide. Kass wants me and Maxwell to do it. Oh – I didn't tell you Maxwell's been seconded to Homicide.'

'Yes, I know.' He looks away. 'Kass must have mentioned it.'

'Anyway, I'm not sure why they're making us wait until tomorrow. Maxwell reckons they're just unbelievably bureaucratic.' She reaches round for her coat. 'I promised I'd only stay a moment and the duty nurse looks like he takes no prisoners.'

She stands up. 'Try to get some rest.'

His smile is exhausted. 'It was good of you to come,' he says, the sort of thing you might say to a not-too-close relative.

'I don't suppose I'll be able to get back here for some time. We'll be working through those files and so on,' she says. 'There's a long way to go, but, as with everything, eventually there's bound to be light at the end of the tunnel.'

'I'm sure you're right, though I can't help but wonder exactly what it will be illuminating.'

She squeezes his good hand again and then, on impulse, leans forward to kiss his lips. There's a moment before he responds but when he does the tenderness of his kiss unnerves her.

She pulls away, turns to go.

'No one mentions Rashid,' he says.

Chan busies herself with her scarf. 'We haven't seen much

of him. I expect he's busy working on something by himself.'

As she's shutting the door, she hears him mutter: 'Gone missing, has he? Now there's a surprise.'

Chan stops Dr Rishi in the corridor. 'I don't want to interfere, Doctor, but I'm a bit worried about Inspector Cavallo.'

'What's the problem?'

She hesitates. 'It's just – well, he seems rather agitated.'

'I'd say that's more than understandable given what happened. Physically, he's doing remarkably well.' The doctor lowers her voice. 'However, between you and me, his latest brain scans continue to show certain puzzling abnormalities.' Her dark eyes seem to see too much. 'I'm afraid neuroscience isn't my specialism. I was hoping by now the problem would have resolved itself, but it hasn't. To be on the safe side, I've sent the scan images to a professor at the university.'

'That seems like a good idea,' Chan says. 'One more thing, Doctor – Inspector Cavallo told me he's requested a replacement stud from DSD so that he can follow the investigation into Sergeant Stefánsson's death. I wonder if that's really such a good idea?'

Dr Rishi shakes her head. 'Thank you for telling me – I think we may need to adjust his medication. In any case, I'll make sure we intercept that stud before he gets it.'

Fifty-Three

Bruno looks around the small room with a pang of regret that he's burning this particular boat. In another life, he might have been able to make something of this opportunity; in the life he's stuck with, those choices have all disappeared.

He stares down at his hands and sees the gashes from the crash have healed thanks to Marty's ministrations: just one of the many reasons he has to feel guilty about all this.

With so few possessions, there's no need for him to pack; all he has to do is stuff a couple of extra things into his pockets and he's good to go.

No fresh snowfall is forecast for tonight. A look outside the window confirms there's a clear sky, though a harsh and bitter wind is rocking the bare branches of the trees and rattling the pinned-back shutters on the pool house.

Over the last couple of days, Bruno's dreams have terrified him. He's already experienced several versions of what's about to happen next and none of them end well.

He's fairly confident that if he, as Salvo, strolls out of the compound this evening, they'll wave him through assuming he's just on a night out.

Though it's not obvious at first glance, his stud – the one Ása's henchman had reluctantly given him – is one of the new AVRs. They claim it performs some kind of sync-up with the neural pathways of your brain – that its sensors anticipate your next wish even before you utter it. He'd certainly noticed something curious and wholly unexpected when he'd received his brief orders from the odious Ása. 'Block all location tracking,' he says aloud, just to be on the safe side.

Although he's now the proud possessor of a credit log, with genuine credit, it's worse than useless to him – they'll trace him the second he uses it. He takes the damned thing out of his pocket and kicks it under the bed. Anyone finding it will assume that, in his haste to leave, Salvo didn't notice he'd dropped it.

He steps outside, closing the door behind him. Though he's wearing every piece of clothing he has, it's not enough to stop him shivering.

Bruno's disappointed to see Frank's not on duty at the gatehouse. He's seen one of these new men before and is pretty certain this sergeant-in-charge is called Lance. The guy's bigger and uglier than Frank. Along with the usual scans and checks, everyone arriving at or leaving the mansion's compound now gets a thorough pat down. Apparently, one or two have even been subjected to a strip search.

Fortunately, Lance's shovel-sized hands never stray beneath his clothing. 'Off somewhere nice, are we?' he asks.

Bruno rubs his hands together. 'Yep – got myself what promises to be a red-hot date.'

'Lucky sonofabitch – you make the most of it while you can.'

Salvo-the-stud turns back to give him a theatrical wink. 'Don't expect me back tonight.'

The guard shakes his head. 'Be sure you don't bring something else back with you – if you get my drift.'

The streets immediately surrounding the mansion are lit up like a stadium, leaving not the slightest shadow unrevealed.

In a show of force, more security guards are patrolling with dogs inside and outside the perimeter fence. As he passes the nearest ones, Bruno flashes his pass and is nodded on his way.

Further out, the lighting drops to more bearable levels. Bruno looks up at the expressway as a train streams by. It's easy to follow the route of the still-humming rails as they plunge towards the city centre. Bruno strides on. He encounters only a handful of pedestrians – all heads down and intent on their destination. Everything seems oddly quiet tonight – like the whole city might be holding its breath.

After an hour's fast walk, he's reached an area he's more familiar with. Up on the hill to his right the main university buildings are in darkness. The shops and cafes he passes are already closed and boarded. Hardly anyone is out on the street and those he passes seem determined not to make eye contact. On normal nights, music and raucous laughter would be spilling out from the bars and clubs, but tonight most of them have already given up and closed their doors.

Once he's clear of the streetlights, the sky above him looks like black quartz. All those billions of stars and who knows how many other worlds might be up there. At this exact moment, in some parallel universe, another Bruno might be looking up at a whole load of doppelganger galaxies.

The streets he's in now are completely deserted. Nonetheless, he ducks into an alleyway and listens for any telltale sounds that might betray him. Nothing. It's time to try this.

She answers with a single word: 'Yes?'

He takes precautions. '*Aunty* Ása, is that you?'

'Hvaða helvítis fáviti ertu! Whatever you think you need to say to me, I don't want to hear it.' Despite the triple encryption she knows is built in, she's spitting nails at this break in agreed protocol. 'Stay put,' she orders. 'Wait for my next instructions. You got that?'

'Wait!' he says. Her end goes silent. Concentrating hard, he enters the maelstrom of her thoughts. Right now, his life expectancy isn't looking too good.

'I know you really wanted me to hold down this job, Aunty,' he says, playing for time, 'but I've thought about it a lot and I've come up with my own plans for the future.'

In the short silence that follows she tells him more than he'd hoped for.

'Stay exactly where you are. If you so much as move an inch from the place, I promise you won't live to regret it,' she says before the connection goes dead.

Along the skyline to the east, the tendrils of the Aurora extend in sea green and purple to feather the whole night sky in a restless dance. Rising above it all, in the far distance, are the familiar white peaks of the two mountain ranges that between them almost encircle the city. Bruno stops walking, gives himself a moment to catch his breath and admire the beauty of it all.

Up ahead in the distance, the Hamrar Bridge is all lit up. He can just make out the soldiers patrolling with their weapons ready. Bruno ducks down inside his coat and takes the path that runs off to one side of the swollen river. The rush of the water drowns out every other sound. He picks out more landmarks up ahead and now he's more or less certain he's heading in the right direction.

Fifty-Four

The door opens and a nurse he's seen before comes in. The man is holding a small box. 'I don't know if you can remember me, Mr Cavallo,' he says. 'You were a little out of it the last time.'

He's young and dark-skinned – probably still in his twenties – with body art adorning his muscular arms and protruding from his collar up his neck and around the sides of his face. His hair is drawn back into a ponytail. 'My name's Nelson and I'm your nurse for this evening,' he says, in a manner more appropriate to a nightclub host.

His wide smile has more sincerity. 'Let's start with the dreaded meds, shall we, Mr Cavallo.' He holds out a tray that contains a beaker of pills and another of water.

'Please – just call me Nero.' Without bothering to look at the latest multi-coloured handful, he swallows the pills two at a time and swills them down with the water.

He's curious about that box. 'What you got there – is it some new instrument of torture?'

'Not this time.' Nelson puts the small carton into his good hand. 'We had to cut off your body armour and your clothes; I'm afraid this is all that survived of your personal effects.'

Nero opens the lid. Inside he finds his "lucky" wristwatch and, tucked underneath that, his old stud.

'I overheard somebody say you were waiting on a new stud,' Nelson says. 'Don't they claim these things are indestructible?'

The small device looks a bit singed but is otherwise intact. Nero's fingers are slow to pick it up. He fumbles before locating the right spot on his ear. It snaps into place.

The glass face of the wristwatch is crazed but not broken. Although he's touching the casing with his bare fingers, for the first time ever, he feels nothing except the coldness of the metal. The blasts had been enough to erase any lingering traces of his family.

'Looks like quite an heirloom,' Nelson says. 'My old grand-dad used to have one like that. Can I take a look?'

There's nothing left to preserve; Nero hands it over. 'It was my dad's and his father's before that,' he says. 'I keep it as a sort of lucky charm.' He grimaces at the irony.

'Did its job though, didn't it – you survived.'

'Yeah, I suppose you're right. Perhaps it's due a peaceful retirement.' Nero leans back against the pillows. 'Could I get a drink of something that isn't water?'

'I can get you a hot drink, but I can't give you alcohol with the meds you're taking.'

'What's the coffee like in here?'

'The stuff we give patients tastes marginally better than the stuff we get but it still tastes like ditch water. Personally, I'd recommend the tea.'

'Tea it is then. Black, no sugar.'

Nelson hands back the watch. 'I'll see if I can find a piece of cake to go with it.'

Left alone, Nero examines his stud. Like him, it's lost some of its pre-sets. It takes a few adjustments before he can break into the department's exchanges. He listens to the chatter. After a few minutes of that, he tries the feed from the patrol units.

Nelson returns with the tea and a slice of pale cake and

puts them on the bedside table. 'Afraid it's decaff – we don't want it disturbing your beauty sleep.'

'I sure as hell need plenty of that.'

'Sorry it took so long. It should be plenty cool enough to drink. Here, let me help you.'

'It's okay.' Nero stays him with a hand. 'I can manage.' He moves the back of the bed until it's fully upright. Reaching for the cup, he feels a wincing pain in his shoulder.

'When they brought you in, you were mostly speaking Italian – shouting would be more accurate,' Nelson says. 'I've got a mate who's Italian, so I recognised some of the words for family. Your file says they were all killed in some sort of accident.' He shakes his head. 'Pretty tough, man.'

'That was all a long time ago.'

Like a crane operator, Nero swings the cup towards his lips. A thin trail of brown liquid dribbles onto the bedclothes but he gulps it down before his muscles give up.

Watching his progress, the big nurse gives a wry smile but doesn't intervene. 'I know how it feels to leave a part of yourself a long way behind.'

The man won't let it rest. 'You spoke about your sister Fede. Isn't that short for Federica?'

'Look. I'm sorry,' he raises his free hand to halt the man's trajectory. 'I know you're trying to help, but I really don't want to discuss all of that. I came to terms

with what happened long ago. And, as you rightly say, mine's hardly an unusual story – half this city came here as refugees or asylum seekers escaping from hellish situations.'

Getting the cup back onto the table is another small triumph. He looks Nelson straight in the eye. 'Chewing over the past is absolutely not what I need right now.' He looks at the cake, its slash of red filling, and decides against it.

The nurse holds his ground. 'Look – I don't want to upset you; I just thought I should mention that taking those kind of things – it's never the answer.'

'Are you suggesting what I think you're suggesting? Do you think I've got some kind of drug habit?'

'Look, man – they found traces of benzodiazepine in your blood when they brought you in. There is no shame in admitting – '

'I don't take drugs, alright.'

Nelson raises an eyebrow. 'The facts speak for themselves – you'd ingested a considerable amount of Benzo less than forty-eight hours before you were admitted to this hospital.' He folds his arms in front of him – rests his case.

'If I did, I certainly didn't do it knowingly.'

The nurse wrinkles his nose like he can smell something bad. 'I'm sorry, but that seems very unlikely. You'd have known – it would almost certainly have rendered you unconscious at some point. Afterwards, your balance, your reflexes and so on would have been noticeably impaired.'

Nero's head is reeling. He flops back onto the pillows. 'I need to rest.'

'You're the boss,' Nelson says, holding up both hands. 'Just for the record, I think talking about what happened to your family might help.'

At the door he turns. 'They're shipping you out of the HDU tomorrow. If you're lucky, they'll put you in a room with a view – or a window, at least. Remember, I can always make the time if you'd like somebody to listen.'

The back of Nero's neck is full of pressure. Had someone else's blood sample got mixed up with his? He wants not to believe it and yet no other explanation fits.

He pictures again the two of them sitting on her small couch, laughing and chatting as they eat. Chan gets up to pour the wine; she hands the glass with its golden liquid for him to take like a promise of things to come.

Voices continue to crackle inside his ear. He depresses the back of the bed and looks up at the shadows of the ceiling. A tired despair weighs down his eyes as the patrolmen's voices enter his sleep.

Fifty-Five

She slips into the building making almost no sound. In seventeen and a half minutes the backup system on the surveillance equipment will kick in. In Free Zone hospitals they try to play down security, prefer not to show any physical presence except for the two officers stationed downstairs by the main entrance. Without their electronic eyes they're blind.

Through her thin soles she can feel the hum from the machines supplying all the building's needs. At this late hour, the whole floor is softly lit and as quiet as a burial chamber.

Rounding a corner, she hears raised voices. She draws closer, can see the noise is coming from the duty medics at the orderlies' station sipping their drinks and chatting.

There are three of them – exactly as expected. Keeping in the shadows, she moves forward, stops about fifteen metres from where they're standing; she tucks herself behind one of the support columns.

They begin a good-natured argument. One of them – tall, black, muscular – raises his voice above the others. 'No, no, no, my friends – you are so wrong. *The* absolutely greatest movie ever made has to be Shawshank Redemption. I'm talking about the original 1994 version. Superb piece of writing, superb performances by –'

'Yeah, yeah,' one of the women – white, skinny, short – 'I

agree it's a really good film but it's damn serious. Depressing even. On a Saturday night in, it's got to be Love Takes it All. A genius of a plot – I mean the way you don't realise at the beginning that he's –'

'The both of you are wrong.' The other woman – black, fuller figured, tall – puts down her cup to hang her arms round their shoulders. 'All-time best movie ever made has to be Witness – you know, that one about the Amish. The original's good but the re-make with Kelo Nassem is even better. You can watch that movie over and over and each time you notice something different.'

While they're finger wagging and laughing, she slips into the corridor that leads to the High Dependency Unit.

So far, so good. She's not expecting any additional security here and definitely no guards. Thirteen and half minutes left. This is almost too easy.

This corridor is lit only by subdued strips at floor level; with movement censors currently deactivated, it should stay that way. The room she wants is on the far left.

Stopping for a moment, she hears nothing except the whir of machines coming from the other rooms.

And now she's right outside. A quick glance confirms the right name at the top of the readout. Through the small glass panel set into the door, she can see him lying in bed. He appears to be fast asleep.

When she presents her pass, the door opens soundlessly. Once she steps inside, it glides shut behind her.

No alert has been triggered; there are no approaching footsteps in the corridor outside. Like clockwork – it's almost an anticlimax.

Right now, should someone peer through the glass, they would struggle to make her out in the darkest corner of the room.

And still no flashing lights, no running feet. She hears the sound of his regular breathing and the purring of the monitor by his bed.

Twelve minutes now: time to act. As she advances towards the prostrate man, his breathing becomes irregular; underneath his eyelids she can see the rolling movements that tell her he's dreaming. Her gloved hand extends to push away the nearest machine – it rolls away just far enough, there's no need to unhook it or any of the other monitors.

She reaches into a pocket for the tiny device and attaches it to the underside of the bed frame. It's been programed to record and then duplicate the same thirty seconds of data over the next twenty minutes – ample time to escape the building and the surrounding area afterwards.

Everything in the room needs to be exactly the same as before. The autopsy report must raise no concerns – his sudden death must raise no suspicious of foul play.

His limbs begin to twitch as if he's running away from something. The movements slow and then abruptly stop as if he understands that any struggle would be futile when it's already too late.

She removes a tiny epijet from her breast pocket. As a final precaution, she checks the dose is exact before stepping forward. Within two minutes of being administered, the drug will dissipate and completely denature. It will be totally undetectable in his corpse.

The building begins to shake. Fokk!

Fifty-Six

Someone is shaking him. Heart pounding, he knows he's in real danger: must wake up and do something.

Now!

He opens his eyes to see a gloved hand. Before he can react, it smothers his mouth, constricting his breath and preventing him from yelling for help. His nostrils fill with an acrid smell he can't identify.

Pinned down in his shaking bed, his training tells him he must focus on the most pressing threat and that has to be the glinting epijet poised over his bare flesh.

From its angle, he can tell it's aimed at his chest.

He grabs the thin wrist with his good hand. With only half a grip on the slippery glove, he concentrates what strength he has on keeping the end of that fokking thing from touching his skin. The pain of the effort threatens to overwhelm him as the epijet moves closer by increments; he can do nothing but watch as the gap slowly and surely narrows until it's almost touching the skin above his heart.

The building shudders, the bed rears. Nero twists his head just enough for the gagging hand to lose its grip.

A gulp of air and then he bellows out for help. If he must die this way he wants his killer to be caught. He shouts again as loudly as he can. Stifling his cries, his assailant wrestles him down. Nero fights back and his flailing leg smashes into the monitor and triggers its wailing alarm. A pulsating orange light begins to strobe the darkness.

The building steadies itself. His opponent's head jerks up. Assured of no immediate danger, his attacker brings the epijet close – this time aiming for the side of his neck. Nero's loose arm dislodges the metal tray and it strikes the floor with a deafening clang. With redoubled strength his opponent makes a frenzied effort to finish the execution. Crippled by pain, Nero grapples the arm but already the power in his muscles is beginning to fade and a wave of weakness starts to overcome him. Registering this reduced resistance, the assailant wrestles the epijet downwards until it makes direct contact with the back of Nero's neck.

He feels the device touch his skin and the last fight goes out of him. He's powerless to do anything but wait for the tiny hiss of pressure that will signal the drug's release and his own demise.

Light floods in. Two massive black hands clasp the attacker's shoulders from behind. In a pulse of orange light, Nero can see that his saviour is Nelson.

He easily overpowers the assailant and for a moment it looks like it might be all over, but then an elbow is jabbed deep into Nelson's stomach.

Winded and groaning with pain, the big man doubles up. Before he can regain his breath, the intruder spins around and the hand still holding the epijet is brought down like a fist onto Nelson's bare throat – then a snake-like hiss as the poison enters his bloodstream.

Nero staggers onto his feet and manages to grab the attacker by the arm. This is swiftly rotated to release his grip before he's pushed in the chest. Unable to maintain his balance, he falls backwards onto the hard floor. A boot swings out to smack straight into the side of his head.

His brain lights up. Another heavy blow is delivered to his skull before Nero loses all consciousness.

Fifty-Seven

Nero is hit in his right side; pain shoots through his body. Opening his eyes, he can see someone's foot. He tries to curl up into a ball.

'I'm really sorry, couldn't see you down there in the dark, Mr Cavallo. Mr Cavallo, Nero, look at me.'

The lights keep flickering on and off. A face floats just above him. One minute it's there, the next it's gone.

'Yes, that's it. Come on, try harder.' Dark hair – good-looking young man. 'No, no, no – don't shut your eyes.' Something familiar about him. 'It's important – what's that word? Crucial – that's it. It's crucial you stay awake, Nero.'

The boy kneels down, peers at him. 'Are you okay? Well, obviously you're not but, you know, these things are always relative. Anyway, I've come to get you out of here. How badly are you hurt? Can you sit in up? Wait – maybe you shouldn't.'

Nero remembers where he is, needs a moment to form a question into words. 'What – what about Nelson? How is he?'

The lights stay on this time. He can see the boy clearly as he shakes his head. 'If that's him over there, I'm afraid he's dead. I already checked several times.'

Nero shuts his eyes, overwhelmed.

'No, please don't do that.' He shakes Nero's bandaged shoulder; seems intent on causing him pain. 'I know how you're feeling – of course I do. And yes, I appreciate that if it wasn't for you he'd still be alive, but this is no time to wallow in guilt and self-loathing. Save it until we're out of here.'

He puts his head on the side. 'I suppose that might have been a bit insensitive of me.' The boy straightens up. 'Right now, this whole place is mayhem, what with the power going on and off and the quake damage and all. That psycho bitch outed the surveillance system and, with one thing and another, the override still hasn't cut in yet. Lucky break eh?'

Nero remembers his attacker – Nelson's killer.

'Got away,' the boy says without being asked. 'And you're right – it was a woman who killed the nurse. We both know it was really you she was after. I can help you track her down.'

'It's over,' Nero tells him. 'Just leave me.'

'Can't do that. You think I'm going to abandon you after I've been to so much trouble finding you in the first place? Listen Nero, what you need to understand in words of one syllable, is that it's not safe for you to stay here – not anymore. Frankly, nowhere is safe.'

The boy looks him full in the eyes. 'They know all about you.'

He waits for that to sink in. 'If we leave before the cameras reboot, they won't be able to work out how or why you disappeared. They'll assume somebody kidnapped you.'

The boy's white-soled trainers walk over to where Nelson is lying. 'I'm sure he didn't deserve to die.' He kneels down by the big man's body and begins to undress him. 'This might look kind of bad – disrespectful even – but I'm only going to put on his overall.' He's struggling to lift Nelson's shoulders. 'And he doesn't need his ID tag anymore.'

Nero groans. 'Then what?'

'I'm going to get everything I need to wheel you out of here – magic you away from right under their noses.'

He stands up and starts to put on the overall on – smiling to himself like this is all one big game.

The lights flicker a couple more times but stay on. 'I know you must be seriously pissed off – incazzato nero – if you'll excuse the pun.' The boy picks a pillow up from the bed and lodges it underneath Nero's head. 'I may seem a bit weird to you; a bit sort of off. I confess to being a bit overexcited but I'm not drugged-up or a psychopath or anything – I promise.'

His dark eyes peer into Nero's. 'This is the first time I've ever met someone like me – a fellow telepatico. Imagine how awesome we're going to be together! You and me – we're probably related. Maybe we're cousins a couple of times removed or something like that.'

Nero grabs the boy's hand and they both feel the shock of the connection. Lightheaded and shaking, he drops it again.

'This is way too dangerous,' Nero tells him, recovering his own senses. 'We've now learnt too much about each other – more than it's safe to know. I'm serious, *Bruno* – the best thing you can do right now is disappear.'

Despite a stab of pain, he pushes the boy away. 'Levati dalle palle! Vaffanculo! Get the fokk out of here. One man's already died today because of me.'

Bruno tut-tuts. 'Such bad language from a senior police-man.' His face breaks into a smile that's too wide for his own good. 'We're from the same worryingly narrow gene pool so we must be related, Cavallo. You're – what – about twenty years older than me? Think I'm going to call you *Uncle Nero* from now on.'

'We're not the same,' Nero says. 'For a start I'm not young enough to know everything.'

The lights flicker again. The boy's expression drops. 'Stay right where you are; I promise, just like the terminator – I'll be back.'

He stands up, walks over to the door. 'Don't look so worried, Nero, I already know exactly how we're going to get away from here.'

The story continues in
No God for a Warrior –
Volume two of Eldísvík trilogy
available on Amazon & Kindle now

Dear reader.

I very much hope you've enjoyed reading 'Until the Ice Cracks'. Thank you so much for buying or borrowing it. The story continues in 'No God for a Warrior' – volume two of the Eldísvík trilogy.

This series of books really means a lot to me. If you would like to help more readers discover them, please think about leaving a review on Amazon, Goodreads, or anywhere else readers visit.

Any book's success depends a great deal on how many positive reviews it gains. If you could spare a few minutes to write one, I would be very grateful.

Thanks in advance to anyone who does.

If you would like to find out more about this book or any of the Eldísvík novels, please visit my website: janturkpetrie.com

Contact Pintail Press at: pintailpress.com

Acknowledgements

First of all, I need to thank my wonderful husband John for reading and commenting on everything I put in front of him without complaining and for helping to give me the self-belief any writer needs simply to keep on going.

Thanks also to my brilliant daughters, Laila & Natalie, for all their love, humour and encouragement, to my lovely son-in-law, Dr Edward Dewhirst for his help and advice with the all the tricky medical stuff and to my mother, Pearl Turk, for her love and belief.

I'm also grateful for the encouragement and support of my fellow writers. In no particular order, they are:

Dr Rona Laycock, John Morrish, Lise Leroux, Wilkie Martin, Gill Garrett, Richard Hensley, Pam Keevil, Liz Carew, Derek Healy, Pam Orr, Meg Davis Berry, Mary Flood, Lianna Pike, Colin Waterman, Rod Griffiths, Susannah White, Sarah king, John Holland, Liggy Webb, Radhika Swarup, Debbie Young and everyone at Cheltenham Alli.

Special thanks also go to Dr Alaric Hall from the University of Leeds for his advice on Icelandic matters – any mistakes are entirely mine – and the extraordinary Magnús Skarphédinsson of the Elfschool in Reykjavík,

Lastly, I'm very grateful to my brilliant editor, Johnny Hudspith, and to cover designer Jessica Reed for all her patience.

72393820R00183